I0764429

YUMURANGO

YUMURANGO

Nicole Mastan

Commercio Press, LLC

New York • London • Rome

Published by Commercio Press, LLC, New York 10019

Direct inquiries for reproduction, permissions, or content usage to
permissions@commerciopress.com.

Printed in the United States of America
16 15 14 13 12 11 10 09 1 2 3 4 5

Library of Congress Cataloging-in-Publication Data

Mastan, Nicole N.
Yumurango / Nicole Mastan.—1st ed.
p. : ill. ; cm.

ISBN-13 978-0-578-01305-3
1. Fantasy 2. Action Adventure 3. Dragons I. Title

Library of Congress Control Number: 2009901870

First Edition

ACKNOWLEDGMENTS

All my gratitude to my family and friends for helping me with this book, with all their input and advice. Dad, with his "loose ends" that constantly kept me on my toes. Mom with her detail oriented mind; I'll never forget a comma again. All the guys at school who pressured me until I finally got this thing published, along with those who actually read it and told me they loved me, no matter how bad the draft was. And finally, my sister, for making me strive to write better just to prove her sarcastic comments wrong. Also, thanks to her for making the cover of my book pretty. Finally, thanks to the great editors at Commercio Press for all their awesome help. Enjoy guys!

TABLE OF CONTENTS

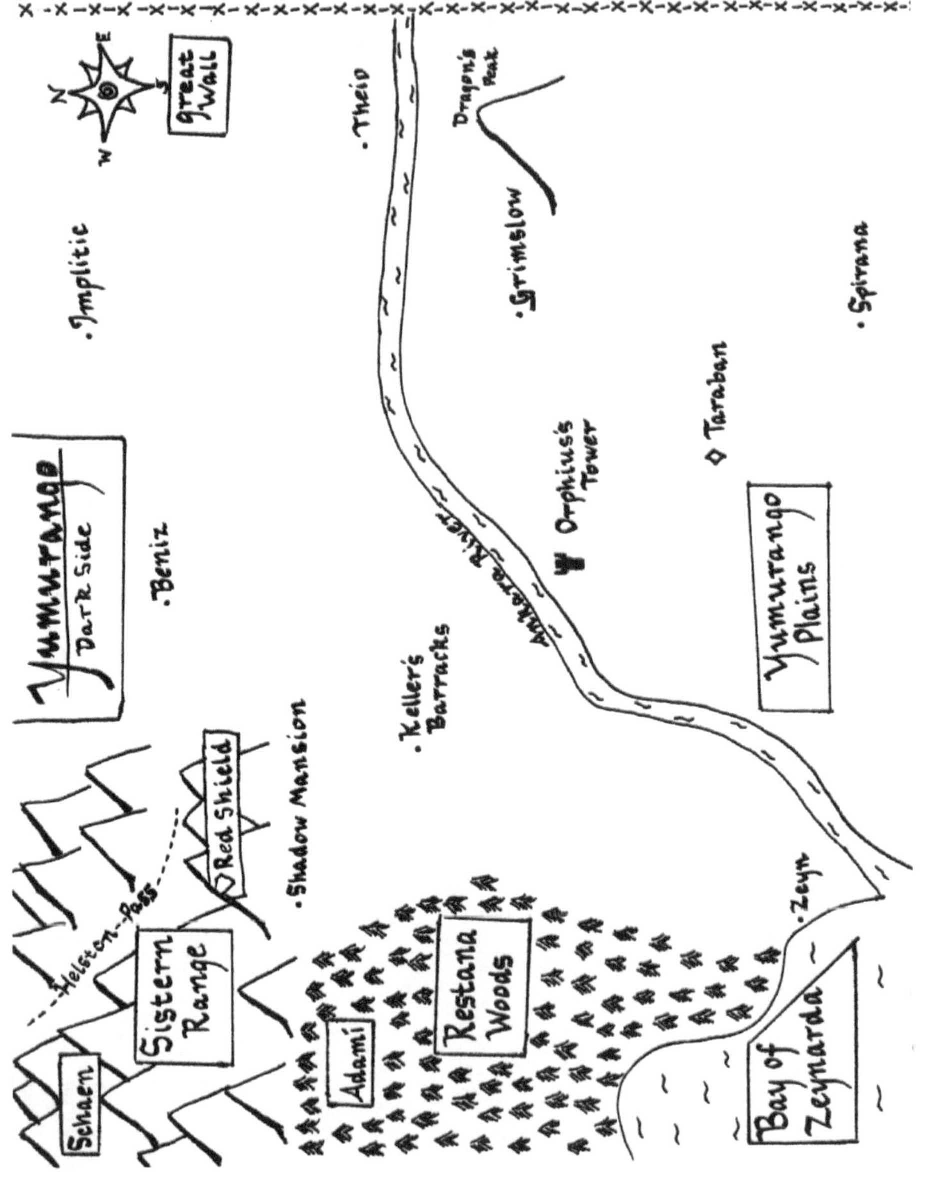

Great Wall
N
E
S
W
Implitic
Theid
Dragon's Peak
Grimslow
Spirana
Yumurango
Dark Side
Beniz
Orphius's Tower
Taraban
Amera River
Yumurango Plains
Keller's Barracks
Shadow Mansion
Red Shield
Helston Pass
Sistern Range
Schaen
Adami
Restana Woods
Zeyn
Bay of Zeynarda

CHARACTERS

Dominique-Girl from Colorado, has purple hair and eyes. She hopes to find a place to fit within society, but seems oddly detached from the others around her.

Tom Horter-Living skeleton with a knack for stealing. Directs yellow fire to emerge from his palms. Wanted in Yumurango for his crimes, dead or alive.

Shayla-Last remaining shape shifter after Keller's purge of her kind. Can morph into a dragon at will, works at a dragon fighting arena as the reigning champion.

Flint-Robot found in the basement of the Shadow family's ancestral mansion. Has no recollection of the time before she was put to sleep. Very handy with all firearms.

Yakimi-Adamean warrior who has been frozen under a spell for over a century. Uses his teeth and sword blade with deadly efficiency. May be the last of his kind.

Keller-Eldest surviving member of the Shadow family. Wears armor to mask his emotions. He is at war with his brother, Orphius, who he hates bitterly. Commands powerful black energy due to his Shadow heritage.

Orphius-Second oldest surviving member of the Shadow family. Hates his brother, Keller, and has built an army to oppose him. Makes a habit of killing officers that fail repeatedly. Like his brother, possesses powerful magic.

Poz-Guardian of the portal linking Earth and Yumurango. Married to Duna.

Duna-Female guardian of theportal between the two worlds. Married to Poz.

Val-Leader of the rebel faction, Red Shield, which opposes Keller and Orphius. Long time friend of Tom's; the only one living to command a Marauder.

Sadiki-Ill tempered Marauder, bound to Val's service. Massacred villages when he was unbound.

Berra-Keller's personal dragon. Has been his companion since childhood. Scar runs through one eye because of fights she has participated in.

Reyzar-Berra's son. Still in training to be one of Keller's top choices for combat.

Vilondra-Red Shield member. Hates Tom and the Shadow family for personal reasons.

Derek-One of Vilondra's twin brothers. Meekly submits to her authority.

Jack-The other twin brother. Resents his sister when she assumes she's the sibling in charge.

Gupper-Orphius's spy. Resembles a man's head on a small metal bird's body. Constantly afraid his master will kill him.

Ethan-Yumurangonian citizen. Travels and trades with his family among the major cities.

Gretchen-Ethan's wife. Lost all of her livelihood because of Keller and Orphius's war.

Amy-Ethan's daughter. Has grown up traveling, ever since her family's home was demolished by soldiers.

Danny-Creature called a Shartan. Pulls Ethan's family's cart around Yumurango. Likes to have his forehead scratched.

Christina-Dominique's best friend. Constantly worried that she'll never get a date.

Sam-Newcomer to the orphanage where Dominique lives. Seems perplexed by Christina's odd behavior.

Serena-Reigning queen of Dominique's high school. Beats up girls who make moves on guys she considers her property. Particularly hates Dominique.

Alan-Sweetheart of the school. Popular, cute, athletic.

Mrs. Magnuson-Orphanage caretaker. Has looked after Dominique for five years.

1

A Strange Girl

How do stories begin, exactly? Does a hero or heroine automatically find themselves in an impossible situation, with no way of backing out? Are they the ones that are born to be ready, who take charge of their destinies-

Pale fingers snapped the book closed in disgust. The girl rolled her eyes and tossed the novel to the other end of the room, glowering at it. Heroes? Heroines? She wasn't buying it. Everything that she had been led to believe had been exactly the opposite; heroes weren't around, but villains were abundant.

The villain in question (at least for today) was knocking on her door right now, demanding that she be up and ready for school in five minutes.

"Dominique, if you don't get your skinny rear out this door VERY soon..." the voice trailed off threateningly, and Dominique gave the voice the finger before she lazily swung the door open.

"Good heavens child, don't you have any other colors to wear?"

It was simple black attire, as usual. Dominique didn't really go for the flashy clothes. Flashing the woman a look as she went by, the girl tossed back her hair and flounced into the bathroom.

Well, there it was. Her reflection wasn't going to get any different anytime soon. Her pale face, with her sharp cheekbones, might have been pretty if it hadn't been for her hair and eyes.

Yes, Dominique thought bitterly as she began to comb through the purple strands. *I'm a freak with purple hair and eyes. That's why I have hardly any friends.*

Mrs. Magnuson, the caretaker, poked her head in to see how it was going.

"You're going to be late," she warned. "And I need you to bring the new kid, Sam, with you to get him signed in at school."

Dominique groaned. "Are you kidding me? I had to do that for the last kid too!"

"Well, you're the one who's been around here longest, so you've got the most experience," the woman said distractedly. Dominique froze inwardly as she watched her walk away, calling for a young child's name.

Of course, Magnuson hadn't meant any offense. She had known Dominique for the past five years, so she wouldn't be too careful about saying hurtful things like that.

Thank you ever so much, Dominique snarled in her head. The orphanage, however, was the only home she had ever known; there was no way to keep denying the fact that no one was going to adopt her. She was too...weird.

Yes, that was the word. The girl looked back at her reflection, and her violet eyes. There was no one in this world who would want anyone like her.

"DOMINIQUE!" Magnuson screamed. She swore and sprinted downstairs, grabbing her bag from her room as fast as she could.

The head of the orphanage was there, along with the new kid, Sam. His parents had been killed in a car crash a few weeks ago. Since he had no known relatives, he had been sent here.

"Welcome to hell," she announced sourly. Magnuson gasped and whacked her across the head.

"Ow!"

"Don't say things like that!"

"Well, it's true!"

Magnuson shook her head and went on her busy way, calling hastily for the same kid who (obviously) wasn't coming anywhere near her.

Rolling her eyes, Dominique returned her attention to Sam. He was staring at her, of course. She was surprised to realize that after so many years of being stared at, she hardly noticed anymore.

Instead, she widened her purple eyes and shook her hand in front of his face.

"Afraid I'm gonna eat you?" she said in a creepy voice. He blinked once and grinned sheepishly.

"Sorry, I've just never seen someone with colored contacts in...they're cool."

Oh. Dominique inwardly gave herself a mental slap. He thought they were fake. Well, let him think that...with luck, he'd think the same thing about her hair. Might as well not rain on his parade.

"Whatever. Let's go," she said, opening the door.

It was an uncommonly hot summer for Colorado. Already, Dominique could feel the heat of the sun breaking over her head and shoulders. Her black clothing made it all the more uncomfortable.

"So...have you lived here for very long?" Sam asked, trying to be conversational. Dominique cringed inwardly.

She had no idea. There was no memory in her head aside from the last five years. At twelve years old, she had been found wandering aimlessly outside the town, crying. The only thing she remembered from before that was a horrible fire.

As though she had cued it, Dominique suddenly heard screaming and the roar of flames. Someone had been shouting at her to get out, get out while she still could, while the sounds of fighting erupted near her.

Dominique shook her head roughly. This wasn't good. Having delusions was one thing, but entirely fake memories? There had been no reported fires anywhere around the area where they had found her, so she must have come from somewhere far away.

A thorough background check had, of course, ensued. The police had crawled all over the place, looking for Dominique's parents. It wasn't a surprise when they were never found. The young girl had been shipped off to the orphanage, where she had been in the care of Mrs. Magnuson ever since.

"Hello?" Sam asked, laughing nervously.

"Oh, sorry. Umm...I've been here since I was twelve."

"And you're how old now?"

"Seventeen. I think you're in my homeroom."

"Oh," the boy said, looking down at the scrap of paper that was his schedule. "Cool. Anyone I should avoid?"

Dominique shrugged. "I would recommend staying away from Serena and her group, but they're usually nice to boys. It's just girls who get found behind the school with black eyes."

"Wow," Sam muttered. Dominique hoped he wouldn't notice the almost healed black eye *she* had. Serena and she weren't the closest of friends, so to speak.

In fact, she only had one really close friend...

"DOMINIQUE!"

"Oh dear," the girl muttered, whipping her head around. They had managed to walk two blocks undisturbed, but this was where her friend lived, and she knew that whenever she saw her...

"There you are!" the girl shouted, jumping up and giving Dominique a huge hug. Sighing, the girl patted her awkwardly on the back.

"Hey, Christina."

Her friend drew back, pushing her glasses up the bridge of her nose with a finger. Glancing toward Sam, she smiled.

"Hi."

He stared at her as though she was insane.

"Don't worry, you actually get that a lot," Dominique snickered to Christina as she again began to walk. Sam followed the two of them dutifully, obviously flabbergasted.

"Hey, how's your eye?" Christina asked, inspecting her friend's face closer. Dominique rolled her eyes.

"It's fine," she snapped. "It happened over a week ago. Serena's forgotten all about it. Today I'll be back to the normal, invisible me."

"You're not invisible," Christina retorted, in the easy manner of an old argument. She turned to Sam.

"She says that all the time," she mouthed to him. Her reward was a smack from her friend.

"Well, if it's worth anything, I don't exactly think you'd blend in with the crowd," Sam muttered. "With your hair and everything,"

Dominique's eyes flashed toward him in a glare, which he laughed nervously at.

"Okay then..."

The girl looked ahead again. School was near, and her head was full...of *Alan.*

"Don't tell me," Christina said, with a twinkle in her eyes. "Looking for someone?"

"No," Dominique snapped. She felt her face turning bright red.

"Whatever. Sam, come with me!" Dominique ordered, gesturing in the other direction.

Christina waved to them as they left, heading off toward her locker. Dominique escorted the new kid to the main office, where she handed him a few papers.

"Just tell them you're new, and you're from the orphanage, okay?" she said. "I've gotta get to class."

"Umm...sure. See ya!" Sam said with a small wave. Dominique nodded back before she continued on her way.

People walked by her in the halls, usually staring as they went. Dominique hardly noticed.

"Hey, zombie chick!" some jerk called. "Come here, I wanna show you something!"

Dominique ignored him as she walked by, keeping her gaze steadily on her locker. That was when someone grabbed her shoulder and spun her around.

His name was Chuck. That was all she knew. But right now, he was really getting in her face. She didn't like that.

"What do you want?" she snarled.

"Aww, you're so cold. What's your problem?"

"Hey, *you're* the one who-"

"What's going on?"

The voice that broke upon her ear was familiar, and Dominique could feel her face heating up again. Chuck broke away and mumbled something under his breath. Dominique turned around.

Alan was standing there, in all his glory. His tanned skin (from his Italian heritage) was a striking contrast to his blinding smile. He had a gorgeous mop of black hair, and he carried himself like a king. His eyes, usually so full of laughter, were cold and angry.

Although he was shorter than Chuck, Alan was obviously in command of the situation. His dark eyes appraised the other boy calmly. It did help, of course, that he was being flanked by three others.

"Don't tell me," he snapped. "She's your girlfriend?"

"I don't think so," Dominique snarled. She rubbed her arm and glared at the hulking monstrosity that had grabbed her. "I'm leaving."

She stalked off, but not before she heard Alan starting to talk threateningly to the other kid.

As she struggled with her locker combination, she saw someone out of the corner of her eye. They leaned up against the locker next to hers, waiting for her to notice them. Yeah...as if she didn't know who it was already.

Dominique turned her head and smiled hesitantly at him. Alan smiled back.

"You okay?" he asked.

"Oh, yeah, I'm fine." she said, grinning wider. "It's not like that was unusual or anything."

"I think *he'll* stop, at least," he said, glaring back at the other boys. They were hanging back, laughing amongst themselves as they glanced her way.

"I'll work on it," he said.

"You don't have to," Dominique interjected, getting her books out for first period. The boy laughed.

"You're right, but I want to."

"Oh? Are things not going well with Jillian?"

It was common knowledge among the schoolyard population that Jillian was Alan's girlfriend, but that things had been rocky of late. Rumor had it that he had cheated on her with Stacy, another girl in their class. Dominique really didn't know, or care, but either way it was fun to tease him...

"Ha ha," he said dryly. "See you later."

"Okay, umm...bye," she called after him. He waved back.

Dominique looked down at the ground, and then, began to laugh. It felt like she was floating the rest of the day.

2

Haunted House

Sixth period. Things weren't exactly going fast in Dominique's book. Staring at the clock with a blank gaze, she didn't notice Christina elbowing her until a few seconds later.

"What?" she whispered. The teacher was in the middle of a lecture, and she knew better than to interrupt him once he got going.

"I heard you were talking to Alan earlier today," Christina murmured. Dominique rolled her eyes.

"Can we discuss this later? He's sort of in the middle of-"

"Dominique?"

She cringed as she turned to see her history teacher peering at her with a crucifying gaze. Smiling wanly, she cleared her throat and made a show of paying close attention.

He seemed satisfied...for now. Glaring at her friend in exasperation, Dominique prepared to ignore her for the rest of the day. Not that that was too long...there were only ten minutes left.

"Oh, come on! You've gotta give me some little teasers before the actual conversation!" Christina, perversely, insisted. "I mean, I haven't had any action with a guy in over a year since Doug dumped me, and-"

"Christina? Come here please."

Ooh, he sounded *pissed.* Dominique gave her friend a sympathetic glance as she trudged dutifully to the front of the room, where he was already filling out a detention slip. A few kids in the back row snickered.

Dominique yawned, wondering how two o'clock could be the worst time of the day. She slumped forward onto her desk, day dreaming. Unlike Christina, who usually daydreamed about her latest crush or had nightmares about failing a project, Dominique always dreamed of another life.

She was younger then, and it was the happiest she'd ever been. A huge mansion was her home, and she was the only girl. Three other kids were always present, along with a couple she assumed were her parents. The thing was...she couldn't make out their faces. It was as if something was always blocking her dreaming mind.

Then, it always turned to the same nightmare. Flames appeared out of nowhere, licking away at the once splendid house while the dream mother called out for her children to get out of the house while they could, to escape and live-

Dominique jerked her head up with a sharp intake of breath. God, she hated when she did that. A few people around her gave her odd looks, which she ignored. There was no reason to get upset over a nightmare...

Oh geeze. She had slept for eight minutes. Hopefully she hadn't missed any homework. Getting up, she packed her backpack full of her books and joined Christina by the door. Everyone else had already herded together by it, waiting to escape as soon as they could.

"So," her friend started suggestively.

"He was just telling some jerk off, alright? It's no big deal."

"I think it is. Do you think he's finally starting to notice?"

"Notice what? Your black eye?" a snobby voice interrupted them. Dominique groaned inwardly. This was exactly why she hadn't wanted to have this conversation in class...

Serena was tall. She was pretty. She had big breasts. She was every guy's dream date. Her glossy black hair and large green eyes were the perfect traits for an object of beauty. If she didn't have two guys fighting over her at once, it was three. And she knew it, too. Every other girl, except for her two toadies, were the enemy to be slaughtered.

"Are you talking about Alan again?" she said with a smirk. Dominique glared at her coldly.

"Mind your own business," she snapped.

"Ooh, the freak's angry," Serena said, laughing. Christina shuffled her feet and backed up a few steps.

"At least Willaker's got the right idea," the prima donna said coldly, tossing her hair. "But you, Dom...You've got an attitude."

"My name is Dominique, thank you very much," the girl said frostily. "And what I do with my attitude is no business of yours."

The bell rang. "Out of my way," Dominique snarled, shoving Serena over and marching out the door. Behind her, she heard shouts of alarm and protest.

"You can't stand for that!" Amy, a girl in Serena's "in" crowd, shouted. Their leader rolled her eyes.

"Did you honestly think I was going to?"

Dominique shoved Serena's absurdly grim thoughts of revenge out of her head as she sped for the door. There was a long walk ahead of her to get back to the orphanage, and Christina had tennis practice today...she would be on her own.

Heat made her shirt cling to her back as she started home, and sweat beaded on her forehead. She had never been one for hot weather, but hey, what was a girl gonna do? They were in the middle of a heat wave and she'd have to endure.

Scenes from the day's events rolled through her mind, from the fight with Serena back to Alan's rescue. Maybe she wasn't as invisible as she thought. Hmm...

But right now, all she wanted to do was go home. It didn't even matter that she was only going back to the orphanage. Next year she would be out in her own place, and never have to get back there again. Senior year in high school could be a plus. She couldn't wait to move to somewhere cold; especially where she might be able to find a type of hair dye that covered up her purple hue...nothing worked where she lived now.

Suddenly, a cold wind blew into her face. Dominique stopped, puzzled. The fresh air was a welcome contrast, but there was one question she had to ask...where was it coming from?

Oh. It was coming from the street to her left. Past a vacant lot and over a fence, in fact. That old house.

It had been there ever since anyone in the small town could remember. An old, rickety building, half rotted and choked with vines that had long since taken over the structure. Dominique half wondered if it was the plants that now formed the house itself. Everyday, odd creaks and groans could be heard from it...people said it was haunted.

That, and the fact that no one had ever lived in it, despite the constant noise complaints from the neighbors, was not a comforting thought as Dominique stared at it. One empty window was a featureless pit in the side of it. Creepy.

But, as she watched, a set of eyes flashed once, reflecting the light from outside. Dominique jumped and clutched her backpack, her heart beginning to pound from an adrenaline rush as she prepared to flee.

They disappeared just as suddenly. Feeling oddly vulnerable, the girl dug her nails into her backpack's straps and walked a little faster. It was just her imagination...just her imagination...

"Hey freak!"

Oh no. Please say she was imagining that horribly familiar voice!

"Yeah, you heard me!"

Whirling, Dominique swore under her breath as she saw Serena coming toward her. And she wasn't alone. She was flanked on both sides by Amy and another girl named Mina. They were armed with bats...and dangerous.

"I don't want any trouble," Dominique warned, but the voice that had supposed to sound fearless ended up being dry and weak. It even cracked at the end of her sentence.

"Aww, what's the matter? Don't wanna play?" Serena sneered, brandishing her weapon as she came closer. "I swear this won't hurt a bit..."

With that, she lunged. Dominique turned tail and ran into the vacant lot, the only place where she could lose them. Old trash littered the ground, and there was a maze of old cars and furniture toward the fence.

Sunlight, of course, was a merciless force as Dominique skittered over the hot metal and dry dirt. It felt like she was in a desert, running from...what, a snake?

That was what Serena reminded her of now. The girl's tongue was hanging out as she laughed at Dominique's attempts to scuttle away, and her green eyes looked more hypnotic and deadly than the girl had ever seen them before. She must have really pissed her off today...

"Where do you think you're going?" a voice snarled in front of her. Dominique skidded to a halt and jumped back just in time to avoid Mina's swing. The bat whistled through the air just a few scant inches from her nose.

"Why are you doing this?" Dominique demanded. The girl tossed her blonde hair and kept coming.

Vaulting over a stack of old tires, Dominique landed sprawled on her back and looked up with despair. She was at the fence. There was no where else to go.

Swearing, she dropped her backpack and began to climb, fear giving her strength she didn't know she possessed. Serena screeched in frustration as Dominique teetered on the top of the fence for a moment before falling down onto the other side.

A mass of bushes cushioned her fall, but needles got into her clothes and skin. Dominique muttered foul things under her breath as she brushed herself off, picking out some of the slivers. From the other side of the fence, she could hear the other girls jeering at her.

"Come on, freak! What's the matter? Scared?" Amy taunted.

"Let's go Dom! You're usually more fun than this!"

"Hello? Are you still alive?"

Dominique ignored them, concentrating on where she had ended up. The house loomed in front of her now...she was pretty sure there was fencing all around it, but also had a gate at the front. Going around the house was probably the safest choice. Plus, it would get her the farthest away from Serena and her posse. She could retrieve her bag later.

Bugs hummed and rustled in the knee-high, brown grass as Dominique started forward, feeling the plants brush against her legs. A few weeds had thorns—she winced every time she felt something scratch her.

"There you are!"

Jumping up into the air, Dominique turned, not believing her ears. Serena was about halfway over the fence, a malicious smile on her face as she looked at her prey.

"We're not done playing yet!" she called.

There was only one place to go now. In desperation, Dominique began to run...*toward the house.*

"You're actually going in there?" Serena asked. Even she sounded shocked. "That place is ready to fall down on its own! It doesn't need your help!"

"I think I'll take my chances!" Dominique snarled back, and kicked the back door in. Motes of dust drifted in the air, receding into darkness.

Dominique felt a twinge of hesitation. What if there really *was* something sinister in here? Would it eat her? Kill her? Oh God, why was she doing this-?

"I'll get you first!" Serena shrieked behind her.

Oh yeah. That was why.

The girl ran blindly into the house, feeling her way through the dust clogged rooms and rotten wood. Several times, her foot went through the floor, and she shrieked. Ivy draped across the hallway slowed her progress; like a crazed animal, Dominique struggled against them.

When she finally broke through the plant-filled hall, Dominique slowed. The kitchen was a mess. Dead animals were lying everywhere, and she covered her mouth before continuing. Who knew what diseases they might be carrying?

Wait a minute. Most of these bodies were skeletons, picked clean of all flesh. Cold terror swept through the girl as she realized that something must have eaten them.

"It's probably just a cat," she told herself, trying to calm down. A cobweb brushed her forehead; she screamed.

Okay, she needed to relax. Closing her eyes, she massaged her temples to help get a hold of herself, Dominique opened her eyes, determined to just get through this-

And found herself face to face with something in the shadows.

Two yellow eyes, slit like a snake's, stared motionlessly at her as the occupant of the house sat frozen. Dominique screamed and scrambled back, blindly feeling around for anything she might use as a weapon-

And grabbed hold of something warm...and scaly. In horror, Dominique looked down and saw that she had grabbed a *tail.*

A terrifying hiss broke through the stagnant air, and with only the dim light from the filthy windows to see by, Dominique let go swiftly and stood up, trying not to hyperventilate.

She backed further into the kitchen, and had no idea how to get away. There were *two* sets of eyes now, and they were coming closer...

The hissing, however, seemed to take on a more urgent note the farther she went into the kitchen. Dominique glanced behind her just once to see if she was about to trod on their nest or something.

She found herself standing on the precipice of a gaping hole in the floor. Swaying back and forth, she tried using her arms to keep her balance, all the while deciding between the hole and creatures...which was worse?

"Oh my God!" she screamed, as she began to fall back into the hole. How deep was this thing? She was gonna die in the middle of a haunted house!

All of a sudden, she heard one of the creatures shout. Although she might have been hallucinating at the time, she couldn't have been sure.

But it sounded like *"NO!"*

By the time that fact registered in her frantic brain, Dominique was gone.

And to where?

She had no idea.

3

Yumurango

There was no bottom. That was the first thing that Dominique realized as she continued to plummet into the hole. She screamed, louder than she ever had before.

Blackness surrounded her, and she wasn't sure where she was. The air whipped her hair up above her head, and there was nothing she could do. Groping blindly with her hand, she tried feeling if there was anything there—anything to break her fall!

A flash of light almost blinded her. Crying out in alarm, Dominique shielded her eyes and squinted. Flashes of white and purple came to her eyes, reminding her of a strobe light.

Disorientation set in rapidly, and soon Dominique couldn't distinguish up from down. She squeezed her eyes shut in an effort to shut out the confusing vortex she found herself in.

And suddenly, light invaded her eyes; solid light, not the flashes she had been subjected to.

Hesitantly, Dominique opened her eyes...and screamed.

She was falling through the air, toward a rough, barren landscape that didn't look too hospitable. Looking beneath her, she saw a few scraggly trees. Oh dear...this was gonna hurt...definitely not hospitable!

The first few branches didn't even break her fall. She whipped through them as though they were toothpicks, smashing them to pieces. A large branch beneath the upper canopy slammed into her back; it slowed her down, but it hurt like hell. Scratches appeared on her arms and face as she plummeted.

Finally, she managed to grab hold of one of the lower branches; her arm twisted sickeningly in her socket, but she held on. Her arm socket realigned after she had swung for a moment.

"OW!"

Then, she let go. The last ten feet were quick, and she ended up sprawled on the ground, facing into the sky.

Despite the pain, Dominique sat up quickly, looking all around for anything familiar. Where was she?

Her head swam, and her cheeks burned. Blearily, Dominique leaned against the rough bark of the tree and tried to steady herself. This just had to be a nightmare she was having. Staring at her arm, she gave herself a nice, hard pinch.

"Ow again!" she swore under her breath and rubbed the now red spot. Okay, fine. This wasn't a dream.

But then, where the hell was she?

In this strange place, it looked as though the sun was halfway set. The trees around her were the only tall vegetation in sight; the brush surrounding her on all sides was scarce, altogether presenting a rather unpleasant landscape.

Dominique took a few shaky steps forward, gauging the distance to what appeared to be structures on the horizon. If there was a way to get to this place...there had to be people, right?

God, she hoped so.

So she walked. Soon, the trees she had landed in (Ow) were small specks in the distance as she began to climb a gentle slope, taking in the barren wasteland. So far, there was nothing promising. A few times the bushes had rustled, causing her to jump and scream, but nothing had revealed itself.

But to her right, the movement had suddenly grown more persistent. Dominique slowed her pace and stared at the shifting brush, trying to work up her courage. Clearing her throat, she called out.

"Hello?"

The movement stopped. In trepidation, she waited for a response, but there was none. Gulping, she tried again.

"Is anyone out there? I can hear you!"

This time, she got a response. A small growl, sounding like some crazed animal, floated back to her.

"Okay, just kidding!" she squeaked, and began to run up the hill, tripping over rocks and brush in her haste.

Scrambling faster, the girl shrieked as she reached the hilltop and went sliding down the other side of the hill. She tumbled along until a rock stopped her.

"Ow! Oh, for the love of...you've gotta be kidding me!" she moaned.

"Are you okay?"

Dominique bolted upright. She had heard someone, hadn't she? Or was she finally going out of her mind with fear?

No, there was someone there. Squinting against the backdrop of light, all Dominique could see was a vague silhouette as the figure came closer to her.

"Hey, can you hear me?"

"Oh, uh...yeah, I'm fine. Just slipped."

"You should be more careful. It's getting dark, and you know what that means."

"Yeah, sorry," Dominique said, noticing the buildings around her. She came closer, craving the artificial light and sound of an obviously populated place. Relief flooded through her as she saw people walking through the streets.

But it disappeared just as quickly when she realized it...

Not all of them were human.

Gasping sharply, she forced herself to calm down as she saw the odd intermingling of her kind and other creatures. Slit eyes and fur were present on some of them; others looked like foxes that had decided to walk on two legs. The rest Dominique couldn't identify, but she could see resemblances to other familiar animals.

Jerking her head toward the friendly persona who had helped her, she could see that it was a woman with ears like a cat. The woman arched her eyebrows.

"You're sure you're okay?"

"Oh yeah, I'm fine," Dominique said quickly, though her face must have said differently. Composing herself, she gave the cat-woman a smile.

It was returned, and suddenly, the woman jumped lightly up onto a balcony above them and began to prowl across the railing. Dominique made a distressed noise as she moved into the crowd. A sign above the street, hung by strings, introduced her to the place she was about to enter.

Welcome to Beniz.

This was gonna take some getting used to.

Okay, she had to get her priorities straight. Number one; find out where the hell she was. Two; find some shelter and three...

Three was to get home. It wasn't the best place in the world, but at least Dominique knew what *planet* she was on. The strangeness all around her was already making her brain ache.

A vendor up the street was selling something; newspapers, Dominique gathered. Cheered by the minor display of normality, she headed toward it, ducking between people and creatures as she went. When she got to the kiosk, she stopped and studied the paper.

It had the same date as what she'd left, so she assumed that time wasn't an issue here. The headlines, however, were in a strange language that she couldn't read.

"English versions for humans are over here," the vendor said, jerking his thumb toward another stack. Throwing him a grateful glance, the girl picked one up.

Battle at Theio ongoing; Orphius gaining upper hand.

That was the headline? Confused, the girl flipped over to read the article.

Well, here we go again. Reports from our on scene specialists seem to be finding conclusive evidence that the tyrant Orphius and his army are starting to gain the upper hand in the skirmishes that have been happening around the small town of Theio, just north of the Ankara. Recent accounts from witnesses have claimed that Orphius's hoards of Rhinox and Horgons have finally begun to beat down the men from Keller's forces. The general has been retreating and has now been pushed back to the plains. Other witnesses, however, claim-

Dominique stopped reading, since she had been lost at the first sentence. She had no idea who Orphius or Keller were, but they obviously didn't like one another. And what were Rhinox? Or Horgons?

Another title drew her gaze; *Yet another theft by the infamous Tom Horter.*

There has been little doubt in everybody's mind that Horter is, of course, the most notorious bandit Yumurango has ever seen, and his theft of the Dygon's shrine is no surprise-

"Yumurango?" Dominique tasted the strange word on her tongue, and sighed. So that's where she was. Now the only question was...*where* exactly was "Yumurango"?

She put the newspaper back onto the stack, neatly folded, of course, and turned back to the street. There had to be someplace to stay, in a town with this many...uhh... people.

"Excuse me," she said, grabbing hold of a woman's arm. The lady glanced at the girl and arched an eyebrow.

"Can I help you?"

"Yeah, is there a hotel around here? I've never been to this town before."

"Go up the street and turn left. The inn's right on the corner."

"Thank you," Dominique said, and started out in the direction given. There was still money in her pocket; she had about fifty dollars, since she never left her money at the orphanage. With so many little kids around, she couldn't trust even her small hoard to be safe. Hopefully, it would be enough.

The inn, when she arrived at it, looked decent enough. Through the windows Dominique could see, lights burned bright, and a cheery atmosphere emanated that seemed to relax her.

Opening the door, Dominique was gratified with sudden warmth, and smiled in spite of her situation. She didn't want anything more than to have a comfortable place to rest her head.

The clerk, who looked like an oversized slug, inspected her politely.

"Shall I find you a room, miss?" he asked.

"Yes please," Dominique said. She was embarrassed when her words slurred slightly. He, however, just laughed.

"Had a long day?"

"Yes sir. Umm...how much are the rooms?"

"Thirty dollars,"

"Here," Dominique said tiredly, handing him the cash. Wow, this was cheap for a hotel...maybe it was like in third world countries; dollars were worth more.

"Third floor, room 108," the clerk instructed, after glomming onto the cash and placing it into the cashier. Dominique nodded and turned away, heading toward the stairs near the corner of the lobby.

They were wooden, and squeaked under her weight. For the first flight, the girl took it slowly to avoid being killed from a fall through potentially weak stair boards.

However, they soon proved they were sturdy enough, so she began to walk up at a normal pace. Paintings of sad looking faces stared at her as she reached the top floor. The dusty, faded colors made her feel slightly claustrophobic.

She opened the door to her room, not even caring that the bed was little more than a cot. She fell onto it in a heap, and closed her eyes before her head hit the pillow.

In the next room over, she suddenly heard a stringed instrument start to play. It sounded like a cello, but who was she to know what instruments existed in this strange world?

Still, the song was relaxing, and Dominique wanted to go to sleep...but her mind wouldn't stop working.

How had she gotten here? What was Yumurango? Another world? Dimension? How was she going to get home? *Was* there a way to get back?

Her eyes slid shut, and the sound of the music enveloped her head.

I'll listen to the end of this song, and then go to sleep. She thought. *Just a little while longer...*

Less than a minute later, she was out like a light.

4

Magic

"GET OUT OF HERE!"

Dominique rolled over with a groan. It was too early to be up for sane people...there had to be a few more hours left till school...

"Five more minutes," she mumbled into the pillow.

Wait a minute.

Jerking her head up, Dominique opened her eyes wide as she realized she was in a strange room. Memory flooded back a second later, and she leapt out of the cot she had spent the night in.

Loud noises were coming from outside her door; crashes and bangs that sounded a lot like gunfire. Swearing, she ducked down behind her bed and decided to wait it out.

How had this happened? The last thing she remembered was falling asleep listening to the mysterious cello player...and now BULLETS?

"Look out!" someone shouted. A scream followed, and the sound of running feet. The lock on Dominique's door flew across the room; something had shot it out.

Smoke rolled in, and Dominique covered her mouth and nose as she smelled fire. She needed to get out of here *now.*

"Anyone in here?" a snarling voice came to her ears.

"Search the room!"

Dominique stood up, coughing. They were here to help her, weren't they-?

Bullets suddenly filled the room, and she screamed. So much for helping...

"You get her?" one of them murmured.

"I think so," was the reply. "I hope Orphius doesn't mind we killed civilians."

Orphius's boys, then. Dominique remembered his name in the paper. So what, now they were targeting innocent people instead of their enemy? Rage filled her, and she suddenly felt the urge to do something.

She stood up, not questioning where the urge came from. There were two masked figures standing in her doorway. One laughed.

"Well, looks like you missed her."

"She must have ducked."

Dominique stalked closer to them. They were obviously having such a grand old time...well, she was about to rain on their parade.

Without consciously knowing what she was doing, she whipped her leg around and slammed one of the gunmen with a kick to his head. He went down like a ton of bricks; his partner gasped.

"Hey, what the-?"

Dominique stretched out her hand, and before either of them knew what was happening, the man was down on the floor, totally encompassed in a cloud of black...black something!

Surprise flitted across the girl's features. What had happened? Where had the black substance come from?

Then she noticed it. A thin trail of the stuff was issuing from her hand. In shock, she raised her hand up to her face to inspect it.

Turning around, she looked into the mirror to make sure she wasn't imagining it. Her reflection, however, made her scream.

Not only was her hand leaking black...stuff, and smothering the man on the floor until he passed out (she could feel it working; it was weird), but her eyes were *glowing white.*

Horror made her lose her concentration; the black energy stopped, and her eyes snapped back to their normal (well, normal to her) purple shade.

Shaking all over, Dominique sprinted out the door, away from the scene of the attack. Outside her room, the hotel was in shambles.

Debris filled the entire hallway, and it took her at least five minutes to navigate her way through the rubble. Muttering under her breath, she finally kicked her way out and walked down the now ruined stairs.

The lobby, understandably, wasn't in much better shape. Outside, Dominique could still hear the sounds of conflict, but it was faint and distant.

She coughed out any dust she might have inhaled during the process of making her way through the hotel to the street outside. It was empty everywhere she looked; everyone must have fled the scene. Blearily, she began to wander down the road, looking for any sign of life.

A few dead bodies met her gaze; she looked away quickly, not wanting to realize the full implications of what had happened. Orphius's men had blown through the town without warning...they had killed *innocent people,* seemingly with no regard for their lives at all!

Gritting her teeth, Dominique gave a wordless shout of rage and slammed her fist into the side of a building. She didn't know who this guy, Orphius, was, but she was ready to go and kill him herself.

Before she could shuffle on, however, a noise drew her ear. Whirling, her eyes raked the surrounding area for anything that would try to hurt her. She had no idea where that black energy had come from, but she knew she could wield it...and *would* wield it.

It sounded like a large animal; a loud, snuffling sound that set off all of Dominique's natural alarms. A roar entered her ears, and she winced; it sounded like a human's scream.

Based on the sound's direction, she expected whatever emitted the roar to come around the corner of the closest building; all her attention was focused on that spot.

So naturally, she was surprised when something scooped her up into the air.

Screaming, Dominique looked up to see her abductor. At first, all she could see was a wall of scales...then she saw the whole picture.

The creature looked like a huge snake, but with wings glommed onto every single ridge of its spine, providing it with amazing speed. Two brittle looking arms gripped her to its belly snugly.

"Let me go!" she raged, slamming her fist into the creature's stomach.

Its head popped down to look at her. Dominique made a disgusted noise at it; it was the leering face of an ape, with a wide grin that made her stomach do little frightened flips.

"Son of a...LET GO OF ME!" she screamed, and bit down on its arm. The creature howled with pain and rage, but didn't release her. Greasy strands of hair on its skull blew hard in the breeze.

Growling in frustration, she began to squirm around. The creature made little huffs of frustration as it began to lose its grip on her. That was when she looked at the ground.

"Oh *crap,*" she choked out.

They were at least one hundred feet up...and there weren't any trees this time to catch her.

"Wait just a minute," she squeaked, and grabbed hold of the creature's arms tighter. It made a sound like it was laughing.

Just for that, she slammed her fist into its stomach again. With an exhale of foul breath, the creature faltered, but didn't let go.

Dominique didn't know how long they flew for; at least ten minutes in this awkward position. The creature was taking her somewhere, but the question was...where?

As she was pondering this, the creature suddenly jerked around and accelerated, alarming its passenger. It was almost like it was running from something...but what?

Glancing back, she gaped, her mouth hanging open.

Two large dark figures were starting to close in on them. Bat-like wings cut through the air with powerful strokes, bringing the dark shapes closer to the fleeing creature with every flap.

"This can't be happening," Dominique said monotonously.

Dragons. Two *dragons* were coming up on her captor and her. Black scales glinted in the rapidly rising sun, while their coal red eyes looked at the creature carrying her greedily. One seemed to smile before it dove down at them.

"PULL UP!" Dominique shouted, not caring that the creature probably didn't understand her. The thing was so stupid...

It gave a squawk of pain as the dragon's jaws closed around it, like a hawk with a wriggling snake in its mouth. Its grip on Dominique loosened, but she clung on for dear life with a tenacity that astounded her.

The other dragon came up behind his brethren, roaring something to the one with the prize in his mouth. That one growled threateningly and began to descend.

Dominique knew it was time to let go...unless she wanted to be eaten with it.

Taking a deep breath, she let go of the creature and plummeted toward the ground. A moment of clarity enveloped her mind before she panicked:

This is the third time I've fallen, isn't it?

She looked down, at the impending doom awaiting her. Nothing was going to save her this time; there was only her, and she didn't have the power to fly or anything...

Wait a minute. If that black force that came out of her hands could smother people...could it smother her?

Concentrating for an instant, Dominique remembered how it had felt when the power had come out of her hands. Sort of a rage feeling that seemed to consume her very being...

When she opened her eyes again, she wasn't falling. In surprise, she looked at her hand.

Bingo. It was completely enveloped by her black energy, and she had stopped falling.

Holy crap...she could *fly!*

Euphoria spread through Dominique's mind as she dropped the rest of the way to the ground slowly; when she reached the dirt, she stopped concentrating, and she was back to normal. In amazement, she laughed and looked back up from where she had come from.

The two dragons were gone, but she could still hear the creature's wailing cries. In triumph, she got up and brushed herself off.

Where to next?

Her first move, she figured, was to go back to the city where she had come from. She was alone, and that could prove to be dangerous. There had to be ways to get around this wasteland (or Yumurango, she guessed) faster. Maybe they had cars? Or horses?

Voices sounded in her ear, not too far away. Immediately, her warning bells rang. Were they friend or foe? Where...there! Just ahead of her, down a makeshift path in the ground, coming her way.

Well, from the look of it...they didn't appear dangerous. They looked like a band of wandering travelers who had happened to cross her path. Odd little instruments played a merry tune as they strolled through the wasteland. An old wagon, resembling a covered wagon from old Western times, was pulled by an enormous, lizard-like creature that brought up the rear of the group. It snorted once in tune with the beat, then lapsed back into silence.

"Excuse me!" she shouted. The leader stopped, staring at her. He looked to be about forty to forty five years old.

"Ah," he said. "So you survived the Rhinox? Impressive!"

"I told you she'd make it!" a little girl shouted. The beaten-up, old cap on her head was far too large and kept falling into her eyes. Pushing the cap up over her eyes, the girl stared at Dominique and stated (matter-of-factly), "She looks like a fighter!"

Dominique grinned nervously at the praise and looked toward the leader again. "Umm...you wouldn't happen to be traveling to anywhere populated, would you?"

"Oh sure, we're headed to Implitic. Largest city in Yumurango!"

"It's also the one where the most fighting's been taking place," another member of the group, a sad looking woman, said. "Keller has got the entire place locked up like a prison."

"We're only going to trade with the people inside; we'll be out in a jiffy," the man scolded affectionately. He turned back to Dominique.

"You're welcome to come with us, if you'd like," he said.

"Oh, thank you!" Dominique said, almost falling over in gratitude.

"No problem, but...you're not from around here, are you?"

She looked up with a sheepish grin. "How could you tell?"

"Well, for one thing, most people wouldn't have been scooped up by a Rhinox to begin with...you must be special. You see, those foul beasts have something of an attraction to power. That's why they all love Orphius."

He had started to move the troupe again; Dominique walked alongside him, listening to his words with growing interest.

"So...this guy Orphius," she stated. "Who is he?"

"Ah, my dear. He is one of the two remaining descendants of the Shadow family, some of the most powerful magic workers of all time."

"Magic?" she asked, dubious. He laughed.

"I'm sorry, but I didn't catch your name before we started chatting back there," he said. "I'm Ethan."

"Dominique," she said, offering her hand. He took it and shook it firmly.

"My wife's Gretchen, and my daughter's Amy," he said. The name "Amy" rang a sour bell in Dominique's mind, but she ignored the thought.

"Nice to meet you," said Gretchen and Amy at the same time, which started them giggling.

Ethan grinned. "But anyhow...Orphius has inherited powerful magic from his heritage, and, being an egotistical megalomaniac and all, thinks he can get away with taking over the entire dark side of Yumurango."

"Dark side?"

"My goodness, dear, where in this good world are you from? Yes, the dark side. You're *on* the dark side. The light side is practicing democracy, or so I hear...you see, the two sides have been barricaded from one another for centuries now. We don't get out into the other's world often."

"I see," Dominique murmured. "It probably doesn't help the light side's impression of this side, seeing it at war and all."

"Yes, but not just any war, mind you. You see..."

Ethan leaned in closer. "Orphius isn't the only descendant left. His brother is still alive as well...Keller."

"But I thought he was fighting him," Dominique said, confused. She cocked her head.

"That's the thing; after their parents and two younger siblings died in a fire, they began a quarrel that soon escalated into this whole war. Rumor has it that the two of them blame the other for causing the flames to consume their family."

"That's sad," Dominique said, staring off into space. "You'd think they would be closer than ever, after that."

"Well, with the Shadows, nothing has ever been what it seems. In my mind, I'm glad that their lineage comes to an end with Orphius and Keller."

"How come?"

"Let's just say, the Shadow family members weren't the most compassionate people around...Orphius and Keller are no different. The younger two siblings, however, appeared to have been on a more positive path...that is, until they were burned alive with their parents."

Dominique winced. "And so we're back to square one with the two surviving sons."

"God only knows what children those two men would have...that is, if any woman would consent to be with them!"

Ethan threw back his head and laughed at the thought of the kind of woman that would go for Orphius or Keller. Dominique shook her head and rolled her eyes. Maybe he was crazy...

"But seriously," the man said, taking on a more somber tone. "For five years now, the fighting's been going on...there has been no stopping. Sometimes I wonder if those two will realize what a mess they're making of this land—their home and *our* home."

"It doesn't seem like they would care," Dominique agreed, nodding her head.

"But of course there's still hope," Ethan said slyly. The girl raised her eyebrows for more information.

"There is a secret organization that has been working to annihilate both Orphius's and Keller's armies. Without them, the two men will be forced to go head to head, *mano a mano,* and end this conflict...they call themselves The Red Shield."

"Nice," Dominique said with a snicker.

"Rumors are even flying about that Tom Horter, *the* Tom Horter, is working for them now. They've become a very powerful force if that's true. I swear that man can steal anything..."

"I heard about him," Dominique acknowledged. "He was in the newspaper."

"Dominique, he's *always* in the papers. Every day it seems he steals something else. The man is a genius when it comes to figuring out creative ways to filch anything valuable. But the thing is he's so *young*. I have no idea where he learned it all from."

The girl smiled. "Maybe he's just a natural."

"Maybe," Ethan agreed.

They walked in companionable silence for some time after. Dominique took some time to take in the surroundings. In the distance, she thought she could see a river; it glittered in the slowly setting sun. For now, the temperature was warm...but the girl could feel it getting cooler by the minute as the light dimmed across the plains.

"Oh, look!"

Ethan came to a stop and pointed suddenly, and Dominique whipped her head around to see what he was pointing at. In the distance, she could see several tall towers.

"Is that Implitic?" she asked, squinting to try and see it better. Not a lot of success.

"Yes indeed; see the things circling around the towers? Those are dragons."

"Yeah...I've met them," she said with a grimace. "They didn't seem to like the Rhinox, though."

"That's because, while the Rhinox are attracted to Orphius...Keller can speak to dragons. It's how he's managed to keep the upper hand in this war. While their foot armies are about equal in strength, dragons always win in the air against those Rhinox snakes."

"I like dragons better!" Amy announced from behind them. Ethan laughed.

"Yes, our little dragon lover. She wants to be a trainer someday."

"A trainer for dragons?" Dominique asked, alarmed.

"Not the black variety. Oh no, those are the ones used for Keller's forces. Just the regular type, mind you...there's still some wild ones up in the mountains, or so I hear."

"Honey, we should take a break," Gretchen called. Ethan nodded and stopped. Amy went and pulled on the lizard like creature's reins, bringing it and the wagon to a halt.

Dominique moved closer to inspect it. Although its slit eye looked suspicious, it allowed her to put her hand on its neck and stroke its scaly skin.

"Wow," she murmured. "What is it?"

"Danny's a Shartan," Amy said proudly. "The best Shartan ever!"

She hugged the creature's neck, who began to sniff her hair. She pulled back, laughing.

"That tickles!"

Slowly, Dominique moved her hand to the Shartan's face and looked at him closer. The creature sniffed at her once, and blew hot breath in her face.

"Where did Shartans come from?" she asked. Amy giggled.

"They've always been here. People found them in the Restana woods, a *long* time ago."

The little girl patted Danny on the neck again, and grinned. "He and other Shartans are faster than horses. You see a lot of them around, 'cause people like them so much. But Danny's the fastest!"

With that, Amy un-harnessed the creature and led him off a ways, watching him begin to sniff around the brush on the plains. Dominique watched them for a while, smiling at the smaller child's contentment.

"We're actually lucky to have one," Gretchen said, coming alongside the girl. "My mother was very wealthy, but she lost most of her money when one of Keller's brigades burned her home...before she died, she gave him to us, so we'd have some way of living on the plains."

The girl frowned. "You were routed from your home, too?"

"Yes."

Anger surged up inside her. Here was yet another example of how Keller and Orphius were making these peoples' lives miserable. There *had* to be some way to stop this.

Dominique went to the side and sat down by the wagon, intently watching nothing in particular on the plain, trying to calm her mind so she wouldn't feel so overwhelmed by all that had happened to her.

Ethan was making some food, she saw. Vaguely, she wondered what it was, and if she'd like it...

A cry overhead made her look up. With a frown, she saw the same two black dragons that had earlier freed her from the Rhinox's greasy claws. They swooped overhead, heading straight toward the city. Their red eyes were smug as they roared in Dominique's direction.

She narrowed her eyes as they quickly became specks in the distance. Whether or not those two brothers were blaming each other for a terrible tragedy, they were killing innocent people in their blind quest for revenge...she didn't like that.

"Food's ready!" Ethan called. "Dominique, come on, you've got to eat something!"

The girl looked toward him.

"Keep up your strength so we can reach the city by nightfall! You don't want to be out in the plains when night comes!"

"Sure," she said, and got to her feet.

After all...the city was where she might find her way home.

5

Tom Horter

They reached the city just as dusk was beginning to settle over the plains. Dominique looked behind them nervously as they approached the city gate...two dragons guarded each side of it, looking bored.

Two men were astride them, and they looked down sternly at the approaching group. One of them urged his mount forward, and the dragon slunk over to them.

"What is your business here?" he asked. His mount hissed lightly, startling Danny. The Shartan backed up a few steps, nostrils flared.

"We come to trade; isn't the market in session tomorrow?" Ethan asked, wide eyed and innocent. Dominique suppressed a smile.

"What have you got to trade?"

"A few odds and ends. Would you like to see them? I have this fine little watch in the back-"

"No," the guard interrupted. He obviously wasn't interested in having a conversation with Ethan. Looking at his companion, he cleared his throat.

"You may proceed. But we're keeping an eye on everyone who comes through here. Orphius's troops have been unusually active in this area."

"I hadn't heard," Ethan said faintly. "Come on," he said, waving his family and Dominique forward.

As the girl passed between the two dragons, one of them snarled deeply in its throat, glaring at her. She looked at it in alarm, and realized that she must smell like a Rhinox, having picked up the scent when the creature grabbed her.

She made a rude gesture toward it while its rider wasn't looking, earning her another growl. Ethan and the others were getting ahead of her; she ran to catch up.

Implitic was much different from the other town she had been to. More people, more noise, and they weren't all on foot. Dominique glimpsed Shartans, among other things. The people riding them seemed to be of a higher caste than the others, given their haughty looks and the imperious way they carried themselves. She made a face, irritated by those that felt superior to others, and made a show of it.

"We have arrangements to stay at the Sign of Three tonight," Ethan announced. "It's a bit cheap, but it's the best I could do on short notice."

"Thank you dear," Gretchen said with a small smile. Amy rubbed her eyes and yawned.

"You three should go to bed after we get there," Ethan said.

"No," Dominique said. "Actually, I want to see the sights...you know, since I've never been here before."

"Hopefully you won't again," said someone who had apparently overheard their conversation. Dominique turned.

Whoever had spoken was already gone. Raising an eyebrow, she turned her attention to Ethan again and cleared her throat.

"So...I'll meet you guys there?"

"Do you know where it is?"

"I know how to read the map you gave me earlier today. And ask for directions."

"Well, if you're sure, I guess that's alright."

Dominique smiled. It was nice to have friends in a strange world like Yumurango. Glancing around, she split off from her new friends and began to explore.

The city was alive with colorful lights and sounds. Crowds of humans and non-humans alike wandered here and there, passing through a multitude of brightly decorated booths selling all kinds of food and goods. Loud music blasted at her from a door as she walked by, making her hair stand on end. The singer sounded like nails on a chalkboard...not her style.

She stopped at a booth to get something to eat. Ethan's so called "Tepfer" had been pretty good, and she saw that they had the same thing on the menu. One thing she had learned quickly about Yumurango, however, was that Earth money wouldn't always work for purchases; Ethan had given her some Yumurangonian money earlier. Apparently, only the small towns, like Beniz, accepted money from both worlds. Big cities only went for the local currency. Even then, the Tepfer cost the rough equivalent of two dollars; not bad.

Pocketing her change, the girl continued on her way. And then, of all things...she heard a familiar tune floating through the air.

It was the same cello as before; the one that had lulled her to sleep at the inn during her stay at Beniz. Curiosity overcame her, and she began to follow the sound. Whoever was playing it had been at the same place she had been yesterday...maybe they knew what had happened there.

A crowd of people was clustered around a street corner, listening. Dominique eased her way through the throng so she could see who was playing.

When she got there, however, the answer she wanted wasn't exactly obvious. The figure playing the instrument was cloaked; she couldn't see its face. Even its hands were gloved.

The song abruptly came to a conclusion, and the figure stood. Dominique couldn't help but marvel at how tall it was; at least six feet, if not more.

With the cello properly stowed in a carrying case, the figure slung it across its back and bowed once to the audience. Dominique swore under her breath as it began to move away. Following, she tapped it on the shoulder.

"Excuse me," she said politely. The cloaked figure turned, apparently surprised.

"You were there, yesterday, at the inn, right?" she asked.

"My dear, I've been to many inns," it responded.

The voice was male, of a medium range. It had a warm tone that made Dominique comfortable with him at once. Clearing her throat, she stepped back.

"What I meant was, do you have any idea what caused the fighting?"

"If you haven't noticed, two madmen are at war. Of course there's going to be fighting."

Dominique frowned. "I was just asking."

He paused, thinking. "How old are you?"

"Seventeen," she answered automatically. Then, she eyed him warily. "Why?"

"You're old enough to understand classical music; did you like my song?"

"Uhh...yeah, you're good," she said, blinking. "Again...why?"

"Because I don't think you're going to hear it again," he said.

And, very suddenly, he grabbed her and spun her around.

"Hey!" she shouted. "What gives? Let me go!"

Out of nowhere, an entire squad of police had appeared, wielding strange and dangerous looking weapons. All the weapons were centered on the cloaked figure; he was using Dominique as a shield.

"Let me go!" she raged, trying to kick him. Somehow, she kept missing.

"Let her go, Horter!" one officer commanded. Dominique froze.

Horter? As in, Tom Horter? In shock, she turned to look at her abductor. This was the infamous thief that had stolen almost every valuable item in Yumurango?

Well, he didn't look like much. Dominique was just about to try squirming out of the thief's grasp when one of the police fired. The shot was aimed right at the thief's head, but he ducked with unnatural agility, and only his hood was shot down, uncovering his face.

What she saw made her gasp.

Instead of an ordinary man's features, as she had expected, there was a skull. Hollow eye sockets stared out at the world, but she saw his mouth was closed, somehow...

"Oh, that's real nice," he snapped. His mouth opened and closed as he talked...some kind of layer...

His eyes, she noticed, also changed shape. Right now they looked angry, and his brow was furrowed.

"What *are* you?" she murmured.

"I think it's time to go," he said.

And suddenly, he tucked her under his arm and ran. Dominique screamed as she was taken through the streets, seeing blurred faces pass by as the skeleton ran with amazing speed.

Through the crowd, she suddenly saw a flash of a familiar face.

"ETHAN!" she screamed. His face was a mask of horror as he attempted to push through the crowd to her, but it was too late. The thief was too fast.

"I'm telling you, let me go!" she screamed.

"Look, just bear with me for a few more minutes," he said hastily. "I'll let you go after this is over; I promise."

Dominique was so stunned by his sincerity that she stopped struggling and stared up at him. He was obviously concentrating on getting out of there alive. After all, he was just a thief, not a murderer...

Right?

Shouts of protest from behind them made Dominique swivel her head back around to see what was going on. The police were trying to get through the crowd, with little success. To her surprise, she found the whole situation amusing.

She laughed slightly, and Tom looked down at her in surprise.

"What?"

The girl just shook her head.

"Ah, here we are!" Tom shouted.

Dominique looked around, confused. What was he talking about? All she could see was the sea of people around them-

Before she could react, the skeleton had bent down and removed a manhole cover. He dove in...with her in tow.

Dominique screamed as darkness closed in around them, feeling the air rush past her face. This couldn't be happening...a *fourth* time? She needed a break from this falling business.

To her surprise, Tom kept hold of her even when they landed (He must have had practice with carrying things down his escape routes before).

They were in a brightly lit hallway. Torches, the source of the light, lined the entire length of the hallway as far as Dominique could see. In amazement, she gaped.

"Can you walk?" the skeleton asked, setting her upright. The girl nodded numbly, but sat down on the ground, hard.

"Umm...about the whole walking thing..." he said doubtfully, watching her. She glanced up at him with a blank expression.

"Where are we?" she asked dully. He arched a bony brow and kneeled down, staring her in the face.

"I think you're in shock," he said, seeming shocked himself. "That wasn't even one of my flashier getaways."

"Shut up," Dominique snapped, and after a couple of minutes of sitting quietly, she rose to her feet. She had calmed herself down now. Tom rose as well, towering above her.

"So tell me," he said. "Since you probably already know my name...what's yours?"

She stared at him in disbelief.

"My *name?* You expect me to tell you my *name?* After you *kidnapped* me and dragged me into an underground tunnel? I mean, God only knows where we are right now!"

"We're under the city, in a secret maze of passages," the skeleton said, sounding bored. "There's no need to freak out."

"Freak out? *Freak out?* Well, excuse me for acting like a normal person would in a situation like this!"

"My God, I've never understood girls..." the skeleton said, rubbing his bony temples and beginning to walk away. With nowhere else to go, the girl followed him.

"Hey, where do you think you're going? You can't just ditch me here!"

"Watch me," Tom muttered.

"That's not fair!"

"Life isn't fair!"

"What's your problem?"

"My problem is *you* being so annoying! Why did I have to pick you?"

Dominique swiveled in front of him, pushing her finger into his ribcage.

"You. Take me back...NOW!" she screamed into his face.

"I don't have to if I DON'T WANT TO!" he shouted back. "Who the hell put you in charge of this operation? I'm the one who started it!"

"Well I'm gonna be the one to finish it! Now *take...me...back!"*

They stopped for a moment, breathing hard from their shouting. Staring each other down, Dominique finally rolled her eyes.

"Please?"

Tom hesitated at her change of tact. She was giving him a sad look now...he had always been a sucker for sad looks...

"Alright, fine," he said with a sigh. He seemed to deflate even as she watched him. "But first I've gotta stash some of this junk I stole today."

"Where is it?" she asked.

Without saying anything, Tom took his cello case off his back and opened it. The instrument was in there...but so was jewelry.

"Not bad, eh? Picked them off people who came too close," he said to himself, looking at the necklaces and bracelets. He inspected a large, green gem with a half smile.

"Wow," Dominique muttered, impressed in spite of herself. She looked at the treasure in the case. "I guess you really are a master thief."

"Why, thank you," Tom said. "Anyway, just wait here while I go-"

"Not gonna happen," the girl snapped. "Like I said before...you're not ditching me here alone. You said you would take me back..."

"Alright, alright," he said tiredly. "Follow me."

With that, he closed the lid to his case and started down the hall. Dominique hurried to keep up with his long strides, muttering under her breath.

"Mind if I ask a question?" she asked.

The skeleton shrugged. "Go ahead."

"Umm...not to be rude, but what *are* you?"

He laughed. "That's a good question, and one I honestly don't know the answer to. Not that it matters."

When he glanced over his shoulder, the girl could see the tense look on his face. Apparently, this wasn't a talk he was enjoying.

"So...how long have you been doing this, exactly?" she asked, in an effort to spark up an easier path to the conversation. Tom turned to look at her.

"I'm not sure, exactly. Since I was a teenager."

"How old are you?"

"Twenty three. Or at least, I'm pretty sure."

"Pretty sure?"

"Well, since I don't have any parents, we can't really be sure, now can we?" he snapped. "Anyway, June fifteenth for a birth date works just fine for me. I sort of picked it randomly."

"Hmmph. Well, happy almost birthday." June fifteenth was a week from now, and Dominique didn't really think she'd see this guy again. Might as well be courteous...

"Why thank you," he said distractedly. "Ah, here we are."

He stopped at a particular part of the tunnel and kneeled down, tracing his long fingers along a point. Then, he pressed down.

The stone caved in, in the shape of a perfect circle. A smile flicked across his lipless mouth as he grinned up at the girl.

"Ta da."

Dominique arched an eyebrow.

The impression in the wall was beginning to grow, the stones simply disappearing. The girl realized she was gawking.

"What's the matter? Never seen a little magic?" the skeleton asked, giving her an odd glance as he stepped into the hidden passage.

"Of course I have!" she said, acting shocked. (It was true, in a way...)

Following him, Dominique looked around suspiciously. She couldn't see him anymore, and it was darker in this tunnel. Gulping, she rubbed her arms against a sudden chill and looked around with a growing fear.

"Hello?" she called. "Hey, where'd you go?"

Since no one answered, she rolled her eyes and started to press forward, wondering how she had lost track of him so quickly. He had been right in front of her just a moment ago-

"HA!"

From out of nowhere, someone grabbed her shoulder. Dominique screamed and whirled around, slamming whoever was there with her strange power.

Tom ducked out of the way just in time, grabbing her wrist and watching the black energy with interest. With some amusement, he turned his gaze to her.

"Well...what have we here?" he asked. Dominique yanked her wrist out of his grasp, shuddering at the touch of bone.

"None of your business," she snapped. Her eyes returned to normal; she stepped back, watching him cautiously.

"Listen," he said. "Are you going to tell me your name, or not?"

"Not unless you've given me a reason to trust you," she snapped. "Especially now. Besides, what can you do? You must know that I can escape anytime I want to."

"Really?" Tom said vaguely, inspecting something on the floor. Dominique glanced down to see a small diamond, glittering on the ground.

"Must have dropped it," he muttered. "Anyway...about you escaping, why would you want to run? If either Orphius or Keller find out about your power, they're going to recruit you into their army."

"I don't use my powers that often," she said. "I've only had them for-"

"Ah ha!" the skeleton said, snapping his fingers. "So you're an amateur. I suspected as much."

Dominique frowned, irked at his words. "What's that supposed to mean?"

"Nothing," he said quickly. "I'm just saying that you'd be safest traveling with me."

She laughed. "Are you kidding? You're the most wanted man in Yumurango. Why would anyone want to travel with you to be *safe?*"

"Why do you think I'm a thief? Prison is a better fate than being enlisted into those armies! No one who goes in comes out...*ever.*"

He stared off into space, and she frowned. There was obviously some personal connection here, but she couldn't see what.

Silence followed his words for a minute. Dominique looked up at him, only to see that he was staring off into space. Finally, she shook his shoulder.

He snapped back into reality. "Oh, uh...sorry."

"That's okay," she said. "Did you know someone who...didn't come out?"

Tom ignored the question. "Come on," he said. "We're almost there."

They walked on in silence. Dominique glanced at the thief out of the corner of her eye, wondering how she had gotten herself into this mess. He was obviously pleasant enough, but the whole 'wanted thief' thing was a little much...

Tom stopped suddenly; Dominique looked ahead and saw they had come to two heavy, wooden doors.

Bracing himself against them, the skeleton pushed; they opened with a creaking sound, and Dominique gasped.

"Oh my God,"

In front of her, inside a huge stone cavern, was the largest store of items she had ever seen; mounds of gold were to the left, accompanied by precious gems and other objects of value. Gleaming suits of armor and swords were stacked carelessly up the entire side of the cavern.

To the right, however, were more mundane items. Books upon books were stacked on top of one another. There must have been thousands of books; easily more than her school library contained. Dominique looked at a few of the titles with interest as she passed by.

Tom dashed over to a corner and began to transfer the items he had stolen to the already swollen pile. Whistling cheerfully, he glanced up at what the girl was doing.

Dominique had somehow been drawn over to the large collection of swords, feeling each of their hilts. She stopped at one. It was in the scabbard still, but the silver symbols etched into the hilt were strangely...familiar.

She cocked her head, staring at it. Grasping the hilt, she drew it from the scabbard and held it up.

Suddenly, the cavern light brightened and reflected from the blade, blinding her. She shielded her eyes from the glare with her arm. Almost immediately, the light died down, and she looked eagerly at the sword.

The blade was silver, and was inscribed with the same type of symbols that were on the hilt. Its highly polished surface reflected her face, and she was well aware of how dirty her hair looked.

She made a face into the mirror-like blade, but stopped when she saw Tom arching a brow at her. Rolling her eyes, she held up the sword.

"Where did you get this?" she asked.

He smiled. "It was one of the hardest treasures to steal. I took it from Orphius himself...it's a family heirloom."

"Of the Shadows?" Dominique clarified, looking down at it.

"Yeah. I heard that Keller had men searching for it too. Too bad I got it first!"

The skeleton snickered once. "He was pretty pissed off when he found out about it."

"How do you know?"

"Well, let's just say that Keller's not very good at controlling himself. I could hear him screaming at his men as I ran away with the sword."

"He's not a fan of yours, then."

Tom laughed. "Not exactly...whatever he wants, I get first. It's kind of a mutual hatred. Actually, I'm a little afraid of what he'd do if he gets his hands on me."

"Clearly, Orphius hates you because you're usually stealing from him," Dominique said.

"Exactly. I'm the odd man out in this war. Another reason to be a thief, I might add."

Dominique just shook her head.

"Well, I'm all done," Tom announced, standing up and slinging his cello onto his back again. "We can get out the way we came in, or-"

He was suddenly cut off. A resounding roar came through the tunnel they had come from...it sounded like a dragon.

"Oh dear," the skeleton said.

"So, about that other way..."

"Yeah. Come on!"

Grabbing her wrist, he began to sprint toward the opposite direction of the cavern, away from the door. Dominique had to grab onto Tom in order to keep up. Looking back, she saw shadows from the pursuing forces beginning to emerge. The sound of scales scraping against the stone wall alerted her to a dragon's sure presence.

"Gotta move faster than this!" Tom warned, and, without another word, scooped her up and ran with her in his arms. Dominique voiced her protest, but she soon shut up as she realized that the dragon was getting closer. She heard snorts and growls, now...it was only a matter of time before it got to them.

"Hey, let me go!" she shouted. "I've got an idea!"

"What do you suggest?" he shouted back. "That thing's *pissed.* When it gets to us, the first thing it'll do is-"

Dominique smacked his head. "Drop me NOW!"

Tom obliged, and she landed sprawled on her stomach as she turned to face the threat. She saw the dragon's head now; its red eyes illuminated the area in front of it in a hellish light as it saw her.

Oh God, it was big. Way bigger than Dominique had thought. Her feeble idea of fighting it back with her powers evaporated in her mind like smoke.

With a roar, it reared its head up as high as it could in the tunnel. Dominique crouched, waiting for it to make its move.

"I hope you know what you're doing," a voice beside her murmured. She turned in surprise to see Tom crouching beside her.

"What are you doing here? The point was for you to escape!"

"Well, I can't do that, you're a girl!"

"Excuse me?" Dominique snapped. "We'll discuss sexism later, thank you!"

"That's if we have a later."

The dragon was obviously working on something spectacular; behind it, Dominique could hear shouts of complaints as it took up the entire hallway. Among the voices, she heard one that was incredibly deep.

"Oh God," Tom said. "That's Keller. Why is he here? The only reason I was in this city in the first place is because he wasn't-"

"Shut up!" Dominique hissed. "Uhh..."

"I thought you said you had an idea!"

"That was before I saw how *big* this thing is!"

"Well that's just great! We're *screwed!*"

The dragon opened its mouth, and within its gullet, the girl could see flames beginning to build up. She swore.

"Alright...here goes nothing!" she shouted, and propelled her energy toward the creature. A black spear lanced into the dragon's mouth, piercing its snout from the inside out. The dragon roared with frustration and pain. Tom watched with a grim expression.

"Only fire can kill a thing like that," he muttered. "Girl! Keep going!"

"What are you doing?" she called, without taking her eyes away from her target. The expenditure of power exhausted her; she fought to keep the flow stabilized.

She winced. "I can't keep this up!"

"Then let me help!"

With that, he stretched both his hands out...and let his own magic fly.

A torrent of yellow fire intermixed with the black energy Dominique had flying from her own body, and she gasped.

"I didn't know you had magic!" she shouted, above the roar of flames.

"Well, I don't even know your name!" he shouted back.

"Dominique!"

"What?"

"MY NAME IS DOMINIQUE!"

And suddenly, the dragon exploded.

Dominique shrieked as pieces of it went flying everywhere, leaving a charred skeleton behind. She felt as if she had just taken a bath in dragon guts. It smelled disgusting.

"This," she said tonelessly. "Is the worst day of my life."

Tom swore and began to run, motioning for her to follow.

"Let's get out of here while we can!"

The girl sprang after him, running for her life. Behind her, she heard the coarse shouts of men, and that one deep one...

Okay, she had to look. Glancing back over her shoulder, she saw one figure standing out above the rest.

He was at least Tom's height, if not taller. Unlike her companion, however, he looked solidly built. What she could see of him was an armor shell; even his face was completely covered-

"Dominique! Come on!" Tom shouted. She realized she had paused, watching the surreal scene and unconsciously wiping off the dragon residue from her body, and all the while Keller had been getting closer.

"You there, stop!" the armored figure shouted, beginning a final sprint toward her and Tom. His voice was a baritone that seemed to shake Dominique's bones. Swearing, she leapt into the air and tried to make her powers work.

In a matter of seconds, she was hurtling through the air, out of control. Up ahead, at the end of the cavern, there was a small opening, where one person might be able to squeeze through.

Aiming for it, she screamed as she rocketed through, barely sliding her body through the small opening.

And suddenly, she slammed into Tom. The skeleton gave a shout of surprise as he was smacked back into the ground.

Dominique blinked in the sudden brightness, realizing they were well outside of the city. The plain was laid out before her, and she bit back a groan at the thought of traversing it again. Rocks crumbled beneath her feet as she moved cautiously.

She didn't get much of a chance to recover. Tom hauled Dominique to her feet and began to run again.

"Hold on a sec!" she gasped. "You can't possibly run forever!"

Tom laughed. Looking over his shoulder at her, he smiled.

"Yes, I can."

Dominique just rolled her eyes.

This guy had to be insane.

6

The Pit

"Okay!" Dominique gasped, stopping and resting her hands on her knees. She was gasping for air; she had been running at full speed for at least ten minutes. "Let's stop!"

Tom skidded to a halt in front of her. He sighed and crossed his arms as she saw how out of breath she was.

"If you think Keller's going to wait to send dragons after us-"

"Let's just find someplace to hide!" she gasped. "My God, you don't always have to run."

"Whatever," he said. But he too, was breathing hard. Since they were on the outskirts of town, there weren't many people...he could afford to relax a little.

They were in the middle of nowhere, by some old remains of a town that looked like it had been burned. The few structures that remained standing were blackened, and Dominique could still smell old smoke.

"What happened here?" she asked. Tom looked toward her grimly.

"Dragons," he murmured. "Carnage sanctioned by Keller."

Going over to a vine covered, old stone wall, he leaned against it and slid down, staring up at the blue, cloudless sky. Dominique joined him.

"So," she started. "What's next? Keep running? Find an inn somewhere? You should be in disguise, you know."

"I sort of dropped my cloak; this cello's heavy enough," he said, patting the case fondly. "But it's my baby; I'm not leaving it anywhere."

Dominique snorted. "I wonder how you remember to carry it anywhere when you're running for your life."

"I'm used to it. What can I say?"

The girl sighed and leaned her head back.

"Dominique," Tom started hesitantly. "How old are you?"

"Seventeen," she said, just as cautiously. "Why?"

"*Only* seventeen? Good God, where are your parents?"

"I don't know," she said. "I don't remember anything from before I was twelve."

"Huh," he said. "So you're an orphan too?"

"Yeah."

She kicked a rock with her foot and watched it skip across the road.

"Sucks, doesn't it?" he murmured.

She nodded. "Sometimes, I just feel like...I don't know who I really am."

"Well, I guess you would feel that way, with no memory."

Dominique snorted. "Thank you ever so much."

"That would be my job. Anyway, can we go now? You've had your rest."

"You needed it too," she reminded him testily. "Where to?"

"Well, unless I can get in touch with some of my colleagues, we could always head toward the capital."

"What city is that?"

Tom looked at her for a long while. "Umm...how do you not know that?"

She stopped, suddenly embarrassed. "Uhh, well, that is-"

"Hold on," he said, a delighted grin suddenly lighting up his face. "Are you from the other side of the portal? Earth, is it called?"

Dominique looked at him. "Uhh...yeah. Do you know about it?"

"Only that a long time ago, the two worlds used to trade using those portals. They've been completely sealed off for ages."

He laughed. "No wonder you seemed so out of it. I was beginning to wonder if you'd just woken up from a coma or something!"

"Shut up," Dominique snapped. He grinned playfully, and she rolled her eyes.

"Are you going to answer my question, or not?" she snapped.

"Taraban," Tom said. "That's the capitol. And the best thing is that Orphius and Keller have no troops there. It's not a tactically brilliant place, so they wouldn't want to waste their men."

Apprehension suddenly filled the girl's mind. She looked back toward the city, thinking of Ethan and his family.

"So, there's no chance of going back to Implitic?"

"Not if you want to get caught."

Dominique sighed. "When do we go?"

"Right now," Tom said, standing. "That is, if you want to stick with me for a while."

Dominique stood up with him. "Yes," she said. "I may be insane, but I actually want to."

He smiled. "Then let's go."

Back in Implitic, three rows of men were standing stock still, even afraid to breathe. Their eyes jerked from side to side in an involuntary gesture, and sweat beaded from their brows. The crowds of Implitic moved away and gave them a wide berth, staring at them with wide eyes.

People moved even faster, however, once they saw the two dragons soaring over the buildings. They knew who rode one of the dragons...and who it was coming to "thank" these men for their failed mission...

Silence, absolute silence, descended upon the entire street as the dragons alighted to the ground, sending deep vibrations through the ground and into the crowd. Their red eyes bored into the men's faces, and they growled slightly.

The figure which had been crouched between the neck and shoulders of the head dragon jumped down. His boots made a loud *thud* that resounded through the still air.

Now, the soldiers straightened even further. Their general's very presence made them all nervous. He was powerful, far more powerful than any of them could ever hope to be.

And Keller knew it. As his hulking silhouette crossed the front line of his men, he could sense the fear in them. His bond with dragons had heightened his senses and perception, making it even easier to detect the slight twitching of their eyes, and the trembling of their hands.

He stopped in front of one; a younger man, who had been recruited recently. His name was Tomar, or so he thought.

"You," he said. The man flinched at the sound of his commander's voice.

"Can you tell me why I'm here?"

Tomar gulped. "Because you came to see why we didn't catch...him."

"And who is this *him* that you're speaking of?"

"T-Tom Horter, sir," he stammered.

Keller stopped pacing. His helmeted head slowly, *slowly* turned in the soldier's direction.

"Yes," he hissed. "Tom Horter...LISTEN UP!"

His sudden shouting made a few men jump, and the fear and dread became even more apparent on their faces.

"If anyone ever, EVER fails me again, your ENTIRE UNIT will be fed to the flock!"

He pointed toward the dragons; they snarled menacingly and seemed amused when the men blanched. One bared its teeth in a silent hiss.

Keller grabbed Tomar by the collar of his uniform and, with one arm, lifted him up the foot that he needed to be eye to eye.

"AM I CLEAR?" he shouted into the man's face. "Tom Horter is an obstacle in my way to killing Orphius! We need BOTH of them dead!"

"Yes sir!" Tomar screamed, his voice shrill with fear. The general dropped him onto the ground, leaving the soldier cowering on the ground in a heap, grateful for his life.

"I'll expect a full report on the pursuit," he snarled, and stalked away. Each and every soldier expelled a sigh of relief.

The general stormed deeper into the barracks of his troops in Implitic, not even noticing the men that dove out of his way to avoid being trampled and crushed. No others in the barracks dared move until he slammed the door to his cabin.

Inside, the man removed his helmet; no one had seen his face for five years now, and it would stay that way. Wearily rubbing his face, he went to the bathroom and splashed cold water on it.

He looked up, staring at his hollow, bleary reflection. Lack of sunlight to his skin had left it nearly bleach white, and his violet eyes were underlined with dark circles from lack of sleep. His dark hair was cut short, and his cheekbones more defined than they had been just half a decade ago.

He shook his head. This entire feud with his brother had escalated into something far worse than either of them had imagined. They were involving all of Yumurango now...how was the winner to restore order when it was over?

And there was little doubt in his mind that *he* would be the victor. Orphius was clever, but he was the younger brother. Everyone knew that he was starting to lose his grasp on several key areas of the plains. It was only a matter of time before Keller crushed his armies and moved in for the kill.

Then, and only then, would his family be avenged. Orphius had caused that fire, had made it spread throughout the mansion.

Keller squeezed his eyes shut and hung his head, feeling the usual gall rise up within him at the memories. Everyone he had cared about, even his sweet little sister, had been incinerated in those flames...

And to see the look on his brother's *face.* Orphius had been jubilant now given the chance to claim their father's throne. It had been too much; Keller had snapped.

So now they were here, surrounded by their own armies, trying to kill one another.

At the least, he thought. *It makes for uncomfortable family reunions.*

Laughing at his grim sense of humor, he shoved himself away from the sink and thought to other, more current events.

Horter. That damnable skeleton had been stealing more things from his brother than usual. Things that *he* needed to aid him in this war. If he wanted to defeat Orphius, then he needed to kill Tom first. And who had that girl been? He hadn't gotten a very good look at her.

No matter. Keller moved over to the window and looked out at his mobilizing troops. A few dragons were beginning to get irritated; he would have to step out and diffuse the situation soon.

Wherever Tom and his accomplice were, he would find them. Whoever they turned to would hand them over out of fear. No matter how long it took, he would find them and make them pay.

That was one of the perks of being powerful.

"Okay," Dominique said, looking at Tom. "Where are we going?"

She had *assumed* they were heading for Taraban, the capitol, but so far, all they had done was cross an enormous river (using a boat Tom had stolen), and had walked across the barren plain for about a day.

"I already told you; to the capitol," he whispered back, confirming her assumption. There were people moving around now, and he had just "borrowed" a cloak. Even with the cloak, he had to talk quietly to avoid recognition.

"We're still miles from the capitol, and it'll take some time to get there."

"So why are we wasting time going to a bar in this dumpy town?"

It was true; the town around them had obviously seen better days. The sign that announced its name, *Grimslow,* was covered in dirt and grime. Dominique could barely read it. Most of the citizens in this town looked unfriendly, to say the least. One man, his skin glinting blue in the midday sun, leered at the girl as she and the thief approached the bar's entrance.

"Because bars can be the best source of information out there. Do you know how many times I've evaded troops because some drunken idiot turns out to be a spy? It's hilarious. This particular one's given me some great intel. We may come across troops on our way to Taraban, and I want to avoid them. So..."

He grinned. "We go in."

"If you say so...but I'm underage. Don't forget that." the girl said, dubious.

"Just stick with me, alright?" he asked, reaching out with a (now gloved) hand to muss her hair. She smacked it away.

"Stop that!"

Laughing, he held open the door for her. Inside, she could hear blaringly loud music.

Looking at him with obvious distaste, Dominique reluctantly stepped in. Tom followed, the door swinging shut behind them.

The minute it closed, Dominique felt claustrophobic. Lights flashed different colors in every direction, and the heat from the sweating bodies was nearly overwhelming with so many people packed in together—she was finding it hard to breathe...or even catch her breath.

"Okay, I don't like this!" she shouted, beginning to backpedal. The skeleton caught her and urged her forward.

"Here, we can go over to the cages. There'll be more room there," he explained, speaking close to her ear to overcome the noise.

"Cages?"

He didn't answer. Grabbing her arm so they wouldn't separate, the skeleton began to quickly make his way through the crowd. Dominique kept up with him just fine. It wasn't as if she wanted to be left alone with the stinking multitude in the bar anyhow.

Tom had been right; there was more room to breathe just to the side of an enormous, underground pit. Dominique gasped in as much air as she could while trying not to hyperventilate.

"Will you be alright?" he asked, shaking her shoulder. She nodded and stared blearily at the scuffed dirt at the bottom of the pit.

"I'm fine," she insisted. He shrugged.

"I'm going to go get a drink; do you want anything?"

She glared.

"Alright, alright...I know...I know...underage. Sorry."

As soon as he left, however, Dominique began to grow nervous. The people around her eyed her with unfriendly looks and murmured to each other. A few of them stared at her with openly astonished gazes.

"Purple eyes," she heard one man murmur. "She has purple eyes."

Why should her eyes matter?

Ignoring the stares, and clearing her throat, she looked at the pit. There was a dome of fencing that spread all the way up to the roof of the building...what was it for?

From the corner of her eye, Dominique saw large, glowing orbs on each side of the dome come to life. Dragons were displayed on each of their surfaces, which she glanced at curiously. Okay then...

"Alright!" someone shouted. "Let's see the worms!"

Worms? Not exactly a fitting name for a dragon. The girl thought to herself as she looked down at the hole again. It was rather large for a wrestling event, wasn't it?

The crowd around her began to roar, and more people began to press in on the edge of the fence, seemingly eager to watch a spectacle that Dominique had no knowledge of. A few of them were exchanging bets, and nearly all were shouting at the top of their lungs.

And then, as if there *wasn't* enough loud sound in the murky air, an announcer came on, and a set of speakers blared.

"Ladies and gentlemen," he announced in a deep and resonating baritone voice. *"Are you ready for the biggest match of the evening?"*

"YES!" everyone roared. Raucous laughter followed.

"Then let's get ready...for DRAGON FIGHTING!"

The roar of approval that greeted his words was astonishing. Wincing, Dominique cupped her hands over her ears and tried to ignore the throbbing in her brain.

But then, over the mind-numbing noise, she heard one sound rise above all else; the roar of a dragon, saturated with rage. Looking down into the gaping pit, her eyes widened.

A large male dragon had tromped into the arena. Orange, with black spikes; its yellow eyes were wide with hate as it looked around at the teeming masses of humans and assorted creatures. Spreading its wings, it roared again.

Dominique shook her head. This was horrible! They put dragons into a pit and made them fight? Nothing like this should be legal-

From the other side of the pit, a gate began to open. A minor hush fell over the crowd as they watched a yawning tunnel present itself.

A single claw emerged. Unlike the other dragon, this one was white, with a slightly opaque sheen. It reflected the light as it twitched, once, experimentally.

Dominique gripped her sword tighter. This dragon was *enormous.*

As it slithered all the way out into the light, a few members of the crowd gasped. Apparently, she wasn't the only one who had been surprised by its size.

It stood about twice as tall as the other dragon, and was more defined in its muscles and stature. The regal way it held its head reminded Dominique of royalty. Large, elegant spikes ridged its spine, ending with a single, spiraling horn in the middle of its forehead. Its scales were white, but she could see numerous scars that had been recently healed. Finned ears quivered in the air, catching every sound. But what held most Dominique's attention were its eyes.

They were a beautiful, turquoise blue, which apparently was a rarity among Yumurango's dragons, and Dominique was startled by the *intelligence* in them. Unlike the other dragons she had seen, those eyes had a sparkle that set this dragon apart.

It pranced into the center of the ring, eyeing the other dragon coldly. Then, without another thought, it spat flame at its opponent.

Dominique watched with amazement at the scarlet flames that licked out of the creature's jaws. Its teeth were easily six inches long...

"There she is," one man near the girl murmured. "The greatest dragon that ever lived, or so they say."

The girl gulped.

Inside the arena, the small orange dragon zipped out of the way just in time to avoid the blast. It sprang into the air, attempting to evade its fate as long as possible. Dominique saw, now, why they needed the fencing to the roof—to keep the combatants in.

The white female dragon roared again and sprang after her quarry, flying just as agilely as the small one. She did a few corkscrews in her pursuit, until she easily caught up with the other dragon.

With a terrified squawk, the orange dragon whipped around and slammed its tail into the white one's face. A hiss of rage followed; the female cocked her head back like a snake and jabbed at it.

Its tail was caught between her jaws; delicately, as though she had expected it to happen, the white dragon swung the other creature around in circles a few times, then threw him down to the ground. The crowd screamed with delight; tonight, they would see blood!

The orange male lay there, stunned, as the obvious victor of the battle spiraled downward toward it. The female's blue eyes never left its fallen form as she landed lightly and pressed one talon onto its neck.

The animal obviously knew what was going to happen next; giving a pitiful mewl, it stared back at her with unblinking eyes.

Dominique held her breath. What would the white one do?

She seemed to think for a moment. Then, surprisingly, the female released her opponent and began to stalk across the arena, back to her tunnel.

Before anyone could begin to applaud her victory, however, the orange one leapt up and lunged at the back of her neck with a horrific screech. Dominique tried to scream a warning, but the words stuck in her throat. That beautiful creature was going to be-

Her thought wasn't yet finished when the white dragon whipped her head around and aimed her spiral horn straight at the incoming target.

The orange dragon squawked with surprise, but its momentum would not allow it to stop. To the huge amusement of the crowd, it impaled itself on her horn, screeched for the last time, and slowly went limp, hanging like meat on a butcher's hook.

Shaking her head, the white dragon let the corpse fall to the ground, but then did a curious thing. Lowering her head, she *bowed* to the fallen dragon before turning around and leaving.

Thunderous applause erupted around Dominique, and she found herself joining them. That dragon was amazing!

A man had run into the arena below; the orange dragon's trainer. With a shout of disbelief, he began to stomp around his dead dragon, shaking his fists in the air with obvious rage, and shouting at the tunnel where the white dragon had gone.

When her roar answered his threats, however, he fell comically back onto his rear with fright, bringing on even more hilarity in the crowd.

Dominique felt a hand on her shoulder; she jumped, but relaxed when she saw it was just Tom.

"Did you see that?" she asked, pointing toward the scene of the match. He nodded grimly.

"I saw it on the orb," he said, jerking his hand. "We'd better get out of here. I think someone might've recognized me."

"Fine by me," Dominique said quickly. The last thing she wanted was to stay here *longer.*

"Are dragons usually that big?" she asked. "You saw that white one."

"No," Tom said. He seemed concerned. "Unless they've got magic."

A dragon? With magic?

Oh goodie.

7

The White Dragon

Why me? The creature asked himself. *Why is it always, always me?*

He was *always* the one to go tell their commanding officer when things went wrong. Everyone always volunteered him, almost automatically. So what if Keller's men had beaten them *all* to their objective? It was the unit's fault, not just his!

Maybe it was because he was a Horgon. He knew that his people weren't exactly the most beautiful people Yumurango had ever been home to, with their slimy skin and yellow eyes. The fangs didn't help either. But still, all those stupid human males had some egotistical issues that needed to be worked out. Being in Orphius's army required being at least mildly compatible with other species. It was the one advantage the man had over his brother; his army worked together, while Keller forced the humans and dragons together in an unnatural allegiance.

So here he was, approaching the center of the camp that had been set up as a temporary base. A few minutes earlier, three Rhinox had flown in from the north. He wondered what was going on.

"You there!" a corporal barked. The Horgon jumped nervously, shedding some of his natural slime. "Where are you going?"

"To report to the lieutenant," he said, confused. "Why? What's wrong?"

The guardsman who had asked him looked worried. "We have a special guest."

A sharp intake of breath was the Horgon's only response. In this place, there was only one man who was a *special* guest.

He jerked his head to the large tents set up for the commanding officers. The Rhinox were crouched outside, snuffling at one another. So, someone had to have ridden on at least one...

"Orphius is here?" he whispered.

"Tread lightly. That's all I have to say," the other man said. "You'd better deliver your report quickly."

Gulping, the creature moved forward. It was only when he was about to enter the tent that he heard the voices.

"Sir, there was really nothing I could do," a young lieutenant was saying, apparently trying to explain something. An angry noise responded.

"I'm sick of being failed, lieutenant! The reason I have you in charge here is because you have proved yourself in the past, but if this continues..."

The voice trailed off threateningly. "Then I will have no choice but to *replace* you. Understand me?"

Outside, the Horgon's stomach made frightened flips. He knew who was speaking in such a raw, forceful tone. Its raspy edge, rumor had it, came from a time long ago when Orphius's throat had been burned by the fire that had destroyed his home.

He risked a peek. Barely opening the flap of the tent, the Horgon adjusted his yellow eyes to the dim light and gazed at the man who was the leader of them all.

Imposing. That was the word to describe him. As far as fearful appearances went, Orphius ranked right up there with Keller...and not because he wore armor.

His skin had been so badly burned that the healers had had no choice but to temporarily freeze his skin. The large extent of the burns had resulted in permanent skin damage, even after the freezing treatment had thawed. His skin now exhibited a smooth, ghastly gray shade. No hair would ever again grow from his gleaming skull, and his features reflected the shame of his appearance. The violet eyes in his face, a common trait among the Shadow family, were always bleak and distrustful. His sharp nose was complimented by a narrow, never smiling mouth. And as was always the case, he was dressed in black robes.

At the moment, his face was twisted with rage. In a quick gesture, like a striking snake, he leaned forward and peered directly into the other man's face.

"You have *one* more chance," he hissed. Then, suddenly, his violet eyes darted to the place where the Horgon was looking in.

"You there! I will not tolerate being spied on!" he shouted. Glad to no longer be the object of Orphius's ire, the lieutenant gathered himself and gave his subordinate a dark glare as the Horgon shuffled in.

"Who are you?" Orphius hissed. The creature gulped.

"A lowly soldier, at your service," he said, ducking his head. Orphius laughed.

"Very funny. What is your business here?"

"I h-have come to deliver a report, sir," he said, regretting his stammer. Orphius arched an eyebrow in apparent amusement.

"Go on. Your commanding officer is present, is he not? And if you owe anyone your report at all, it's to him."

"Yes sir," the soldier said, raising his gaze apprehensively. For the moment, Orphius, his master, seemed calm. He had even gone to sit in one of the cheap chairs laying about, in an apparent attempt to set the room at ease. He brought his hands together, interlocking his fingers, and pressed them to his mirthless lips.

"What is it?" the lieutenant growled, jerking the Horgon back into reality. Clearing his throat, he saluted.

"Sir, you instructed us to go to Implitic and try to seize Tom Horter, but, umm...we were too late. Keller's forces beat us to it."

The lieutenant swore under his breath, and the Horgon glanced toward Orphius; the man's gray face was like a stone, but his eyes flashed with rage and pinned the lieutenant with a homicidal glare.

The Horgon lost his train of thought at the horrific look on Orphius's face, but hesitantly continued.

"We, umm...engaged them, when they were withdrawing from what we believe was Horter's initial hiding place. After suffering heavy casualties, we pulled back and returned to base. However..."

He cleared his throat nervously again. "There were post-battle reports of the skeleton escaping, accompanied by an accomplice. We might be able to track them down before Keller."

"Thank you, corporal," the lieutenant said, obviously preoccupied with the man sitting in the chair beside him. "You may go."

Nodding once, the Horgon hastily exited.

No one would believe this.

A few minutes after the soldier had left, the camp held its breath as their lord exited the tent. He was inspecting his hands as though they were unclean. Orphius's violet eyes flashed upward, and everyone worked on their tasks twice as hard.

He seemed to take no notice of the noise and activity around him as he strode through the camp, back to his Rhinox. The three creatures grunted in tandem, acknowledging his presence, as he crouched down between two of them.

As if on cue, a small creature, no larger than his hand, darted over from another tent, stopping in front of him.

The creature, Gupper, looked very dignified, even if it appeared to simply be a man's head fixed onto a metallic bird's body. Orphius couldn't help but be amused by his little spy.

"I assume you heard all of that," he said. The man nodded.

"Yes sir! What would you like me to do?"

"I would like you to follow these two upstarts—Horter and his accomplice. See if they pose any serious threat to us, and tell me of their position,"

"I can do that."

"And make sure Keller doesn't get his hands on them. If there's anything I hate more than him, it's him getting what I want."

"Yes sir. Is that all?"

"I believe so," the man said, standing up again. As he was climbing onto the back of the largest Rhinox, however, he paused.

"Oh, and Gupper? One more thing."

The bird man turned and waited, expectant.

"I need a new lieutenant. One who's still breathing."

"I guess this isn't...bad," Dominique stated, easily combining sarcasm and cheerfulness together in one sentence. Tom gave her a flat look.

"Next time, I'll let *you* pick the inn, alright? Seeing as how you don't like it-"

"I didn't say that!"

"You were *thinking* it."

Great, Dominique thought. *Now he reads minds.* Allowing herself a small smile, she flopped down onto one of the two beds in the microscopic sized room. It was worse than the first inn she had stayed at...and that had been pretty bad...

They were still in Grimslow. After the fight with the dragons, Dominique had insisted on finding a place to stay. Tom, using some more "borrowed" cash, had purchased a room at an inn not far from the bar where the fight had occurred. It had been a few hours since the battle, but scenes of the titanic clash of the two dragons still flashed through Dominique's mind.

"I get the shower first!" the skeleton shouted, dashing to claim the bathroom. Dominique sat up abruptly.

"Hey! That's not fair! You should let the girl go first!"

She pounded on the door. "TOM! You don't even *need* to wash! You're *bone!*"

A cheerful whistle was his answer; rolling her eyes, Dominique flopped onto her bed again and lay down, closing her eyes.

He can't be that slow, she thought. *I'll kill him when he gets out. I'm not gonna fall asleep...*

By the time she had listened to the shower water running for about a minute, she was out like a light.

The fire loomed up in front of her, always there, always barring her way from escaping. From the other room, she could hear her mother screaming her name. Somewhere off in the house, her family was trapped.

Someone scooped her up; the girl shrieked and clung to her brother's familiar form. He uttered a string of foul words that their mother never would have approved of as he hoisted her up through the window.

"Go!" he shouted. The girl shook her head, reaching down to him...

Something happened, then. The fire blew between them, walling them off from one another. She heard her brother scream in pain as the fire licked at his skin.

"NO!" she screamed.

"Make hassste, child! You mussst get away!"

The silky voice was familiar, somehow. The girl whirled around, trying to decipher where it had come from-

When she started falling. Falling into nothingness, away from everything and everyone she knew.

"DOMINIQUE!" her mother shouted.

And then, there was nothing.

Dominique woke with a start, screaming. Her violet eyes were opened wide, with pupils dilated.

"What the hell!" Tom shouted, sitting up. Shaking his head, he noticed the girl.

"Are you okay?" he asked, abruptly sliding out of his own bed and sitting by hers.

Without thinking, the girl lunged forward and buried her face in his coat, sobbing. The skeleton seemed surprised, and cautiously hugged her in return.

"Shh," he said, rocking back and forth. She was in hysterics, still. He wondered what it could have been...probably a nightmare.

"It's over," he murmured. "Dominique, it's okay."

The girl had stopped crying. Pulling back, she sat up and cleared her throat, drying her eyes with her sleeve.

"Sorry," she said, voice thick. "Just a bad dream."

"I did sort of get that impression," Tom said with a half smile. Then, he sighed. "Do you want to talk about it?"

She shook her head.

"Alright. Try to get some sleep."

Patting her once on the shoulder, the thief collapsed back onto his own bed (more of a cot, actually) and in short order was again sleeping. Dominique, however, remained wide awake, watching the street below from the window.

It was oddly peaceful at night here. During the day, Yumurango was hectic and chaotic, with the war and everything. She wondered why no one, absolutely *no one,* ever went out at night.

Hmm...Perhaps that wasn't completely true. The girl sat up straighter as she saw a band of figures tromping down the street. Confusion lit her gaze as she saw they had guns.

Immediately, her self-preservation instincts took over, and she ducked down so they wouldn't see her. Soon, though, they appeared to have passed by the inn.

"Tom!" she hissed. The man turned over with a snapping sound. She winced at the sound of it, but went over and shook him. "Tom Horter!"

"What?" he groaned. "This is the second time you've woken me up."

"Shut up. There's something going on," she said, gesturing to the window. The skeleton looked out questioningly.

"I don't see anything."

"Well, there was a big group of men. I'm gonna go check it out. I'd rather find out what they're up to first, rather than wake up to a war zone again."

"You can't go alone!" he protested, getting up and rubbing the sleep from his eye sockets. "Come on, we'll go out the window."

He grabbed his cello before they left; Dominique grabbed her sword. Before leaping down, she glanced back. Aside from the messed up covers on the beds, it was as though no one had been here. It suddenly struck her that, other than the sword and the clothes on her back, she had no other possessions here in Yumurango.

Sad, she thought. Regret colored her thoughts. In addition to having nothing, no one knew who she was, or even cared, besides Tom, she hoped. More fiercely than anything, the girl wished that someone would miss her when she left somewhere. The curse of being an orphan had reared its ugly head yet again.

"Come on!" Tom hissed. The girl returned her attention to their situation. Gathering her energy, she used her powers to float down silently to the street level.

"Nice," he said, beginning to walk off. "Look...their tracks lead this way."

With that, he began to head off down the street, monitoring the way the men moved.

"They're obviously in a hurry," he noted. "Must be doing something they're not supposed to be doing, then...but why go here?"

He had stopped at a street corner, looking down the dead end curiously. "The only thing that's back there are the dragon stables."

Dominique's eyes widened. "That man, in the front! He was the trainer of that orange dragon from the match today!"

"And revenge isn't an uncommon thing among these barbarians," Tom muttered. "So...what do you say?"

He looked back at her. "Ready to save a dragon?"

The girl grinned.

Propping up his cello, and using the case as a ladder, Tom climbed up and leapt nimbly onto the eave of a nearby roof, walking casually along the edge, grinning down at Dominique's shocked face. Then, just as easily, he leapt across a ten foot gap separating the roof from the dragon stables, and swung inside the stables.

A shout of surprise came from within it; Dominique winced as she heard a single gun shot. But then, her friend reappeared, a new revolver in his grasp.

"Come on!" he hissed, waving her forward. She didn't need to be told twice.

"What'd you do?" she asked, looking at the comatose guard.

"A roundhouse kick to the head never hurt anyone. Permanently, that is," he added with a wink.

With that, they pressed onward. Dominique looked at each of the stalls as they passed by, and was disturbed to see they were empty.

"Where are the dragons?" she asked.

"These are for Shartans; the dragons are kept below. You don't think they could keep them in open stalls, do you? They'd burn down the entire town!"

He stopped. "Right here," he said, and dragged her down a sudden flight of hidden stairs. She grunted in protest at the rapid change in direction.

As soon as they reached the bottom, the skeleton stopped, pressing a finger to where his lips should be, and cupping his other hand at the spot on his head where one might normally find an ear. She nodded and listened intently.

"That worm couldn't have just disappeared!" the rival trainer was shouting. "There's no way something that big could have been moved without anyone seeing her!"

"Her trainer didn't have anything to do with it; we found that out easily enough," one man said. Dominique shuddered as she heard the sound of knives being re-sharpened.

"We have to take these guys out!" she hissed to her friend. Tom nodded grimly, but didn't make a move.

Softer sounds were getting to them now; small whimpers of pain, from a man. Dominique gritted her teeth with hate. These people were just like the kids who had picked on her at school. No consideration for other people, just their own selfish desires filling their minds. But what these men were doing was ten times as horrible. It *had* to stop.

"Are you *sure* you don't know where your dragon is?" the other trainer said with false sweetness. The girl risked a glance around the corner.

The orange's trainer from the bar was crouching, face to face with a man who was on the floor. His victim was bloody, and, as she looked closer...missing two fingers.

She almost gagged when she turned away, looking at Tom with a shake of her head. He nodded once and cocked the revolver off safety.

"Hey, did you hear that?"

Two of the men had been closer than they'd realized; they had heard the click of the safety being released. Dominique and Tom readied themselves as the pair approached their hiding place.

"Three...two...one..." Tom whispered.

They were almost on them now, just reaching out to see if they had missed something in their initial inspection-

"NOW!"

Dominique sprang out and slammed her dark energy into one of the men's faces. Tom pumped a bullet into the head of the other.

He whirled quickly, and began to fire into the mob, nailing the trainer and possibly others. A few men screamed and ran for cover, but the majority held their ground.

The girl drew her sword; she wanted these men to be afraid before they died. She was going to have to act quickly, especially if this wasn't all the men-

She swore as someone slammed into her from behind, grabbing her tightly in a vice-like grip.

"Tom! Run!" she shouted.

He wasn't listening. Turning briskly on his heel, he fired at whoever it was that had hold of her. Dominique felt the arms around her loosen and drop away as her captor slumped to the floor, bleeding from a bullet hole right between the eyes. She hurriedly got up and held up her sword to defend against another approaching man.

Fear must have shown in her eyes, because he laughed. Bad move.

Angry now, the girl swung with all her might, cutting him on the forearm; he fell back with a cry of pain, his eyes livid.

"You little-!"

"DON'T EVEN THINK ABOUT IT!"

The shouting voice came from an unknown female, whose location was not readily apparent. The voice rang with an air of command, and had a silky edge that reminded Dominique of a snake's hiss.

Hearing this voice, the combatants froze, pausing the battle momentarily.

"Who's there?" the trainer demanded. Tom and Dominique backed up until they stood together; she gripped his arm tightly.

The trainer was getting to his feet, motioning to his men to grab Tom and Dominique. Tom had shot him in the wrist, but he seemed able to shrug off the wound somehow.

"I'm out of bullets," the skeleton murmured. The men began to close in, ready to kill them both-

"I said *don't,*" the woman said again.

"Tie them up!"

"YOU'RE NOT LISTENING!"

And all of a sudden, the white dragon came bursting into the room. Shards of wood flew out from the rather small cargo bins she had been hiding behind. Something clicked in Dominique's head...

How could something that large have hidden behind those?

With a savage roar, the dragon spat flame at the men who were furthest away from Tom and Dominique; they went down screaming.

Two swipes of her powerful talons were enough to gut another half of the remaining mob. The surviving half screamed and ran; she let them.

Dominique dove out of the way as the renegade trainer came hurtling toward the dragon, sword in hand, his wrist seemingly healed from the gunshot wound. He held the weapon up and brandished it in her face.

"You're a demon!" he screamed. "No one could have beaten my orange!"

Blue eyes tracked the waving weapon for a second, and then, the dragon batted it out of his hand and picked him up gingerly, as though he would try to bite her.

"Hell spawn!" he shouted. Spittle ran down his chin.

Then, of all things, the dragon *smiled.* It was a dragonish version, no doubt, but a perfect rendition of one.

That was when she popped him casually into her mouth and swallowed, not bothering to chew. A burp followed up her meal. She picked at her teeth with one dainty claw.

Tom maneuvered in front of Dominique as the dragon turned to face them; she gulped and prepared to make a run for it.

Just as the skeleton began to dash away, the dragon whipped her tail around and slammed it down in front of him. She held up a paw.

"Is she...trying to talk?" Dominique murmured, amazed.

And then, before their disbelieving eyes, the dragon began to shrink.

Her wings shriveled and melted into her sides; the horns along her spine and on her head disappeared. She reared up onto her hind legs and watched with satisfaction as fingers appeared instead of claws. Clothing appeared on her scaled form as she shrank even further. The clothing was exotic, to say the least. Black pants, shining like black dragons' scales, were complimented by a creamy tank top with red ribbon lacing up the front of it. Black boots with thick soles adorned her feet.

Finally, after all this, a young woman stared back at them. Her scaled skin was white, and her eyes were an icy blue hue, with slits down the center. Voluminous black hair cascaded down her back. Even as they watched, she pinned it up with a hair band she had in her pocket.

"Hi," she said. She tossed back her head. "I'm Shayla."

8

The Shadow's Mansion

"Umm...wow," Tom squeaked. He closed his mouth with a conscious effort and cleared his throat. "I had no idea shape shifters still existed, uh, around here."

"Well now you know," Shayla said with a dazzling grin. She flipped her hair back. "You're Tom Horter, right?"

"Uh, yes," he said, blinking once. "Can I just say...*wow?*"

"Holy crap," Dominique murmured. Her violet eyes were wide as she looked at the woman. Shayla grinned.

"What? Never seen a dragon fight before?"

"Actually, I was there when you won that fight in the pit," Dominique said. The woman knit her brow and made a face.

"Oh. That. Sorry you had to see. God, I *hate* it when they throw weaklings like that at me!"

"You're pretty good," Tom agreed. "But it looks like you're out of a job."

"True," Shayla mused. She looked at the prone form of her trainer. The man was lying on the floor, dead and cold. "I'm a fugitive now, aren't I? You don't just walk away from killing people here, even when it was for a good reason."

The three of them exchanged looks. Finally, the shape shifter cleared her throat.

"Where are you guys headed?"

"Well...we *were* headed for Taraban, but at the rate we're being attacked along here..." Tom looked at Dominique. "And with the magnitude of your power, Orphius and Keller are going to be hunting us twice as hard."

"You're saying we're not going to the capitol?" Dominique asked, glancing at Shayla. The woman was listening to their conversation, watching with curious eyes.

"I think it's a better idea if we head for the Sistern Range. That's where Red Shield is hiding...somewhere."

"Red Shield?" Dominique asked. "The rebels?"

"I didn't know you knew about them," the skeleton said, seeming pleased. "But yes. They're in the Sistern range, hiding somewhere."

"Uhh...right." Dominique tried to keep her ignorance hidden, but Tom wasn't fooled. He grinned as he explained.

"The Sisterns are a range of mountains, too high for anyone, even dragons, to get over."

"I wouldn't bet on it," Shayla muttered. But she pressed her lips together as Tom and Dominique looked at her.

"Please, continue."

"Well, to answer your question, we're going to the mountains."

"Ah," Shayla said, nodding. Then, she bit her lip, looking at them imploringly.

"You two wouldn't mind if I, uh, tagged along, would you?" she asked in a pleading voice, smiling nicely.

Tom and Dominique exchanged glances. The girl had a frown on her face at the way Tom was obviously in awe of the shape shifter.

"I really don't have anywhere else to go."

He looked toward his companion. Dominique looked at him, and they seemed to just communicate with their eyes.

Tom turned away, motioning for the girl to follow his lead. They put their heads together and deliberated quietly.

"What do you think?" the thief murmured.

"I don't know..."

She looked back at the shape shifter. Shayla was wringing her hands nervously, glancing around to keep from staring at them.

"We don't know anything about her! Why was she working as a fighting dragon?"

"Shape shifters used to do that all the time," Tom muttered. "It used to be hard to tell whether an animal was a shape shifter or not...that is, until Keller wiped them all out."

Dominique stiffened. "What?"

"Keller. He killed all of them. None of them wanted to join his army, so he sent his troops out and had them eradicated. I'm not sure how *she* survived."

Tom jerked his head in Shayla's direction. Dominique felt sympathy well up in her. She looked at Shayla again, who had begun to pace. The shape shifter met her gaze.

"Please?"

Looking to Tom, Dominique sought the answer in his eyes. He twitched; it could have been a nod.

With a deep breath, she nodded back.

Tom turned to Shayla. "Sure, why not?"

"YES! Thank you thank you thank you! You won't be disappointed, Mr. Horter, I'm an excellent addition to your, uh...group."

Dominique laughed.

"Now," Shayla murmured, suddenly serious. "I don't think we want to be around by the time Keller or Orphius's troops come sniffing to see the cause of the trouble. You know those guys...every time something unusual happens, they always see if there's anyone with enough power to recruit."

She scowled darkly. "And if there's anything they want, it's a shape shifter."

"You're right," Tom agreed. "We'd better go."

The three of them left at a quick pace to get ahead of their enemies; so quickly, in fact, that they didn't notice the small shadow watching their every move.

"Yes," Gupper snickered. "You'd better go, alright."

With that, he spread his metal wings and zipped quietly after them, wondering how his master would reward him for this.

At the moment, however, Orphius wasn't too keen on what Gupper was doing, or his mission. In fact, the main problem concerning him at the moment was the date.

It was always on this day, every year, that he forced himself to do something he *really* didn't like to do. Today was the anniversary of the worst day of his life, hands down.

The anniversary of the fire.

Gulping down his sudden emotion, Orphius turned to the window of his home and looked out at the forsaken plain that made up most of Yumurango. In the distance, he could barely see the snow capped peaks of the Sistern range, the alleged hiding place of the Red Shield organization.

It was there, too, where the Shadows had once dwelled. Where he had grown up and where he had spent the happiest days of his life, learning how to wield his inherently powerful magic and playing with his siblings-

Enough, he told himself severely. *There's no sense in living the past over again.*

But for today, he was going to visit the site. It was the one day of every year that he forced himself to do so.

He descended the stairs of his tower. The tower was the current pride of his life. To honor his parents, he had formed it entirely out of black stone, but leaving the inside barren and open to remind him of the loss he had suffered. And the pain and rage that filled him.

Because that was what kept him going...and what would make Keller pay.

At the mention of his brother's name, even in his head, Orphius narrowed his eyes to slits and gritted his teeth. Keller had a lot to answer for. After all, *he* had started the fire.

Each brother blaming the other...it made Orphius sick. Why wouldn't Keller just give up and admit he'd done it already? That was what half this war was about, anyhow. All he had wanted was a straight answer from him. But instead, he had been attacked, starting this ridiculous conflict.

Wrenching his thoughts away from his brother, and adversary, Orphius stalked down the stairs of the tower and flung open the door. Troops upon troops were milling about outside; he casually walked among and through them, heading straight for the Rhinox stables....time to go visit his family.

"Shayla," Tom complained. "Can you set us down? It's getting cold. I think we're nearing the mountains!"

The dragon beneath him growled an affirmative and began to descend, bringing a little warmth back to his bones. Behind him, Dominique tried to keep her teeth from chattering, but with little success.

"Cold?" Tom teased. She smacked him one and curled into an even smaller ball.

"I didn't know Yumurango w-was t-this c-cold," she chattered.

"It's because we're near the mountains," he said. "See those peaks? Well, it's cloudy, so...never mind."

Dominique just nodded and tried to bundle herself up warmer. She was dressed for a *heat wave,* damn it. She hadn't expected snow to come blowing through in the middle of summer-

She stopped right there. Thinking of home wasn't the best ploy right now, especially when she thought the odds of getting back were pretty slim. Maybe, if this war between the two tyrannical men died down, she would be able to concentrate on getting back. Everyone in Yumurango was too busy fighting, hiding, running or otherwise preoccupied with the war to aid her return.

And as of now, she was a marked target. This war was directly affecting her as well.

Shayla glided the rest of the way down to the ground beneath them; frost coated the plants in fantastic shapes, making gorgeous little sculptures. Dominique, however, didn't have time to appreciate the beauty of it.

The dragon blew gently on a patch of grass, to try to generate some flames for heat, but had no success. When the grass thawed, it became too wet to ignite. With a huff of frustration, she began to shift back to human form.

"Alright, it's officially cold," Shayla muttered, rubbing her scaly arms. Tom's bones creaked from the chill wind that blew down the mountains.

"Where are we?" Dominique asked.

"I don't know," the skeleton admitted. "This isn't where I thought we'd end up."

He stared pointedly at Shayla, who held up her hands in surrender.

"How was I supposed to know? It's not like *I'm* in with Red Shield."

"I think I see something over there," Dominique said, pointing. The shape shifter squinted.

"Yeah...hey, good find, Dom,"

"Don't call me that," the girl said, shuddering at the memory of Serena's taunts. Shayla nodded and began to walk.

Tom, with his cello on his back again, looked fit to travel more than any of them. His coat tapered to fit his slim physique, and his boots were soft and light, built for miles of walking. When he turned, Dominique saw that he even had his gloves on again.

He caught her looking. "You can have my jacket, if you want," he offered. She shook her head. A nice offer, but she wasn't that weak.

Nevertheless, he kept an eye on her as they walked. She was only seventeen, after all. The girl needed to be taken care of.

"Where did you find her?" Shayla murmured to him. Dominique was farther out ahead of them now; they could talk. "Not many girls can hold their own like that. I saw her in that fight with those guys."

"She's from beyond the portal," Tom said. He narrowed his eyes against the whipping wind. "But I think being here is what's awakened those powers. Other than that, I think she's just an ordinary girl."

"Umm, pardon me if you haven't noticed, but her eyes are *purple.* Do you have any idea what that means?"

Tom opened his mouth to answer, but then, he stopped.

"Do you hear something?" he asked.

Shayla cocked her head, listening. Her blue eyes closed as she concentrated, and then, they snapped wide open.

"Rhinox!" she hissed. "Dominique! Get back here!"

The two of them ran for the girl, now fully aware of the fact that those monsters weren't far away. She turned around, confused as to why they were calling for her.

"What?" she snapped. Then, her jaw dropped.

"Oh."

Right behind her friends, she saw a silhouette behind a cloud. She waved her arms frantically, pointing toward it.

"There's a Rhinox!" she shouted.

The serpentine form of one of the creatures was twisting its way toward them, clearing a shallow hill and beginning to descend into the small valley. They had about a minute before they would be spotted.

"Get to those ruins!" Tom instructed, grabbing her wrist as they ran by. Dominique gave a squeak of protest as she was flung over his shoulder.

"Hey! I can run by myself, you know!"

"Save it for later!" Shayla snapped. "For right now...RUN FASTER, HORTER!"

The ruined mansion up ahead of them had likely once been amazing. It was perched on a shallow hill, overlooking the small valley. Much of the original framework was still intact; flying buttresses, columns, and multiple gardens met their gazes. The entire structure was overgrown with vegetation that glistened white with frost.

Dominique stumbled through one frozen garden, barely having time to note what plants were in it before Tom pulled her roughly along. There were roses, she saw...violet roses. She raised her eyebrows, but continued to move swiftly.

They moved through one of the great hallways; icicles greeted them at the entrance archway. Snow followed their hurried movement as the three companions sprinted inside, unseen by the Rhinox.

Gasping, the skeleton and shape shifter sank to their knees, relief making them temporarily weak. Dominique, on the other hand, suddenly froze, looking around.

"What place is this?" she hissed.

Everywhere she looked, she saw something that jogged a memory, deep in her mind. Standing slowly, she began to walk away, seeing how much of the house was *burned.*

She put a hand over her eyes and tried to blot out the images. The fire, screaming, yelling...calling for her mother, being scooped up by someone...falling into nothingness-

"Dominique, stop!"

Why was Tom shouting at her? Opening her eyes, Dominique prepared to scold him about not interrupting when she was having a moment-

When she realized she was about to wander into an enormous hole, caused by...what? A blasting of some sort?

She was on the hole's very precipice; flailing, she tipped backward, but somehow her momentum had already carried her past the threshold-

Someone caught her before she could fall through. Looking at her savior, Dominique caught a glimpse of Tom before he set her down on the floor, hard.

"You. Have. Got. To. Be. CAREFUL!" he snapped.

"Sorry," she mumbled. "This is just...I don't know, okay! There's something weird here!"

She sprang to her feet, looking around. "It's like I've been here before,"

"Umm...people?" Shayla said, jogging up. "Hate to interrupt, but we've got trouble. *Orphius* was on that Rhinox, and I've got a dragon on the edge of my senses!"

"How do you know?"

"Because I'm a *dragon* half the time. I know these things. And there's only one man who can communicate with dragons peacefully, and that's-"

"Keller," Tom said grimly. "Let's move. We've gotta get out of here and fly as fast as we can."

"Works for me," Shayla said, already seeming to flex invisible wings. "If either of those two get their hands on us, we're gonna be in deep, *deep-"*

Something landed on what used to be the roof. The three of them went absolutely silent.

Tom motioned for them to follow, and they did. Dominique looked up with growing fear at the shadow blotting out some of the light that shone through cracks of the roof.

Something evil was up there...and she didn't want to be around to meet it.

Keller crouched down, staring at the old ruins of his former home. He clenched his hands into lethal fists and stood up, feeling wrath course through him.

A squawk reached his ears; a Rhinox, of course. Even his guilty brother was pressured to come visit this forsaken place on this day.

The general sneered. *For once, I beat him here.*

Fog was starting to roll in; Keller was grateful that his armor protected him from the chill air as he began to take his usual path off the roof, signaling the dragon to stay put. The creature huffed once and carefully laid down for a nap.

Slowly but surely, carefully avoiding the now dangerous areas of the crumbling ruins, he made his way downward. Finally, his boots slammed into the ground with a thud, oddly muffled by the fog surrounding him.

Stones crunched under his feet as he walked through the familiar grounds. The burned trees, once so green, were now wilted and blackened beyond recognition.

Sometimes, he swore he could still hear laughter weaving throughout his old yard. Echoes of a time long past that would never be again. Heaving a sigh, he walked around a corner...and froze.

In the middle of his sanctuary, he saw three figures moving quickly through the mist, looking this way and that. One was Horter;

Keller would have recognized those lanky bones anywhere. Another was a scaled woman, with black hair and a sour looking face. The third one must have been the girl from before, Tom's accomplice...

"Hold it," he heard the scaled woman whisper. "The dragon's not moving anymore; he must have gotten off."

The armored figure ducked around the corner again, listening intently.

"Shayla, can we get moving? I'm just a *little* anxious to get out of here," Tom said. Keller grabbed the small gun he had at his side; no way was he letting them escape.

"It's dangerous to take off in such a crowded area," the scaled woman snapped. "With my wingspan, I could hit the edge of the roof. And after that, we still have to deal with Keller's dragon!"

"You won't have to worry about the Rhinox?" a different voice asked.

As the shape shifter replied, Keller froze. He knew that voice. How did he know that voice? Turning the corner again, he stared feverishly at the trio.

They were moving again; he swore and padded after them, keeping his footsteps light.

Ah, there they were. He looked to the right and ducked behind a bush as they walked by.

"Why are both of them here at the same time?" the third, mysterious voice asked. Keller stiffened.

"Because this was the day the mansion burned down," Tom answered. "It's the only place where they'll never fight. Rumor has it that when they're here, they meet peacefully."

Keller almost gagged. He, meet Orphius? Ridiculous.

"It's kind of sad," the girl said again. The armored figure wracked his memory for any recollection of that voice. "I mean, I know they're both evil, but they lost their *entire* family in one night!"

"Actually," Keller heard Tom mutter. "That may not be true."

What the hell was he talking about?

A shout of alarm came from the girl; Keller heard the squealing of a Rhinox as it leapt out of its hiding place, looking for food.

He made his move at the same time. Springing out, he prepared to capture all three of them himself. There was no sense in letting such three prizes go to waste-

Suddenly, he froze. In a very un-Keller gesture, he tripped on a rock and fell flat on his face. Still, he didn't move his head.

Because there, battling a Rhinox in what remained of their home, was his little sister.

He would have recognized her anywhere. The same purple hair, the violet eyes...she was older now, obviously. If he was correct, she would be seventeen. And now she looked even *more* like their mother.

Tom and the scaled woman were flanking her on either side as she pumped black energy at the creature. The skeleton added a blast of yellow, illuminating the area with a sickly light-

"Oh crap!" the scaled woman shouted. Keller jerked his head up and rolled to his feet. She'd seen him, hadn't she?

Actually, she hadn't. The cause of her alarm had been the dragon; it leapt from the roof ...straight onto the Rhinox. Dominique screamed as the two creatures rolled toward her, shaking the ground beneath their feet.

The girl swore as she jumped back, barely avoiding a lash from the dragon's tail. A shriek of pain from the Rhinox heralded the crashing of its face into the ground.

"Dominique, run!" she heard Tom shout. She tried to run in the opposite direction-

But saw a hulking figure standing in the narrow path, watching the battle. She swore again.

"It's Keller!" she shouted. "Guys, go!"

She heard a loud roar; Shayla, ready for battle, had shifted to her dragon form. Alerted to the bigger threat in the premises, the black dragon discarded the nearly dead Rhinox and roared a challenge.

Shayla roared back, a threat lacing her tone. The two dragons squared off in the courtyard; their claws scratching the ancient stones.

Then, they leapt at each other. The vibrations throughout the courtyard caused Dominique to lose her balance; she stumbled and began to fall.

Someone caught her. At first, Dominique thought it was Tom, and she tugged at his arm, expecting him to follow her-

With a jolt, she realized she was tugging on *someone's* arm...but not Tom's. Looking up, she screamed.

Keller grabbed a hold of her wrist, and he wasn't letting go. Swearing, she tried to twist out of his grasp, slamming kicks against his side.

She might as well have been a gnat. But the man seemed taken aback by her display; he hesitated.

"Dominique?" he asked. "Are you alright?"

Her name, stated in his baritone voice, was shocking to the girl. She stopped struggling, staring at him.

"How do you know my name?" she demanded.

"What are you talking about? Don't you know who I am?"

"Of course; you're Keller; one of the most evil men Yumurango has ever known-"

"Besides that!" he said, obviously frustrated. She watched him with wide eyes. To their right, the dragon fight continued.

"Let me go!" she screamed, and blasted the man with energy from her palm. He flew back and landed on the ground, stunned.

She ran for it, trying not to think about what he had said. Her legs felt weak; but she ignored the feeling and kept moving.

Around her, the scenery was changing. Instead of the twisted, burned trees and massive columns that dotted the outside landscape, she was entering the wreckage of the building again...the Shadow mansion.

She couldn't believe what was happening to her. For God's sake, she had simply been an ordinary girl on her way from school. What had happened? Why had fate decided to place her in this extraordinary situation? She was no one special, and she didn't understand why all this was happening to her.

Stairs were ahead of her; risking it, she began to climb, wincing every time she heard the half burnt steps groaning beneath her weight. The entire structure was very unstable, but hey...she could fly if necessary.

Looking back over her shoulder, she breathed a sigh of relief as she realized Keller wasn't behind her anymore. Maybe she had knocked him a little harder than she'd thought.

How had he known her name? She gulped and tightened her hands into fists. Maybe he had overheard, since he had obviously been spying on them, coming out of nowhere like that.

As she tried to put the pieces together in her mind, she tromped heavily up the stairs...it wasn't really a surprise when they gave way beneath her. Shrieking, she was almost too shocked to use her powers until she was very nearly crushed on the floor, but she recovered in time, using her powers to slow her fall. She landed softly on her rear with a small jolt.

Breathing hard, she blinked several times while she righted herself. The heavy wooden beams and chunks of stone falling with her had created a new hole in the floor. Curious, she drifted in.

Beneath the ground floor, there was a tunnel. Adrenaline raced through her system as she slowly alighted on the wet floor, listening to the water drip off the stones around her. Spongy green plants hung down thick enough to bar her movement. This place hadn't been used for years.

She started in, pushing her way through the plants, while the mantra *curiosity killed the cat* chanted in her head. Suddenly, she yelped as she felt something brush against her back.

It was just a plant. Glaring at it, she unsheathed her sword and began to hack at the rest of the foliage to clear a path. She stared at the blade for a moment.

Was it happy to be back here, in its home? Not that it could think, or anything. Dominique just thought the blade shown brighter here, even in the murk. Maybe it was some weird kind of magic...

After what seemed an interminable time, the plants she had been swiping at finally ended, and abruptly cleared. Sheathing her tool again, Dominique peered into the room she had arrived at.

Roars sounded above, and she jerked her gaze upward; the dragons were still going at it. Fervently, the girl hoped that Shayla would be the winner.

As soon as she stepped into the room, lights flooded on. Dominique jumped at the sparks of electricity emanating from an unplugged machine at the rooms opposite end. Gulping, she looked around.

It had to have been some sort of lab; the entire room was painted completely white, though it was now dirty from years of no use. Curiously, scientific equipment still hummed expectantly in a corner, seemingly waiting patiently to be used again.

Dominique grinned as she stepped further into the room. What was this place? One of the Shadows must have been obsessed with science. She grinned as she noted a few vials that still contained strange looking chemicals.

Of everything she had seen, this dirty lab seemed the most...normal, to her. It could have been a professor's lab, back at her high school.

"Wow," she breathed.

Her voice echoed throughout the entire room; clapping her hands over her mouth, Dominique waited breathlessly as, finally, the echoes faded away.

Okay, she thought. *Total silence could be useful.*

Still, she couldn't help but look around some more. Crossing the lab quietly, she hesitantly pressed a button on the side of one of the tables.

The appearance of a light startled her; turning, she saw a corner of the room had been illuminated, and in it...

In it was an examination table, with a vague form covered with a thin, green sheet. Her heart pounded harder as she realized it must be human underneath there...a cadaver? If that was the case, it must have been almost rotted by now.

She gritted her teeth. But what if it was something else? Maybe it was just a trick. Inching closer, she peered at the covered figure.

There was something wrong with its form...it didn't seem to be entirely human. Confused, she hesitantly reached out and poked it.

"Oh my God!" she hissed. Her voice echoed throughout the room; she didn't care.

The thing was *metal.* Curiously now, the girl reached out and pulled the sheet down from the figure's head.

Blank, dead eyes stared at her, but not the type of eyes she had been expecting. This was a *machine.*

The face was of a simple design; no nose or mouth, but with two unseeing eyes. On either side of the head, there were ear-like appendages that reminded Dominique of music headphones. Pulling the sheet back farther, the girl saw the entire robot/android/thing was clothed in black leather. She also noted, with some amusement, that the chest marked it as a feminine design.

*Okay...*she thought, weirded out. With a final flick, she uncovered the rest of the robot; enormous boots were over its feet, and its fingers ended in points that were sharp as a knife's.

All in all, an impressive feat of engineering. Dominique even spotted a pair of gloves on a nearby table, probably used to cover up the machine's deadly hands.

She waved her hand in front of its face; nothing happened. The eyes remained dull and gray in its metallic face. Clapping didn't do anything, either.

Shrugging, Dominique turned away and opened a cabinet, not far from the android. She gasped at the sight.

An enormous rifle, of the sniping variety, was hung delicately inside, along with about twelve ammo clips. Closing the cabinet quickly, she decided to pretend she *hadn't* seen that. Guns she could deal with. Huge guns? Not so much.

The ground shook; the girl gritted her teeth. She needed to get back to the surface, no matter who was chasing her. Tom and Shayla needed her help-

Footsteps echoed on the wet stone. Dominique froze, straining her ears for anything else. They were getting louder.

Desperately, she cast around for a suitable hiding place, and finally decided on hiding behind the robot's table. It had one large column that held it upright, which might just be large enough to hide behind.

She scrunched up into a tight ball and hoped whoever was coming was a friend.

An audible gasp came to her ears as, whoever it was, came to the room. She heard a laugh...it wasn't a voice she had heard before, even Keller's...

That left only one man.

Dominique hesitantly peeked around the table's support beam. The man examining the room was terrifying looking. His gray skin and bald head weren't helping matters, along with his sharp features.

But she was drawn to his eyes. They were violet, like hers. For a split second, Dominique was surprisingly happy. She wasn't the only one in both of these worlds.

Orphius was clearly ecstatic about something. Rushing over, he opened a few of the vials that Dominique had seen and inspected them, laughing.

"More than I'd ever hoped for..." he murmured. Then, he whirled, looking straight at the corner Dominique was hiding in.

She shrank back into the shadows as far as she could as he came closer. Gulping, she was sure that he had seen her-

When he leaned down and inspected the robot. "My God..." he whispered. "Thank you, father."

Father? So it had been the master of the Shadow family who had created all of this. Vaguely, she wondered what he had been like, to sire sons like this.

Orphius threw his head back and laughed. Dominique made a face. How much did this guy laugh, anyway?

He whirled around, muttering under his breath. "Where is that thing?"

Dominique glanced toward the tunnel. It wasn't that far, she told herself. If she could only get there before he noticed she was running...

No. Not yet. She gritted her teeth. She needed to wait until he was farther away...

Her hands clenched her sword, white rimmed. Orphius was preoccupied at the moment. Now was her chance!

Hauling herself up over the table, she whipped her sword out as she began to sprint away. Orphius whirled, suddenly aware of her presence.

"You there, stop!" he shouted. All of a sudden, Dominique felt her legs halt; she couldn't move.

She screamed; it echoed all the way through the tunnel, and she was glad. There was a small chance, if any, that someone would hear her.

"Who exactly," Orphius asked, his voice soft and dangerous. "Are you?"

Even if Dominique could have turned, she wouldn't have. She clenched her jaw and gripped her sword, prepared to defend herself. It wasn't as if anyone would miss this man when he was dead.

The spell yanked her around before she could do anything. Her eyes were narrowed; she was ready to fly at him before he could work anymore magic on her. When she tried to use her powers, some kind of barrier prevented her from reaching the energy within her; she kept her horror from showing.

She hung her head, masking her face with her hair. Orphius lowered her down to the floor again, but kept her still.

"Who are you?" he asked suspiciously. He looked at her piercingly; she returned his gaze through her hair.

"No one of your concern," she snapped.

"I think it is; you're trespassing on private property,"

"I didn't think anyone owned this place anymore. Especially after the fire. Who would want it?"

The man's eyes narrowed. Dominique gulped. She had obviously offended him...his family had died here, after all-

"It's interesting that a mere slip of a girl would be in league with a fugitive like Tom Horter," Orphius said, his voice laced with rage. "There's no reason that I can see."

Dominique didn't say anything.

"What? Not interesting in talking?" the man asked.

"Not really," she snapped.

"You know, you are awfully sassy. Most people would be out of their minds with fear."

"I'm not afraid of you," she snapped.

He laughed. "Not *yet,* anyway."

At that moment, opportunity presented itself.

The ground above them shook once, dangerously; Orphius looked up, and simultaneously, the spell on Dominique's legs weakened.

She lunged forward with her sword, aiming for his chest. The blade found its mark, but he was wearing some type of protective armor; the blade didn't penetrate. Orphius smacked the blade away; she went spinning across the room, and didn't stop until the sword was impaled on something else...the android's arm.

Dominique swore as she tried to work the sword free. Orphius, furious now, began to advance on her, his lips beginning to form a spell-

The blade suddenly came loose, throwing the girl back. With a shriek, she plowed into Orphius, and they both fell to the floor.

He grunted heavily as she landed on top of him, and prepared to retaliate...when he saw her face.

Her eyes. They were full of a misty, violet shade. In disbelief, he looked at the rest of her face...this couldn't be possible...

The girl, however, was looking rather intently at something else. Orphius reluctantly tore his eyes from her and looked in the direction of her gaze. Oh dear.

On the table, the robot was beginning to move. The eyes on its face flickered to life, giving off a yellow light that illuminated the area in front of it.

Slowly, almost majestically, it sat up and turned toward them. When it spoke, Dominique could tell that the slightly buzzy voice belonged to a female.

"Alright," she growled. "Who the hell stuck the sword in my arm?"

9

Red Shield

"Is anyone gonna answer my question?" the robot asked again. Dominique and Orphius exchanged glances.

"She did it!" he said, pointing.

"He did it!" she said, at the exact same time. Both of them glared at each other as they pitched to their feet.

The robot looked between the two of them, as if deciding who to believe-

That was when an angry roar broke through their confrontation. Dominique screamed as the ceiling began to cave in around them.

"Get out of here!" Orphius shouted, shoving her toward the door.

"Don't touch me!" she shouted, lashing out with her sword. He jumped back and looked at the robot suspiciously. She had gotten out her gun, now. With the tenderness of a loving mother, she made sure it was in working order.

Eyes wide, the girl glanced between the man and the robot, not knowing what to do. The ceiling of the room cracked dangerously; the machine was right beneath where it was going to collapse!

Something snapped inside Dominique. She didn't know why, but she didn't want this robot to be harmed. With a quick, decisive motion, she burst into action.

Dominique ran for the robot. "Come on!" she shouted, tugging on the machine's arm. "We've gotta get out of here! The roof is-"

"Alright, just hold on!" the android snapped. "I have to get my ammo-"

"No time!"

Indeed, the roof was collapsing all around them now. The robot seemed to realize their predicament.

"Umm...maybe you're right-"

That was when the dragon fell through. Instead of the white dragon Dominique had hoped to see, this one's scales were a mass of darkness. Red eyes raked the room as the black dragon landed awkwardly on the floor.

With it, an avalanche of rock and wood rained down toward the three people imprisoned in the room. One large boulder began to fall toward Dominique; the girl tried to use her powers, but there was too much strain.

"Oh no," she murmured. The rock began its descent toward her.

Suddenly, she felt something slam into her, and yelped as she was knocked onto her back. The robot crouched above her, and braced herself for the impact-

The rock smashed into pieces as it collided with her metal body.

Dominique scrambled to her feet, looking at the robot with wide eyes. When the falling debris finally subsided, the dragon raised its head and growled.

It hissed in anger as it narrowed its focus to Dominique and the robot. The girl swore and readied her sword; the robot crouched, seeming to think hard about something.

"A little help wouldn't be unappreciated!" Dominique said, in an almost panicky tone. The robot nodded.

"Watch this!"

Without another word, the android sprang at the dragon. Dominique gasped; even the dragon seemed surprised.

The robot climbed with an easy, fluid gait up the side of the dragon, all the way to its head, and grabbed hold of the two large horns that grew there. In a rage, the dragon tossed its head back and roared, seeking to throw her off. Fire licked from its jaws.

Dominique ducked as its tail came whistling over her head. The robot, however, seemed perfectly calm. Suddenly, she swung her legs up and over the dragon's head and landed on its face.

Two homicidal red eyes bored into her as she suddenly reached down and grabbed something from her calf. Dominique started as she realized it was a knife.

Then, the robot plunged the knife deep into the dragon's nose and swung down, hanging by an arm from the knife's handle. A screech of pain nearly deafened the girl's ears.

With a quick, deft flick of the wrist, the robot shook the glove off her free hand and swiped her razor sharp fingers across the dragon's throat.

An agonized din came from the beast, a dying moan. Blood pooled quietly out of the wound as the dragon slid to the ground, its red eyes dimming and sliding shut.

For the first time in what seemed like ages, there was quiet in the Shadow mansion. Dominique gasped as she collapsed to her knees, staring at the scene in disbelief.

"Oh yeah! In your face!" the robot shouted, pointing at the dead dragon. "Wrong girl to mess with!"

Dominique couldn't help but laugh; she was reminded of Christina. Shakily getting to her feet, she wobbled over and put a hand on the robot's shoulder.

"Okay," she said. "I have a feeling we're going to be friends...what's your name?"

The robot hummed. "Flint," she said. "And you?"

"Dominique. My friends are somewhere around here..."

"Was that guy one?"

"NO."

With that, the girl walked across the ruins of the lab, disappointed that it was destroyed. Flint began to follow, hesitantly.

"So...you're a Shadow," she said, eyeing her. Dominique turned, surprised.

"No, I'm not."

Flint shrugged. "Whatever. Denial works for me."

From the tunnel, Dominique heard a shout; Tom's voice, calling for her.

"Over here!" she shouted back. Looking back to the android, she jerked her head in the tunnel's direction.

"Come on. Tom and Shayla are waiting for us."

When they got to her waiting friends, Dominique grinned wider than she thought possible as she ran into Tom's waiting embrace.

"Are you alright?" he demanded, standing back and looking her all over. "We heard the roars and shouting, but they suddenly stopped, and I didn't know if you were..."

Dominique rolled her eyes. "I'm fine," she said. "You?"

"Just dandy."

When he finally let her go, Shayla had a hug waiting for her, too. The girl winced as she saw the gash on the shape shifter's forehead.

"Tough fight?" she asked.

"You're telling me," Shayla said, rolling her eyes. Then, she stopped smiling.

"What is *that?"*

Flint was standing at the edge of the tunnel, staring at their reunion. Dominique jogged back to the robot and dragged her forward.

"Guys, this is Flint," she said. "Flint, this is Tom, and that's Shayla."

She pointed to each person in turn, and Tom offered his hand. Carefully so she wouldn't hurt him, Flint shook it.

"Hi," she said uncertainly. "Umm...I've been out of it for a little while."

"Where did you find her?" Tom asked Dominique. Flint crossed her arms.

"I've been shut off," she snapped. "I don't remember much from before I was. Lots of fuzzy flashes."

She shrugged. "No big deal."

Shayla arched an eyebrow. "Pretty convenient, how you don't remember anything."

"Would you prefer it if I did?" Flint asked, looking directly at the shape shifter. Dominique thought she saw the shape shifter's lips twitch in a smile, but she couldn't be sure.

"She saved my life," the girl put in. Tom and Shayla exchanged glances, and the skeleton grinned.

"I don't see any reason why she can't come along with us, then."

"But she was in the Shadow's *mansion,*" Shayla protested. "Who knows what she's used for? She could be a huge bomb for all we know!"

"Oh, lighten up," Dominique interjected. "She saved my life. She comes with us."

Shayla sighed. "Fine, but if she starts beeping like she's gonna blow-"

She broke off. From inside the collapsed tunnel, they heard the sound of running feet.

"You've gotta be kidding me," Dominique said in disbelief. "That collapse didn't kill Orphius?"

"I vote we go," Shayla said. "I vote we go *now.*"

With that, she began to shift. Flint backed up with a shout of surprise, but soon realized what was happening. Dominique laughed.

When the white dragon crouched before them, the robot sprang on lightly, followed by Dominique. She almost slipped; Tom caught her as she fell back.

"Geeze, you're a klutz," he said, helping her the rest of the way. She gave him a smile.

"I would have loved to have seen you when you were growing into those legs; you must have been like a stork."

"What's a stork?"

"Never mind."

In front of them, Flint was laughing to herself, looking back at the two of them.

"What?" they demanded unanimously.

"Oh, nothing."

Three hours of flying, Dominique soon learned, was not fun on the back. She was sore, stiff, and ready to get off.

"Can we land now?" she asked, her voice edging onto a whiny tone. Tom sighed, rubbing his head. The girl glared at his show of annoyance.

"Shayla!" she shouted. A questioning growl answered her.

"Set us down!" she said. The dragon nodded in affirmination and began to descend. Flint turned around.

"So," she said. "Where are we headed?"

"To Red Shield," Tom answered. "I have some contacts there. We need to regroup...that's the best option."

"So you do work for them?" Dominique asked.

"Well, I wouldn't say *that*...but I know some people who do."

Making an unhappy noise, the girl looked impatiently at the incoming ground. Just a few more seconds...

Shayla landed, and the girl slid down before she knew what she was doing. What she didn't gauge, however was how cramped her legs were. The instant they hit the ground, they crumpled. She swore as muscle spasms ripped through her.

Someone grabbed her arms and hauled her to her feet. Tom looked at her in concern.

"You okay?" he asked.

"Yeah, just dandy," she muttered. The minute he let go, however, she stumbled, only to be caught again.

"I just need to walk it off," she insisted. Raising his hands in surrender, the skeleton let her walk.

"Don't push it," Flint advised him under her breath. "Let her come to you."

Tom looked at his new companion in surprise. Before he could question what she meant, she had followed Dominique.

Shayla came over, dusting off her jeans. "What was that about?"

"Honestly?" Tom asked. "I have no idea."

Violent coughing erupted from the dust surrounding the destroyed room; a hand through the rubble groped, and an armored figure emerged.

It had happened very, *very* fast. Keller had been standing on the courtyard, watching the titanic duel between the two dragons, while still trying to find and put an end to Horter. The next thing he'd known, he was falling through space and had ended up buried in a pile of broken rocks, splintered wood beams, and dust.

He had heard voices; Orphius, and Dominique. Apparently, the girl wasn't just hostile to him. Then had come that machine's voice, and the sound of them getting away with his brother in pursuit...

Swearing, he pounded on the ash and dust. How was this possible? How was his sister still alive? He had spent night after night, lying in torment remembering her screams from inside the house.

And now? She was alive and kicking...literally. He winced as he felt the bruise on his tailbone where she had knocked him down. Her powers had really matured since he'd last seen her.

Part of him was ecstatic to learn she was alive, even if something was obviously wrong with her. She hadn't recognized him or Orphius...

Of course, both of them had changed drastically over the last five years. Grief was a major player in that, along with the hate they felt for one another now.

Slight movement made the man raise his head; someone was coming out of the tunnel, climbing up a mound of debris. Hauling himself out of the hole, the man hastily stood, prepared to defend himself.

Orphius, of course. His brother hadn't noticed him yet. Keller stood stock still, watching his younger sibling traverse the pile.

He looked to be deep in thought, but Keller had a mind to change that. Taking a step forward, he cleared his throat.

The other man whirled, hands going to something at his side. Keller's experienced eyes spotted a rapier before Orphius's cloak hid it from sight.

"You," he said, hatred saturating into his voice. Keller crossed his arms.

"I'm not going to mince words; you saw her, didn't you?"

"Perhaps."

The two of them were silent, bristling like two dragons about to fight. Finally, Orphius broke down.

"Do you realize what this means?" he asked. "Our family isn't-"

"Dead," Keller finished calmly. "But she doesn't remember us, apparently."

"Maybe it's because she doesn't recognize us-"

"Our names are possibly the most famous in all Yumurango at the moment; she'd know who we were."

"But-"

"Good bye."

Keller spun on his heels and walked away, signaling a nearby dragon with his mind. Behind him, his brother's hand went for his sword-

He had whirled before Orphius could do anything. A gun was cocked and ready in his hand. A cruel smile curved his lips as he realized that he could kill him, right then and there.

Orphius knew it too. His eyes were a mixture of hate and fear as he stared at the weapon. Then, of all things, Keller lowered it.

"That would be taking the easy way out," he growled. "Especially for the person who burned our family."

Before his brother could protest his innocence, Keller's ride arrived; the dragon gave a bellow as it circled above them, slowly angling toward the courtyard outside. The man grinned as he recognized her.

Berra, his first dragon, was the leader of the flock of black dragons he commanded. The female gave a roar of recognition when she saw Keller and rumbled deep in her throat. Her red eyes, uncannily intelligent, impatiently watched him.

"I'll see you soon, *little* brother," he said. Keller left the room, approaching Berra and mounting with the ease of practice. He patted her neck once, and they took off, leaving Orphius standing in the ruins of their former home, hands clenched into fists.

Orphius let out a cry of rage as Keller left, disappearing into the snowy sky. Flinging a broken piece of wood across the room, he watched it splinter on the opposite wall before he stormed out into the front yard. A moss covered fountain met his gaze, along with a still intact driveway. The fog was beginning to lift, exposing the nearby mountains to his sight.

A cold wind blew in his face; he grimaced. Somewhere in the Sistern range, those buffoons at Red Shield were beginning to acquire more power than he'd intended them to. That could be a problem.

But what was even *more* of a problem was the fact that his *sister* was alive, and extremely powerful. The only issue with that was...*she didn't remember anything*. It was obviously the work of some blow to her head, or a sinister spell. Orphius cursed inwardly. If he didn't find some way to restore her memory soon, she could be an ally to Keller, working with the very man who had burned their family! If that happened, Keller would easily be able to overpower him with her aid.

He had wanted to see his family again, so badly...the nights he had stayed up, longing to just talk with one of them, were innumerable. Even Keller, he knew, had his days.

To think that Dominique was right there, *right there* and yet so far away...he put a hand to his head with grief. She was running with the wrong crowd, this girl. At this rate, she would get hurt.

Neither he nor his brother could allow that to happen. Orphius looked up again, determination blazing in his eyes.

His little sister *would* be safe.

Even if he had to kill her friends to reach that goal.

Snow, snow and more freaking SNOW!

Dominique grumbled under her breath as she trudged on through the freezing ice, thinking of warm fires and hot chocolate. Ever since she had insisted they land, Shayla had refused to shift back into a dragon, claiming that her "wings were exhausted". That would have been fine, but two hours later, it was getting ridiculous.

"Sure she's tired," she muttered, casting the shape shifter a dark glance. Shayla seemed just fine to her.

It was starting to get dark. Dominique apprehensively thought of how cold it must be at *night.* If they didn't find whatever it was they were looking for *soon,* she was going to throw a snowball at the would-be guide's (Tom's) head.

Finally, just as she was about to begin scooping snow to launch her attack, they stopped.

"Ah," Tom said happily, spreading his arms high in the air. "Here we are!"

"Umm," Shayla said, arching an eyebrow. "Sorry to burst your bubble, but I don't see *anything.*"

The skeleton gave her a flat look. "How can you not?"

Ahead of them, a gigantic mountain loomed upward toward the sky, covered with snow. The only things visible amidst the ice encrusted mountainside were a few rocks and trees, stark contrasts to the white.

Dominique scratched her head, looking around for some sign. Beside her, Flint crouched down and began to study the snow.

"Gee," the shape shifter drawled, answering Tom's question. "Maybe because we're facing the side of a mountain? There's nothing to see!"

"You'd be surprised," he said smugly. "*Very* surprised."

Shayla rolled her eyes, mirrored by Dominique; rubbing her arms for warmth, the girl surveyed the barren landscape. A whipping wind had started up.

"Wherever these people are, can we go meet them now?" she asked. "I don't like it out here."

The skeleton tapped his lip. "If you're cold, have my jacket; this could take awhile."

He shrugged out of the coat as he spoke, and handed it to the girl. Slowly, she put it on, surprised at its smooth texture. An unexpected smell came to her nostrils; peppermint?

Her mind, however, wandered back to that isolated house, down in the valley below them. Orphius had been there, along with Keller. And somehow, they had both known her name...how?

She frowned, deeply puzzled. Although Orphius hadn't used her name outright, it was obvious he had recognized her from somewhere. Keller had been even more insistent, screaming her name in her face-

"Hey," Flint said. "I think I found something."

The robot was still crouched down, looking intently at something on the ground. "There's a mild signature here," she said, and began to move slowly, keeping her eyes down. "Footprints are what I'm guessing."

Tom seemed impressed. "Nice," he murmured. "Let's go see where they lead."

Flint led the way into a small grove of trees, covered in snow. Feeling wetness on her face, Dominique looked up; snow was beginning to fall in little flurries, pushed every which way by the wind.

Shayla sneezed; the dragon side of her didn't like the cold. Dominique smiled at her friend (she supposed they were friends by now) as she approached to walk by her.

"I would really like to know why you were a fighting dragon back in that cage." she said, her eyebrows arched. She hadn't had the chance to ask yet, and she was very curious.

The woman grinned. "When you're a dragon, you don't need money," she said in a matter-of-fact tone. "But there are always people who do. My "trainer" was one of the poorest men you'd ever see before I came to him. I made his life better."

Dominique blinked. Somehow, she had been expecting a greedy response involving the money that came with the pits. Shayla was much kinder than she had expected.

"But you wanna know the reason he was poor?" the shape shifter asked, whirling around. Snow was clumping in her long hair; it looked like she had crystals in it, giving her a cold veneer.

Out of her entire face, though, her eyes were the coldest. Their blue sheen stared out at Dominique angrily.

"Why?" the girl asked quietly.

"Because of those two scumbags we just left," she snarled, pointing back to where they had come. "His farm was burned by one of Keller's brigades marching through the area. They didn't even need to do it! But you know how men can get, just do anything they damn well please-"

Tom cleared his throat.

"Sorry to interrupt your little rant, but Flint's got something here," he said, waving them over. Shayla and Dominique approached them swiftly.

Flint had uncovered something in the snow which appeared to be some sort of padlock. A few more swift swipes of her metal arms, and there was a door. Satisfied, she stepped back.

"That's gotta be the crappiest hideout I've ever seen," she observed.

"Oh? And how many have you seen?" Tom snapped defensively.

"Good point."

Without another word, the machine raised her leg and slammed it down into the door. Metal sliced through metal; a hole was left.

Reaching her arm into the hole, Flint concentrated as she bent her elbow...the opposite way than usual. Doing so, she could get to the lock on the other side of the door...

A click followed, and then snow tumbled into the slightly angled passageway revealed as the door slid open.

Nothing but darkness met their gaze; Dominique gulped.

"Who's first?" she asked, looking in. The four of them exchanged glances.

"Alright, fine," Tom said, squaring his shoulders and marching straight in. The girl smiled, and followed.

As the girl stepped in, she sighed with relief. Although the tunnel smelled somewhat moldy, it was still warmer than the snowbound landscape outside. A steady dripping sound came from above them. Dominique found the sound oddly comforting with its regularity.

"This tunnel used to be an emergency exit," Tom explained, snapping his fingers; Dominique jumped as a small flicker of yellow flame appeared. Using his own finger as a candle to illuminate the passage, the skeleton turned right at an intersection leading them down another dark tunnel. Dominique gripped her sword tight, ready to use it...just in case.

"Huh," Shayla sounded very unimpressed. The thief turned around and frowned.

"No comments," he snapped.

"I didn't say anything!"

For a few minutes, silence descended upon the group. The only sound came from their soft footfalls, muffled breathing, and occasional curses as someone banged an elbow on the side of the tunnel.

Finally, just before Dominique was ready to throw a fit from the suspense and start running in the opposite direction, they came to a door.

Tom evaluated the door's surface. "Hold on," he said, turning to Dominique.

"Look in my right jacket pocket; there should be a small tool in it."

Dominique nodded and began to shuffle through the contents of the pocket; finding nothing like a tool, she kept searching. There was a rubber band, something that felt like a ball, and a-

Someone grabbed her wrist and pulled it out, and she looked up in surprise to see Tom standing beside her. He reached his hand inside the pocket, needing to lean over slightly due to Dominique's petite stature.

His closeness made her blush slightly. No guy had ever come that close to her before, and she wasn't prepared for it. Even if that "guy" wasn't really human. Finally, his hand closed on something and he turned away, seemingly oblivious to her.

"Okay then..." he muttered, starting to twist a knob on the small thing. It looked like a drill. When he stepped back, the three females could see there was a wire attached to it, along with a remote control that was in the skeleton's hands.

"Why does it need that?" Flint asked dubiously.

"Watch this," Tom said with a grin.

He pressed a button; the drill went haywire. Sparks shot off in all directions as the small machine began to tunnel its way through the metal.

The instant it did, however, an alarm pinged its way through the air; a loud sound that made everyone jump. From out of nowhere, red lights descended from the tunnel ceiling and began to flash in front of them.

"Security breach, emergency exit junction C-5," a cool voice instructed.

An instant later, the door opened...and a mix of rifles and bows were all aimed in their direction, all wielded by six powerful looking men.

"Well," Tom said nervously. "I guess they were here after all."

One of them stepped forward. "All of you, hands up!"

Dominique instantly did as she was ordered.

"Search them."

The entire squad moved forward, and Dominique frowned as her sword was unbuckled from her hip. She liked that blade. Flint made an unhappy noise as her rifle was taken from her.

Shayla, surprisingly, had two slim knives strapped to each of her calves, plus the one she reluctantly slid out from beneath the back of her shirt. She shrugged as she saw Dominique staring at her.

Tom, however, seemed perfectly at ease as the men turned to him. Suddenly, they all saluted.

"Sir!"

The skeleton sighed. "Hey guys."

Dominique stared at her friend with a mix of resentment and surprise on her face. How come *he* didn't have his weapons taken away? But no...all that "the guys" did was take his cello case so he wouldn't have to carry it.

"What are you doing back so soon? I heard that you weren't due to return to base for another month at least," one guard said with a happy grin. Tom nodded.

"That was the plan, but as you can see...I've met some people."

As the conversation was directed back to them, the guards' faces became stoic again, and they faced the intruders with scowls.

"Who are they?" one asked Tom.

"Friends of mine. Could you let them go?" he asked.

"Sorry sir, you know the rules."

Tom sighed; he had expected no less. "Fine then," he said. "Let's bring them to Val."

"Move," one guard said, jerking his gun in one direction. Shayla bristled at his tone.

"I'm not an *animal* to be ordered around, thank you very much!" she snarled. "You'd better not talk to me like that ever-"

Without missing a beat, the man slapped her across the face, hard. Tom's eyes widened, and he grabbed the guard's wrist tightly.

Dominique watched as the skeleton screwed the human's face in close. Anger simmered on his entire body, and fear shone brightly in the other man's eyes.

"Don't you ever do that again," Tom hissed.

From behind the commotion, Flint slowly eased her hand back into her glove. Better to leave her concealed weapons for another, more convenient time.

She glanced toward Dominique; the girl nodded slowly and signaled her to wait. Flint nodded back and stared coldly at a guard who came too close.

Their small train began to move; Shayla stared coldly ahead, rubbing her cheek where the man had smacked her. Tom fell in beside his friends, and Dominique looked toward him.

"What's going on?" she hissed. "Where are we going?"

"Val's the head of Red Shield," he murmured back. "He'll decide what happens to you. If he says you can stay, then great. If he doesn't...I'll help you guys escape."

The girl nodded, trying to be brave. Around them, the air had become much warmer; lights from other tunnels shown through doors that undoubtedly led to what was known as Red Shield. Through quick glances as they moved along, she saw a kitchen, a lounge, and even office spaces.

"I don't understand," she whispered. Tom had to lean in to understand her. "What does Red Shield do?"

"They fight," he said simply. "Their main objective is to stop Orphius or Keller from taking over after their war has ended. They've already been on raids to weaken their armies. So far, it's been working pretty well-"

"Stop," one guard snapped. Dominique slammed into Shayla's rigid back; the woman had stopped instantly.

"Hey," she murmured. "Are you okay?"

The shape shifter merely nodded, keeping her gaze straight ahead. Dominique threw a piercing glance toward the abusive guard, who was skulking by in the corner. He met her glare with one of his own.

"Who is that guy?" she muttered to Tom, still keeping her eyes on him. The skeleton looked.

"Oh, him? That's Edward."

He looked at her with concern. "Stay away from him."

Gulping, Dominique nodded, and returned her attention to the front.

The door they had stopped in front of was ornately carved; multiple scenes, all laid out in historical progression, depicting epic battles. Larger than anything else, however, was the symbol in the center; a strange sign, exactly like the one on Dominique's sword.

"What does that mean?" she asked no one in particular.

"It's the Shadow's crest," Flint said. "In a forgotten language, it's said to mean *despair.*"

"Hmm. How nice," the girl said absently. She kept staring at it.

"The three of you, come in!" one guard ordered, waving them forward. Tom slipped through before them, quickly beginning to speak

"Val, before you do anything hasty, I really should explain things..."

"Tom? What are you doing here?"

Dominique entered the room cautiously, hearing the strange man's voice and not really caring to know who it belonged to.

To her surprise, the room was an enormous office; bookshelves, numerous desks, and even scrolls met her gaze, along with an entire wall that was covered with a variety of different swords and weapons. The entire wall facing them was an enormous window. Outside, the snowfall had thickened and was continuing its job of blanketing the world in white.

But it was the man sitting behind the room's only desk that most surprised Dominique. Taking in the appearance of the room, one might have expected the room's owner to be a quiet, conservative person, perhaps with glasses and a classical manner of dress.

Not this guy. He was leaning back in his chair, feet propped up on his desk. He wore a black trench coat which spilled to the floor. His pants were of a casual beige color, while his shirt was a rich, dark red. The entire outfit was topped off by a black hat that shaded part of his face, but didn't hide the patch that covered his right eye. It was a nice patch, obviously crafted for long-term use. His other eye was brown, and had a naturally cynical glint to it. Long, black hair (slightly curly), hung down to his shoulders, and a cigarette was lit in his mouth.

As the man stood, the girl heard a small jingle; looking at his waist, she saw that he had an entire arsenal of weapons attached to him, even in this seemingly most protected of places.

"Welcome back," the leader of Red Shield said, obviously surprised. "I wasn't expecting you for another-"

"Month, I know," Tom said. "But Val, these guys behind me-"

"Are your friends," the man finished with a slightly impish grin. He smiled at the three women.

"Hi ladies," he said. "Sorry for the rude reception, but you were in our emergency tunnels. At first, we weren't sure what you were...or what you were up to."

"That's *his* fault," Flint said, pointing toward Tom. "He told us that it was an emergency exit, but we didn't know-"

"Hey! You're the one who found the thing!" the skeleton snapped.

"Yes, but you could've told us what we were getting into before we ended up in the faces of six really pissed off guys!"

"People!" Val said, holding up his hands in surrender. "I realize things are a bit strained at the moment, so..."

His voice trailed off. He had been sizing up Flint and Shayla first, since they were the largest of the trio and made a strong first impression. But now he was looking at Dominique. The girl shifted nervously, hoping the focus of his gaze would move elsewhere.

"Umm...Tom?" he asked quietly. "May I...May I talk to you alone for a moment, please?"

The guards marched the three outside again, while Val paced in impatience as they left the room. Tom looked determined as the heavy door slammed shut.

Outside the room, Dominique once again felt her eyes drawn to the symbol at the center of the door. She felt as though she had seen it somewhere before...maybe it had been on a doodle she'd made once-

Her head snapped up as she heard shouting coming from inside. Tom's voice was loud and easily recognizable, and Val's was even louder. Maddeningly, she couldn't make sense of what they were saying.

"It's a spell on the door," Shayla muttered discretely. "You might be able to hear them talking, but not understand a word they're saying. Pretty sneaky."

"Don't bother trying to listen in," Edward suddenly said. "There's a listening spell on the door-"

"Yeah, we're not stupid," Dominique snarled.

The man frowned, and looked as though he was ready to smack *her* as well, but at that moment, the door opened. Tom came out, looking worn out.

"Well?" the girl asked, glaring at the skeleton. He muttered something under his breath and looked down at the floor.

Tom took a deep breath. "You guys can stay."

Dominique grinned. Without thinking, she launched herself at him and hugged him tightly. A few of the guards were taken by surprise; one even half drew his sword.

Drawing back, the girl cleared her throat and crossed her arms.

"So," she said evenly. "Where are our rooms?"

The room was nice, she had to admit. Simpler than her room back home, perhaps, but it still had a kind of homey feel to it. There were two beds; one for her, one for Shayla. The shape shifter had already claimed the bed closest to the door, which of course was the one Dominique had wanted as well.

Giving her new roommate a sour glance, she put her sword carefully on her bed and sat down beside it, blankly staring at the bed's white pillow. Shayla noticed.

"What's wrong?" she asked.

"Is this what life is here?" Dominique murmured. "Constant fighting?"

Her violet eyes remained fixed on the pillow. Shayla frowned and came to sit by the girl, her arm going around her thin shoulders.

"Hey," she said, shaking her lightly. Dominique looked up, her eyes moist with tears.

"You're a fighter, Dominique. I know it in my bones. You're different from any other seventeen year old I've met. Haven't you realized that by now?"

Dominique blinked once, looking away. "What do you mean?"

Shayla sighed in exasperation. "I mean that you're...different."

"This sucks!"

Both of the females started as they looked up. Flint had barged through the door, stashing her rifle in a corner before sitting on Shayla's bed, arms crossed.

"They don't have enough rooms for me to have one of my own," she snapped. "I'll have to share one...with..."

Her voice trailed off. For the first time, she noticed the despondent atmosphere. "Umm...what's going on?"

"Nothing," Dominique said, standing up. Shayla hastily nodded in agreement and rose as well.

Flint shrugged and looked around, swinging her metallic feet on the side of the bed for a while before she realized something.

"Where's my bed?"

Two beds for the three of them complicated the sleeping arrangements; in the end, the robot was lying on the floor, complaining that her circuits would freeze up from the cold air emanating from the stone. Shayla and Dominique told her to shut up.

A sudden knock on the door caused them to tense; it was late, and they weren't exactly expecting any visitors. Flint's hand was out of its glove as she opened the door, just in case.

She relaxed. "Don't worry," she said, swinging it open wider. "It's just him."

The *him* she was speaking of (Tom) gave her a look as he poked his head in.

"Everything okay?" he asked. "I know the first day here might seem a little overwhelming-"

"We're fine," Shayla said airily.

"Are you sure?"

Shayla snorted, though she seemed complacent. "Don't worry about us. And Horter," she continued, tossing her black hair back. "Don't you need to go see anyone around here? Old war buddies that you're just dying to share stories with?"

Tom seemed uncomfortable. "I don't believe that's any of your business," he muttered. He glanced toward Dominique.

"What?" she snapped.

He held up his hands in surrender. "I was just gonna ask if you're alright!"

"Well I'm fine, thank you very much," she said, drawing her sword and beginning to polish it with a rag.

"Could I borrow that?" Flint asked, eyeing the way the blade began to sparkle as it was wiped, thinking her gun could use some shine as well.

"Anyway...good night," Tom said, turning on his heel and swishing out the door.

When it shut, Dominique fell back on the bed, staring at the ornately carved ceiling. Shayla sighed and dove under her covers.

"Good night."

Dominique followed her example. The bed felt comfortable and inviting. With any luck, a good night's sleep would bring a better day to them tomorrow.

"Night," she mumbled.

"Don't bother trying to wake me up," Shayla advised. "Dragons sleep hard and only wake up when they want to."

"Fine by me," Flint groused, and Dominique heard the robot mutter something else under her breath.

"She could stand to rest her jaw for a change."

The girl burst out laughing.

"You have a problem?" Shayla asked. Her voice already sounded half asleep.

"Nope," Dominique said, with a small smile.

And at that moment, it was true.

10

Assignment

The next day, however, brought on a whole *new* bout of problems.

An alarm woke Dominique up at an absurdly early hour; her bleary eyes tried to focus on the clanging wall clock, and she finally realized that it was only five-thirty in the morning.

To her right, Flint sat up on the floor. "What the hell?" she muttered, shaking her head as her systems slowly booted up. "What time is it?"

"I should think you'd know, given you're a machine and all," Dominique groused. "I'm going back to bed."

Even with the commotion, Shayla hadn't woken up; the shape shifter's mouth was slightly open, and she was snoring softly and drooling. Even when Dominique jokingly threw a pillow in her face, she didn't stir, although it did soak up some of the drool.

"Guess she wasn't kidding."

"Let's see what they have for breakfast here," Flint said eagerly.

Dominique looked at her oddly. The robot stared back at her, confused.

"What?"

"Umm...you eat?"

Flint rolled her eyes. "Oh. It's not like I *have* to, but its fun."

Her eyes glowed slightly brighter; Dominique guessed that it was what passed for a smile. Grinning back, she shrugged and got up.

When she opened the door, there was a pleasant surprise waiting for her. On a dresser in the hallway outside the room, new clothes had been laid out for them, including black pants that seemed to resemble riding breeches, but were softer to the touch. There was also a simple white shirt made out of light, airy material that seemed impervious to tearing. A pair of soft, brown boots easily slipped onto her feet and fit her perfectly, automatically self-adjusting to her size. The numerous buckles ensured that they would stay snug during travel.

And best of all, Dominique saw a tight fitting, black jacket, displaying on its front a symbol for a shield, entirely red. She arched an eyebrow.

"Their standard uniform?" Flint asked, looking her up and down.

The girl looked at her reflection. The new clothes were comfortable enough, and she had needed new ones. Buckling her sword to her side, she was pleased to see she looked like she belonged in this world.

"What about you?" she asked the robot, who was still wearing her black outfit. Flint looked at her blankly.

"I'd rather die than wear one of those," she said simply.

The subject of her wearing the new clothes never came up again.

Flint led the way through the twisting, turning corridors of Red Shield. Apparently, the robot had managed to memorize the route and the rooms they had passed by the previous day.

She paused at one; Dominique nearly ran into her back as the robot suddenly skidded to a halt. Blinking once, she looked at her friend with mild irritation.

"What?" she snapped.

"Mess hall," she replied, and swung the door open.

Bright light, different from the torch-lit main tunnel, greeted Dominique's eyes as she stepped in. Loud noises of eating, talking and shouting came to her ear.

In front of them, three extremely long tables were laid out, stretching to unusually long lengths for furniture. Dominique blinked once. The light was coming from several orbs of light floating in midair, as bright as any electric lamps she had known back on Earth. It was sort of unsettling to watch them bob up and down, unattached to any type of supporting structure.

At the back of the room, there was a small line of people running by a kitchen built into the wall. Chefs wearing white aprons atop their Red Shield uniforms passed food onto trays as the people in line walked by.

As they stood and took in the scene, few in the room casually looked up from their food and suddenly stopped eating and stared. More and more people soon realized their presence, and a hushed silence fell over the entire room.

"Gee," Dominique muttered. "Guess they're not used to newcomers."

Flint made the first move. Boldly walking past two of the tables, she marched right up to the counter where the chefs were working.

"I'll have what everyone else has," she said. Her eyes never left them as they prepared her food dutifully. Dominique scampered up to her friend.

"Same here," she said. Her voice broke; she was sure her face was the same shade as the emblem on her jacket.

Behind them, conversation started to bubble up again, and the noise that had greeted the two of them soon lapsed back to the normal cacophony. The members of Red Shield, however, couldn't stop from constantly staring at them.

Most of them were human, but some were more...exotic. Some looked like crosses between wolves and humans, while other fanged creatures sported spiny crests along their spines and scales. Regardless of any differences in physical appearance, there was one thing that they all shared, the expression on their faces and in their eyes.

They were certainly all battle hardened warriors. The way they held their eyes in a steady gaze, even when speaking casually, spoke of confidence and hard battles won. There was no way to mistake the proud bearing of a soldier, or to miss the tense set of their jaws. Dominique wondered if she would end up looking like that one day.

Flint and she had taken seats at the very end of the middle table, keeping to themselves. To their left, a large man was talking across the table to a woman who looked as though she had just gotten back from a recent raid; scratches that still hadn't fully healed covered her jaw.

Flint and Dominique politely ignored the others in the room, as the others ignored them. They didn't have anything in common to talk about anyway. Dominique kicked Flint under the table.

"What?" the robot asked.

"Don't you think it's odd that everyone here treats us like pariahs?"

Flint shrugged. "It's probably because you've got purple eyes."

"What's wrong with that?"

The robot just shook her head. "Let's just say, in Yumurango, purple eyes aren't exactly omens for good fortune. More like the opposite."

"Oh," Dominique said, suddenly self-conscious at her appearance. She stared at her food, acutely aware that people here weren't particularly fond of her; even Val had seemed shocked...

"Well, looks like two of the three little piggies are up," a familiar voice said. Dominique's head flew upward, glaring, but broke into a smile as she realized it was Tom. He sat down beside them, minus a tray.

"I already ate," he explained. "How was your first night?"

"Fine. I slept great." Dominique said. Flint just snorted.

"Yeah right. Great if you're actually sleeping on a bed."

"Hey, how long had you been asleep down in that basement?" Dominique snapped. "I wouldn't think you'd mind being awake a little bit more."

The robot shut up, but her yellow eyes flashed brightly beforehand...Dominique got the message that flashing could mean anger as well.

"Hey," the girl said. "What was all that with Val yesterday? He seemed really surprised when I came into the room."

"Hmm? Oh, that," Tom said, seeming to be surprised. "That was nothing. Just the fact that I'd brought three new people in at once-"

"Tom," Dominique said reprovingly. She could tell when he was lying in a second. He sighed.

"It's just that you're a little...unusual," he muttered. "Your eyes, for one thing-"

"You know, I would have thought that when I'd somehow transported myself to another *world,* my eyes wouldn't be such a big deal!" Dominique shouted, getting to her feet. "But here it's an even *bigger* one!"

Furious, she whirled around and began to stride away. As she walked, her sword swung dangerously from side to side, but Dominique didn't notice, or care, until she opened the door to the main hall.

The sword's scabbard swung forward and hit someone directly in the face.

Now, she hadn't really been expecting that to happen- it only had swung up to about even to her waist, and it would have struck a normal sized persons leg...but the little creature with the growing lump on its nose wasn't normal sized, and seemed even smaller having been knocked down by the scabbard.

It wore a silver cloak, which immediately offset it from the black and red garbed Red Shield members in the cafeteria. Its hood had been knocked back from the blow, and it was squinting and rubbing its nose.

Being a newcomer, Dominique couldn't help but feel she was a little out of the loop on this one. Its skin was as white as Shayla's, but smooth like a human's. Its ears were enormous for its small head, sticking out on either side like fans. Around its neck, a cord sported a single silver stone that gleamed in the bright light shining from the ceiling. When it finally opened its eyes, they looked positively enormous for its head. They were a dazzling green.

"And a fine good morning to you, too!" it snapped, rising to its feet. It spoke with an accent she had not yet heard in Yumurango, not unlike that of a person from England. "I expect you haven't quite awoken yet, since your sword has just gone and banged into my face!"

The creature, obviously a male, jerked his head up to glare at Dominique. When he saw who she was, however, he gave a little squeak of fright.

"Oh, dear," he murmured. "Umm...I'm sorry, if I've offended you in any way!" he yelped.

Dominique raised an eyebrow. "Uhh...I think it's the other way around. I'm the one who hit you in the head. You've got every right to take offense with me."

He, however, had other ideas. Sidling alongside of her, he sprinted away as fast as he could...and slammed into Tom's bony shins. The skeleton had been about to tap Dominique's shoulder, and went down with a hard *crack* himself.

The small creature was clearly very shocked. His ears stood up at the sides of his head as he realized who it was he had just knocked over and shared the ground with.

"Oh no," he squeaked out, pulling his ears down from the sides of his head and covering his eyes with them. "Not you."

Tom rolled his eyes. "Sadiki, you're not gonna freak out again, are you?"

Dominique looked at the bizarre little creature, who had hesitantly lifted his ears from his eyes.

"No," he snapped. "I'm just trying to remember if there was ever a time in my life where I've loathed someone this much!"

With that, he pulled himself to his feet, turned on his heels and left Dominique very confused and Tom on the floor.

"Umm..." she started.

"Don't ask," Tom said with a huge sigh. "That's Sadiki...not exactly one of my most noteworthy fans."

"It's actually refreshing," said a voice from the other side of the doorway. Shayla came into view, in her new Red Shield outfit. "I was beginning to think that you could do no wrong here; it was sickening."

"True," Dominique muttered. Out of the corner of her eye, Dominique saw Tom get to his feet. "What *is* he?"

"Right now, he looks like a Doggarth," Tom said, frowning. "That's what his bound form is meant to look like."

"Bound form?" Dominique asked in alarm.

"It's what happens sometimes when something's put under a spell. They take on a different physical appearance than they actually have."

"So...that's not what he really looks like?"

"Yes...don't ever, *ever* take that necklace off of him. He'd do it himself, but Val's got a powerful charm on it; someone else has to."

"Why? What's wrong with taking it off of him?"

No one answered her question. Shayla's scaly arms bristled subconsciously, and she stared at the little creature moving quickly away from them and into the cafeteria with a little more intensity.

"Tom...that thing's not a...not a *Marauder,* is it?"

The skeleton didn't answer. But a telltale tightening of his mouth told everything the shape shifter needed to know. Her eyes widened.

"What?" Dominique demanded. "What's a Marauder? Are they dangerous?"

"You don't want to know," Shayla said hollowly. "Let's just stay away from him, shall we?"

Flint came clomping up to them, looking very edgy. "I just felt something really, *really* nasty come into the room," she said. "Don't ask me how, but where is it?"

Dominique crossed her arms as Shayla pointed to Sadiki. The Marauder was helping himself to some food at a table, talking with a small group of Red Shield members.

"Yecch," the robot said. "I hate those things. It's a good thing they're almost extinct."

"What are they?" Dominique demanded. She fumed silently as no one answered her query...*again.*

"He seemed apologetic to me," she snapped. "He said he was sorry for no reason."

"Marauders don't apologize to *anyone,"* Shayla said, but she seemed surprised. "You must have heard wrong."

The girl just shrugged. "Whatever."

"Hey, I'll show you guys the training rooms," Tom said hastily, motioning them to leave the area outside the mess hall. Since she had eaten, Dominique was feeling more awake, and left without complaint.

As Tom led them away, she glanced back at the odd little creature. He was staring after them, his green eyes fixed on her.

She was grateful when the door shut between them.

Clang! Clang!

Dominique gritted her teeth as she moved to parry the blow; instinctively, she stepped back and performed a series of complicated movements allowing her to bypass her rival's blade. But this maneuver bought only seconds, and her opponent immediately came at her again.

Sweat was dripping down her forehead; blinking furiously, she tried to clear the drops from her eyes, even as her opponent swung down at her again. With a final grunt of effort, she parried the offending blade away and flicked her sword up to her enemy's throat.

Tom laughed. She grinned as well and went to sit against the wall, gasping for breath. He was breathing hard as well.

"You're good," he gasped, chugging some water. They had been dueling for the past two hours now. Given their exhausted state, it was pretty conclusive this was their last match. Dominique shrugged.

"I don't get it. Maybe I learned it before, the time that I can't remember," she said. "Fencing lessons or something."

"Sure," the skeleton said, though it sounded like he doubted it. Dominique elbowed him lightly.

"You're not too bad yourself!"

"Well, *I've* had ten years experience," he said. "I can hardly believe I'm being bested by a teenager."

"Oh yeah? You talk pretty big for a twenty three year old."

"Shut up."

Dominique took in the room. Well, not really a room...more like an arena. The entire sparring area was covered with sand to cushion the landings of practicing soldiers. Above them, the ceiling was darkness. It was almost like it was an entire world of its own, sitting by itself in a vast expanse of space. Farther down, toward the room's far end, there was an obstacle course set up. (Flint was going through it for the fiftieth time, it seemed)

The three of them weren't alone, either. Red Shield fighters were practicing their archery at a makeshift range, and sparring amongst themselves. In her mind, Dominique secretly thought she was better than any of them. Shayla was there as well, and a crowd had been attracted by her fire breathing abilities, which she was exhibiting on a pile of wooden stakes. The dragon gave a satisfied snort as the flames reached a good height.

"It's not bad here," she decided. Tom didn't reply. Looking at him sharply, she was ready to snap at him for ignoring her when she realized he had fallen asleep.

Laughing, she waved her hand in front of his face, just to make sure. But the eye sockets stayed closed behind their odd covering.

She felt like hugging him. If it hadn't been for Tom, she would have never met Shayla or Flint...most likely, she would still have been traveling with Ethan and his family band.

Smiling, and tired, she sat back to rest and stared vacantly across the room. Her brief respite ended, however, as she noticed a trio of people approaching her.

They looked unique, even among the Red Shield. It wasn't just their appearances, (The apparent leader, a young woman, had blindingly red hair, and the two men that flanked her were obviously twins) but also the regal manner in which they carried themselves. It felt to Dominique as if she had been brought into the presence of royalty.

"So," the woman said coolly, sizing her up. Dominique raised an eyebrow. "You're the newcomer, then?"

Her eyes, Dominique noticed, were a vibrant green. The twins flanking her had green eye coloring, and their hair was just as red. Siblings then...she suppressed a frown.

"I suppose I am," she said politely. She rose to her feet, ignoring her cramping muscles, and stretched out a hand. "I'm Dominique."

The woman took her hand gingerly, and the girl suspected, reluctantly.

"Vilondra," she said, and pointing to the twins, stated, "These are my brothers, Jack and Derek."

Dominique couldn't really tell who was who. She supposed the one with the slightly longer nose might have been Jack, but she couldn't say for sure.

"I heard your journey here was quite something," Vilondra said, sniffing derisively as though she really didn't think the journey's adventures amounted to much of anything at all. Dominique's insides churned with anger.

"I guess it was," the girl said, careful to conceal her emotions. She eyed the woman cautiously. "Did you want to ask me something?"

"Is it true you escaped from both Orphius and Keller?" one of the brothers asked, his green eyes alive with curiosity. "What was it like? Were they fighting? Did you see any of their powers in-?"

"Shut up," Vilondra snapped. The twin shut his mouth, but cast his sister an irritated glance as he did so. She took no notice.

"We wanted a word with him," she said, pointing to Tom. The skeleton was still slumped against the wall, breathing with deep, even breaths. "But seeing that he's back in his natural state-"

"What's that supposed to mean?" Dominique snapped. Defensiveness, along with her hidden anger was now also rising up inside her, and she had no idea why.

"Don't you know?" the woman looked falsely shocked. "Your bony friend here is only kept awake by a spell-"

"Thank you, Vilondra, for spilling lies about me for everyone to hear," Tom snapped suddenly. He had risen to his feet now, and he looked awfully mad. His fists were shaking as he clenched them tightly.

"I think it's time you left and did your disgusting business elsewhere," he said calmly. The woman's green eyes flashed.

"Since when have you been able to order *me* around, you old corpse?" she spat. "I'll have you know that I'm the next in line for the-"

"Yes, yes, to the *Collins,*" Tom sneered. "Vilondra Collins, heir to their long empty throne. Have they not found your parents bodies yet? Won't let you seize power because everyone suspects you've murdered them and hidden the bodies in the snow? There's an awful lot of it outside-"

"SHUT UP!" the woman screeched. "How *dare* you!"

"Easily enough,"

"You-you-"

"Hurry up your insults; I don't have time to spend all day here," he said, yawning.

Then, without warning, Vilondra drew out a gun and cocked it at Tom's head.

"Give me a reason not to," she snarled.

"First off; you'll get evicted from this organization before you can say *Shadow*, and-"

"DON'T SAY THAT NAME IN FRONT OF ME!"

She fired the gun.

Dominique reacted on instinct. Reaching out with her power, she focused all of her will onto the bullet, and she focused all her energy on stopping it. She felt something wet trickle out of her nose...what was it-?

What seemed like an instant later, Dominique opened her eyes. Strange...she didn't seem to remember closing them...

She bolted upright, suddenly remembering. Tom! That bullet! And that awful woman! Ooh, when she got her hands on her-

"DOMINIQUE!"

Before she could react, she was being hugged by someone familiar. Her eyes widened as she realized it was Tom. Why had she been lying down, while he seemed just fine? And *why* was he *hugging* her?

"What happened?" she asked, blinking. He just shook his head.

"You're an idiot!" he said, but his heart wasn't in it. "Do you know how stupid that was, trying to stop that bullet?"

"What? That woman was shooting at you!"

"Yes, but I was already dodging it. Not like it would have really done a lot of damage, anyhow...but that's not the point!"

His face suddenly turned fierce. "Your powers may be strong, Dominique, but stopping bullets is well beyond you."

"My personal suggestion," said another voice in the room, "Would have been to have made you a shield between the bullet and Tom, but seeing as how I wasn't there..."

Dominique looked beyond the skeleton to see Val, leaning against the wall. He pushed his cowboy hat up to see her clearly with his one eye.

"That was reckless," he said. "It took a few hours to fix you. You were bleeding badly from your nose for a while there...you strained yourself too hard."

"When you shouldn't have even tried!" Tom snapped.

The girl blinked.

"Where are Shayla and Flint?" she asked.

Tom seemed aghast.

"Where are-where are- WHERE ARE SHAYLA AND FLINT? HAVE YOU GONE COMPLETELY INSANE?"

"No," she said truthfully. "I'm just wondering where our other friends are. Surely you're not the only one who's been worried about me?"

The closed door on the other side of the room banged once, hard; she heard Shayla's roar.

"Well then," she said, smiling smugly. Tom massaged his bony temples, muttering darkly to himself.

"Now that she's better," Val said, addressing Tom. The skeleton eyed him stonily. "We might consider discussing what I brought up earlier-"

"It can wait for a few minutes, can't it?" Tom snapped.

"Actually, it can't," Val said insistently. "This could be the most important mission I've ever sent you on."

"It can wait!"

"NO."

"Tom, hear him out. I'm fine." Dominique said, rising from the ground and slightly alarmed at her friend's behavior. He gave her a look, but grudgingly held out a hand in Val's direction.

Val's boots clicked over the floor as he crossed the room and gave him a small slip of paper, which Tom perused quickly, then froze in surprise.

"You've gotta be kidding me," he exclaimed, going over it again. He screwed his face right up to the paper and looked closer.

"Now you see why it couldn't wait," Val said.

"You're not telling me this is actually *true,*" Tom said, his jaw unhinged. Dominique peered over his shoulder at the paper. It had a short, scribbled message.

Knock thrice on the tree with the silver bark, and be shunted into the Shadows' heart.

"We found it, just a week ago," Val said with a touch of pride. "And we need our best to go and get whatever that spell is hiding."

"The key to breaking Orphius and Keller..." Tom murmured, a skeletal grin playing on his face. "A way to end this horrific war!"

"Exactly. But you've gotta go fast. Here, that's a map for you."

He handed Tom a yellowed scroll, and the skeleton took it eagerly and laid it out, studying it intently. Dominique frowned.

"What's this tree thing?"

"Well," Val said, smiling at her. "It's supposed to hide the Shadow family's most ancient secret, which would ultimately let us control their actions...if they wanted to survive. That source is the thing that keeps them alive."

Dominique raised her eyebrows. "So you're gonna use it to end the war? What if you wanted to take it for yourself?"

He laughed good naturedly. "You're a funny one," he said.

"Val's been all for the people for years," Tom muttered without looking up. "He'd hand it over to the government straight away."

"Oh. Well then," the girl said.

"But," Val said. "Along with your newly acquired trio, Tom-"

"We're going too?" Shayla shouted from outside the door. An unmistakable eagerness was in her voice.

"Yes!" Val called. Then, he seemed to address the door. "Let her in."

The door swung open, and both Shayla and Flint nearly fell over in their haste to get to the paper in Tom's hand. The robot even snatched it away from him as she scanned it.

"Oh dear," she murmured. "I never thought this would be found."

"You know where it is, then?" Val asked eagerly.

"Hell no. I've been asleep for about fifty years now. The family seems to have moved it from the last location I was aware of."

"There's also a small hitch," Val said tentatively. Tom looked up slowly.

"What?"

"I...well...have to send Sadiki with you."

"What?" Tom snapped, enraged. "You know that thing's had it out for me since the moment I met him! What's gotten into you?"

"He's concerned that the girl is untrustworthy! It's not my fault! You know how he gets sometimes..."

"You're the leader of Red Shield!" Dominique said, frowning. "You should be able to control him, shouldn't you?"

"Marauders can be a little hard to handle," Val muttered. He stared moodily at the ground as he kicked it, scuffing the polished white surface. "That little turd's gonna pay one day."

"But anyway," he said, brightening up. "There's no way he'll give you trouble on *this* mission. It was due to Shadows that he was originally bound...he'll be out for blood."

"Quite right," an English tinted voice said from the door. Everyone turned to see Sadiki striding in, looking very dignified despite his small stature. Dominique suppressed a snigger.

"When are we leaving?" he asked.

"Right now," Val said, flashing a glare at the creature. "You'll need horses, of course...we'll need to get to the tree before Orphius or Keller realize what we're doing-"

"I could get them there in half the time if I was unbound-" Sadiki started.

"Don't even think about it!" Val snapped. "Do you even realize how much damage you caused before you were bound? Hundreds of people in that village *died* because of you!"

Sadiki looked at the floor, muttering something foul under his breath, as Val cleared his throat and looked toward the expectant quintet.

"You'll find horses in the stables," he said. "Shayla, I would have you be their primary means of transportation, but knowing that you're all too easily recognized these days..."

"No, its okay," she said, although her tone had a bit of dragonish huff about it.

"Once you've gathered your belongings, set out," Val instructed, once again pulling his cowboy hat over his good eye. "This might be the only chance we've got."

And with that, the leader of Red Shield strode away, already moving down the hall to deal with another important problem.

"Git," Sadiki said casually.

"Come on," Tom said, waving them forward.

Only Dominique seemed hesitant. "But..."

"What?" Shayla snapped.

"I don't know how to ride!"

11

First Challenge

Gupper's metal feet seemed too loud; he desperately tried to quiet them as he clicked his way up the winding stairs of his master's house. Everything was completely silent. Nobody wanted to attract Orphius's baleful gaze.

Ever since he had returned from the mansion, the man had shut himself up in his room and had not emerged to speak to anyone, even about plans for attacking Keller. Each day, screams could be heard from somewhere in the house; from those that had been unlucky enough to cross him.

But he *had* to make this report. It was pivotal to their reign, and his lord would just have to hear him out. He was still young, though he didn't show it...he and his brother and been through the ringer, aging his appearance beyond his true years.

He heard his master's muttering from inside his room; a constant hissing noise that made Gupper think of leaking things. It was as though poison was seeping out into the room.

Taking a deep breath, he knocked quietly.

The hissing noise stopped. Painful silence fell, without so much as an intake of breath from the bird man. Finally, he knocked again.

"Master?" he called, in a quavering voice. "Master, there is something important I must tell you-"

To his surprise, the door opened a crack, and a long, gray hand beckoned him in. Gulping, he hopped in and stared up at Orphius's face. If it had been horrific before, now it was absolutely *terrifying.*

Orphius's glare seemed to penetrate his very feathers as he locked his gaze onto the bird creature. Gupper gave a small whimper and flew as far away as he could in the spacious room. His master, however, simply grinned horribly.

"Come here," he hissed.

His servant had no choice but to do as he was told. Reluctantly, he came over to Orphius and fluttered in front of him.

"What is this report?" the pallid man hissed. "I am not in the mood for trivial news."

"No no!" Gupper nearly shrieked. "It's about Tom, and those others you told me to keep an eye on. They've just been spotted on horses, racing across the plains...sir?"

Orphius had seemed to lose his train of thought at the mention of the rebels. No smile played across his ravaged face, and then he looked up at Gupper.

"Well? Where are they headed? *Why are you here reporting to me, when you should still be following them?"*

"Well, umm..." clearly, what followed was not a bit of news Gupper wanted to give. Orphius's hands twitched, itching to throttle his spy.

"Tell me," he ordered in an icy tone.

"They must have realized that I was following them. There's an odd little creature with them now, I sensed a lot of power...whatever it was probably told them that it sensed me, so..."

He gulped again. "I lost them. I don't know where they are."

"WHAT?"

Orphius screamed the word into the bird's face. Gupper was sent reeling through the air, turning end over end-

"WHAT DO YOU MEAN, LOST THEM? I CAN'T HAVE THOSE PEOPLE RUNNING AMUCK IN MY KINGDOM!"

"Sir, please..." Gupper whimpered.

"HAVEN'T YOU REALIZED WHO WE'RE DEALING WITH? THE GIRL, GUPPER, OPEN...YOUR...EYES!"

With a final shout of rage, Orphius extended a hand, and a crackle of black energy leapt out and hit Gupper squarely in the eye. A furious, burning pain began, and Gupper screeched as the eye began to burn white hot-

Orphius watched coldly as Gupper flew uncontrollably in endless circles, attempting to throw off the spell. Finally, he withdrew the energy; it left the spy's eye smoking, but seemed to have done no permanent damage.

"Now," he hissed, throwing Gupper onto the floor and resting his foot lightly on the metal chest, knowing he could easily kill him if he wished to do so. Gupper knew this as well, and shivered.

"Tell me what you're going to do," Orphius said calmly, expressing none of the anger that he had previously displayed.

"I'm going to find them!" Gupper squeaked. "And then I'm going to bring your sister-"

His master stared at him blankly.

"Ah," Gupper said. "I know, sir. The girl has the same eyes as your father did-"

"ENOUGH!" Orphius screamed. "You are not to lay *one feather* on her, understand? It's her friends that have to go!"

"But she's going to try and kill me too-"

"Let me put it this way," Orphius said coolly. "Are you content with your current plate of *two* Shadows, Keller and Dominique, as your enemies, soon to be just Keller, or would you like me to upgrade that to *three?* Your choice."

His violet eyes were stone cold. Gupper knew he would kill him instantly if he harmed his sister...

"I'll stick with two," he said, starting to wheeze from the weight of his master's boot. Orphius gave a satisfied snort as he released him. Gupper flapped up to eye level, looking winded and scared.

"This is your last chance," he remarked casually. Gupper nodded, shaking, and flew away as fast as he could.

Orphius stood still for a few, long minutes, staring blankly ahead of him. It seemed as though he was hardly even breathing.

Then, whirling around, he focused a glare on an old family picture. The younger, unscarred version of himself stared back at him, a carefree smile playing on his young face.

"Pathetic," he hissed, seeing the way he had his hand clapped on Keller's shoulder. Dominique was between them, staring up with her big, misty eyes.

One small life, miraculously restored, out of a thousand casualties...Orphius stared at the girl in the picture for a moment before turning away, walking to the window.

He stared listlessly out at the plains, murmuring something incomprehensible to himself.

Without warning, he whipped his hand around and sent a narrow stream of energy at the picture of his family, neatly burning out his brother's face.

That was better.

Two dragons wove their way across the sky's blue expanse, enjoying the feeling of freedom as they patrolled the perimeter of Keller's controlled territories. The female among them watched the male with a wary gaze; her son was young, and had not mastered his natural fiery temper yet. Glimpsing five horses on the ground beneath them, she roared an order to him to circle in a holding pattern, and she inspected the animals' handlers carefully.

One of the riders had extremely long legs, nearly dangling to the ground off the horse's sides. The animal didn't appear too happy with his draw; it flinched with each step, as though the rider's bones were digging into its back.

Two of the horses were having an easier time of it. Their riders, for the most part, seemed normal. In a sharp contrast, the trailing horse struggled to keep up with the others, neighing repeatedly when they strayed too far. Its legs trembled as though it was carrying a heavy weight.

A flash of metal caught the dragon's eye; she hissed with suspicion. She could sense power emanating from each rider; even the horse that appeared to be carrying supplies was scented with magic.

She squawked a request to her son; that he bring Keller word of these five strangers so near his land. The male flew off, happy to do his mother's bidding. She watched her son fly off, then, returning her attention to the intruders, swooped down to take a closer look.

"Heads up," Tom murmured, pulling the cloak's hood further down his face. "We might have trouble soon."

"I know her," Shayla hissed back. "She's one of the toughest dragons in Keller's flock."

"And the first one, actually," Tom said. He eyed the incoming dragon, subconsciously tensing. Underneath him, the horse began to fidget and prance.

"What's her name?" Dominique asked.

Tom snorted. "I don't think you need to know *that*," he sniffed.

"Actually," a sarcastic voice said from inside a saddlebag. "Her name is Berra. If you're going up against her, you should at least know that."

Tom glared at Sadiki, though he was aware the Marauder couldn't see him. He still wasn't happy that the creature had been assigned to come with them.

"Berra..." Dominique muttered. To her, the name sounded oddly familiar.

"It would be my advice to clear your heads of any thoughts of our destination," Sadiki added. "Berra is...talented."

As the dragon swooped closer, Dominique cleared her mind, concentrating on the stark contrast of the incoming dragon's black scales among the blue. As she did so, she thought she felt something brush her mind, like a feather inside her head...

Above them, Berra hissed in frustration. They were admiring her, (she didn't mind that) but there was no useful information in their minds. Finding the lack of any useful information suspicious, she dove down through the air toward the troupe, now intent on cutting them off.

"Oh dear," Flint muttered, pulling her horse to a halt. The animal nearly collapsed with relief as she dismounted. The dragon had landed in front of them, hissing.

"What should we do?" Shayla asked, getting off her horse as well. Her ice blue eyes tracked the dragon's every movement; she would be able to tell when she decided to attack, if that was her goal.

"I guess there's no choice," Tom said. His voice was tense, alerting everyone to start preparing themselves for a fight.

Dominique subtly connected a few threads of energy at her fingertips, waiting for Berra to make the first move.

Keller's favorite dragon, hmm? She'd see how good she was.

But still, her name was *so* familiar, like an old friend's identity she now just recalled. Glancing toward the saddlebags, she saw Sadiki's enormous green eyes staring out at the dragon. A curious look was on his face...was it envy? The girl couldn't tell.

A sudden pressure alighted on her mind; she furiously concentrated on the green of Sadiki's gaze, determined not to let the dragon enter her thoughts.

She slipped up; Berra caught a glimpse of her friends, learning who they were. Rearing back, the dragon roared in surprise and breathed fire.

Shayla transformed; her white bulk being about the same size as the black female. Sizing up her opponent, Berra crouched, her eyes narrowed to slits.

Tom let loose yellow fire from his fingertips. The flames licked at the dragon's scales, but had no effect. Berra roared angrily, causing the horses to panic, running wildly in all directions.

Dominique raised her arms, feeling her energy beginning to course through her arms, the blackness becoming visible in her hands. Just a few more seconds, and she'd-

Sounds of a struggle reached her ears, breaking her concentration. Swearing, she looked at the two dragons. They had leapt into the air, launching themselves at each other. Shayla gave a snarl as Berra raked her claws across her shoulder.

Shayla tossed her head; the horn growing out of her forehead slashed the underside of Berra's stomach. The two dragons spiraled higher in a tight formation, each seeking to kill the other.

Dominique felt helpless as she watched from the ground. A few warm drops of blood rained down by her, and she jumped out of the way. It was blue blood...huh.

Up in the air, Shayla's blue eyes tracked her opponent carefully. This worm was good...she had experience in fighting. The scars on her scales were enough to show it. One of her eyes, in fact, had a thin scar running through it which likely obscured her vision. There was her weak spot.

Diving down, Shayla was careful to stay on Berra's right as she prepared her attack. Berra growled suspiciously as she wheeled to follow, but was unable to see anything but a large white blur out of the corner of her eye.

Then, without warning, the blur was gone. Looking around in confusion, Berra hissed angrily and looked down. Had the white dragon lost altitude? Or...?

Just as that last thought entered her head, something slammed down on her back. Shayla plunged her neck down...and bit into the other dragon's spine.

Berra screeched in pain, red eyes widening with disbelief. With a savage yank of her jaws, Shayla released her.

The black dragon fell. The four friends watching from the ground witnessed the grim scene. When the dragon landed on the ground with a loud crunch, Dominique gulped.

"You okay?" Tom asked, without looking away. She nodded once and ran to go throw up.

"Very classy," Sadiki commented as she retched all over the ground. She wiped the remnants from her mouth and gave him a baleful glare.

"Shut up!" she snapped.

"Oh? And who are you to command me? As far as I'm aware, only Val's in charge of me."

"But you'd switch loyalties in a heartbeat," Tom snarled, starting over. His eye sockets watched the marauder carefully. "If any of the Shadows got hold of you, I wonder who you'd serve then."

"I can't help it; I like to be on the winning side," Sadiki said, sighing dramatically.

"Go die in a hole," Flint remarked casually, coming over. Shayla was circling above them, on the lookout for any other threats. "Come on, if we're gonna catch those horses-"

"Leave them," Tom said. "They'll do fine, and if that other dragon makes it back with his report, I'm pretty sure Keller will be looking for horses. We'd better keep moving."

The robot shrugged. "Whatever,"

Shayla landed a fair distance from them, rustling her wings before shifting back.

"Shall we continue?" she asked, grinning at them. Sadiki groaned.

"We don't have any supplies!" he complained. "How are we going to survive?"

Dominique glared at him. "Let's just go," she said. "I'm sure there's something to eat on these plains,"

She looked toward Tom for confirmation, and he nodded. "There's wild Tepfer around," he said. "And if we fail to catch those, we can always get those spiky blue frog things that are everywhere."

"Sounds good," Shayla said, fiddling with a strand of her hair. "Can we go now?"

"Seriously, you people talk too much," Flint complained, shouldering her rifle. Without further adieu, she began to walk away.

Tom and Dominique exchanged glances. Then, for no reason whatsoever, they burst into laughter and followed their friend. Shayla rolled her eyes, and Sadiki just continued to glare.

As they left, the girl glanced back at the dragon's fallen form. Berra appeared to be dead, but she couldn't be sure.

After all, who knew what powers Keller's personal dragon had?

"Sir!"

Keller looked up, vaguely interested, as a nearly hysterical soldier burst into his command tent. The man's eyes were wide either with fear or excitement; he couldn't tell which.

"Yes?" he rumbled. After the incident at the mansion, he didn't have much patience. The soldier's very appearance was already irking him.

"A dragon's come out of the plains with a report of five strangers on horses, just outside our boundaries."

"What's so special about that?" Keller snapped. "We have travelers in the area all the time."

"But sir, it's Berra's son."

"Reyzar?"

That made a difference. Keller frowned as he pondered why Berra might have needed a messenger. Usually, she came to speak with him directly.

"Bring me to him."

The armored figure followed the soldier as he moved swiftly to the center of the camp, where a dragon was crouched. Reyzar's blood red eyes glared at the humans, but brightened as he saw Keller.

"What is it?" Keller asked. A few soldiers exchanged fearful glances as the dragon responded with hisses and growls. Reyzar seemed proud of himself as he finished his message.

Keller listened, and then nodded. "Take me to her, then."

He mounted the dragon's back, feeling Reyzar's muscles lurch beneath him. The crowd parted like a wave before the dragon as he took a few steps forward and launched into the air.

Keller was anxious. Berra had been given to him by his father when he had been a child, and remained a faithful companion. Even now, with everything at stake, he still didn't like sending her out on potentially deadly missions. But still, this had only been a patrol...

Beneath him, Reyzar's breathing seemed slow and steady. His mother had obviously been working with him; Keller smiled.

It was a short flight, but as the two of them began to descend, Reyzar stiffened. He had caught a whiff of something he didn't like.

Keller recognized the tension, and as they came closer, saw what was clearly a large hump rising from the moor. He strained his eyes, trying to see what it was.

Suddenly, realization and horror descended upon him as he saw the glint of black scales reflected by the setting sun.

"Get down there!" he ordered Reyzar. The dragon complied instantly, fear showing brightly in his eyes.

The minute they touched ground, the dragon was galloping toward the unmoving hump. Keller leapt off and sprinted the rest of the way, moving toward the fallen dragon.

Berra had obviously fallen from a great height; her neck was oddly angled, and her entire left half was crushed. Her legs had been broken. Two red eyes, once so proud and valiant, now stared emptily into space. Keller knelt down by her head and murmured a rite as he closed her eyes.

There was only one person who could have done this; his eyes glared at the teeth marks that had ravaged his dragon's spine. No black dragon would dare to betray him, and the mountain dragons were hidden away in their caverns, never to return.

Shayla. His mind burned with the thought of her and the rest of that pitiful little band. Gritting his teeth, he gave a shout of frustration and slammed his fists into the hard packed dirt. Beside him, Reyzar gave a low roar of mourning, craning his head up to the sky.

Keller's eyes showed murderous anger. Tom, Shayla, and that robot would be dead before another sun rose. His sister would be with him, and Berra would be avenged.

He would personally see to it.

12

Interruptions

"Hey Flint, take it easy!" Dominique whined. "The rest of us aren't robots!"

"The way you people walk, I could have made it to the tree and back again before you could get to a mile marker," the android retorted, looking through her scope to scan the area. "Stop whining."

"I can whine if I want to!" the girl snapped. Sweat dripped into her eyes, and she irritably wiped it away.

"All I've got to say is I'm happy I don't sweat," Tom said, striding alongside her with his rangy gait. His cello was still strapped to his back, doing nothing to slow him down. Behind them, Shayla shuffled just in front of Sadiki, trying to ignore his constant pessimistic comments. Both of them were saddled with the supplies they had managed to find on the plains, thrown from the runaway horses' backs, which made them all the more irritable.

"We're all gonna die," the marauder was saying. "Just release me, and I'll be able to get us all there in half the time!"

"Oh, shut up!" the shape shifter snapped. "I'm sick of all this *release me* crap. WE'RE NOT GOING TO, SO LIVE WITH IT!"

She was flinging the words at his face as though they were a physical force, and he winced. His muttering, however, continued as she turned away.

"Will someone *please* shut him up?" she growled.

Without warning, Flint whirled around and shot a bullet at the marauder; it flicked right over his head, knocking his hood down. Everyone stopped and stared at the creature, whose eyes were now as wide as saucers.

"Shut up," the robot said simply, and continued walking. Dominique, Tom and Shayla exchanged alarmed glances.

"Shadow stuff..." Tom muttered, earning him a glare from the robot. He laughed nervously and shrugged.

"So...what's this whole tree thing?" Dominique asked her friend. He looked toward her with surprise.

"I keep forgetting you're new here," he said with a smile. "Well, gee, how do we start...?"

"The tree is the Shadow family's one really big weakness, should it ever be destroyed," Flint explained. "It's their source of magic. Their forerunners found it on the plains when Yumurango was a young world, and it imbued their bodies with magic."

"Why would it matter if it was destroyed?" Dominique asked. Flint looked at her curiously.

"Because if the source of their magic is killed, then they all die too. Their bloodline has become so saturated with it that they can't possibly survive without it. No Shadows, no Orphius or Keller, no war for the dark side."

"It's as simple as that," Shayla added. "But, the trick is to *find* the damn thing. It's supposedly stored in a chest at the base of a silver tree. Rumor has it that only a Shadow can find it without a map; it's believed that all the copies have been destroyed."

"Except for this one," Tom said, holding up the piece of paper. Dominique looked at the scrap of parchment with new respect. "This thing's hundreds of years old," the skeleton said, opening it to inspect it again.

"Why would they hide it at the base of a tree?" the girl muttered. "There are a lot safer places I can think of."

"The tree's bewitched," Tom said bluntly. "We'll have to find it, and then get past any defense it might have in order to get to the chest. After that, we have to see if what's inside of the chest can be dealt with using the weapons or powers we have."

He gestured to their swords, and one gun. "I don't know if magic will work either."

"Fun," Dominique said. "Sounds just dandy."

"Dandy?" Sadiki muttered. She ignored him.

"Where does the map say we have to go next?" Flint asked, looking ahead. "I can see the river from here."

"The Ankara River?" Dominique asked eagerly. She smacked her lips in anticipation of water.

"The one and only," Tom said, squinting to see if he could see it too. "And just in time; it's getting dark."

It was indeed beginning to grow steadily grayer, with the sun almost below the horizon. Somewhere in the distance, a strange animal trilled its call to the evening. Plants swayed in the breeze that blew over the plains, bringing goosebumps to Dominique's arms.

Shayla yawned, shifting the gear on her back. "I vote we make camp there."

"Works for me," Flint said.

"Same here," Dominique added.

"Me too," Tom finalized.

Sadiki didn't say anything, but his face showed that he agreed.

When they got to the river, Dominique scooped up some water from it, eyeing it suspiciously.

"Do you think it's safe to drink?" she asked. Flint stuck a finger into the water, analyzing the liquid.

"Yeah, it's fine," she said. "Just don't drink from that bend,"

She pointed downstream, and Dominique cocked an eyebrow.

"Why?"

A second later, a spiny, many segmented leg hauled itself out of the water, twitching in the air experimentally. Dominique gave a shriek and backpedaled, nearly knocking Tom over.

"I'll get it," Shayla said eagerly. She transformed and swooped down the river, giving a roar as she skimmed the surface and suddenly snapped something up.

The leg had belonged to a creature that looked like brown jelly propped up by many legs. She circled around once and then began to eat, mercifully too high for the rest of her companions to see.

"That's all of them," Flint said, her voice sure. Hesitantly, Dominique cupped some liquid in her hands and drank, thankful for the water.

A fire was lit, and they began to unpack supplies and set up their tents. As they did, Dominique felt herself yearning for a bath. She looked at the swift water wistfully, and stuck her foot in.

Finally, she rolled her eyes.

"I'm gonna go take a bath," she announced. There were a few scraggly trees upstream, forming some cover. She marched toward them with conviction.

Shayla glanced toward Tom. To her surprise, his bones had turned a faint shade of pink, and he was hurriedly rifling through his bag as a distraction. She smiled and shook her head.

Men.

When Dominique came back, clean but freezing, food was being served. It looked vaguely like meat, but she couldn't be sure. She gave Sadiki, the cook, a suspicious glare before taking a bite. He didn't seem to care.

"How far did we go today?" Flint asked, settling herself down for the night as she watched them eat. Shayla shrugged.

"I'd say fifteen, maybe twenty miles," she said. Tom nodded and yawned through his food, covering his mouth.

"We got to the river from the mountains. Even if we started with horses, that's not bad."

"Go us," Dominique mumbled through her food.

"Getting past the dragon was fun," Shayla said brightly. "Don't you guys think?"

Everyone stared at her as though she was insane.

"Oh, alright, be cowards then."

She yawned. "Who wants to do dishes?" she asked, motioning to the river. Flint got up and took the bowls.

Shayla turned over, pillowing her head with her arms, and began to snore. Dominique watched in amazement. How could anyone fall asleep that fast?

Sadiki had fallen asleep even before her; soft coos came from his mouth as he breathed in and out. Dominique arched an eyebrow. When he was asleep with his mouth shut, he wasn't too bad.

Tom poured water on the fire, watching the smoke billow up into the now dark sky. Dominique could hardly see him as he returned to his spot.

"Good night," he said.

"Night," she mumbled. She returned her gaze to the heavens above them; the stars were much brighter here than where she had come from.

It struck her like a blow; she was so far away from home that she felt like a completely different person. There was no Christina, no Alan, and no orphanage...not even a Mrs. Magnuson.

She sniffed once, realizing she was crying. *Stop it.* She snapped at herself. *This is stupid.*

But as those stars beckoned overhead, she thought about how vast the distance was between her home and here. Sitting up, she returned her gaze to the ground and tried not to look up again.

Movement to her left made her jerk her head up; Tom had sat up as well, though he was watching the sky.

"Pretty, aren't they?" he asked. Dominique nodded, not looking again. His eye sockets glanced toward her.

"What's wrong?"

"Nothing," she said, but her voice was thick. She angrily wiped the tears streaming down her face and sniffed again, trying to control herself.

"Dominique, you're crying. Of course there's something wrong."

"It's just...I'm so far away from everything, and I can't..." the girl tried to explain the emotions running through her, without success. Tom frowned and moved over to her side.

"You're homesick," he stated. "It happens to the best of us. You should have seen me when I was finally brave enough to leave Theio!"

He grinned encouragingly. "You're handling it much better than I ever have. I think you've gotta be twenty times braver than me."

"Yeah right," she said, still attempting to quiet her tears. "I've been here for what, less than a week? And I'm crying. That's not brave at all."

Hesitantly, Tom put his hand on her shoulder and shook her gently. "You've got to stop putting yourself down," he murmured. "Think about all the positive things that have happened."

"Like what?" she snapped.

"Well, for one thing, you're alive."

"That's true," she allowed, smiling slightly.

"We're not in Orphius's or Keller's clutches,"

"Yet," she added darkly.

"You're on a mission to *save* this Godforsaken place,"

Dominique didn't say anything. He blinked once.

"And you've met them," he said, gesturing to their sleeping companions. "You've met *me.*"

The girl arched an eyebrow, looking at him. He was staring straight ahead when he said it, and she smiled.

"Yeah," she said. "I'm glad that happened."

He looked at her and smiled. She smiled back.

Patting her shoulder, the skeleton kept his smile in place. "You should get some sleep," he instructed. "Tomorrow's another big day."

Dominique nodded, but she gulped. "Could you-?" but she stopped, turning bright red in the dark. He waited patiently.

"What?"

"Never mind."

"No, tell me!"

"I'm not. It's too stupid."

"Dominique, nothing you can say to me will be considered stupid," he said, raising one hand in the air. "Cross my heart and hope to die."

"You're already dead," she pointed out. He simply raised a bony brow.

"Well, I was wondering if you'd sleep closer," she said. "It's kind of scary, being in a strange world out in the middle of plains that I didn't know existed until about a week ago,"

She looked down as she said it, and she felt him tousle her hair.

"Of course."

With that, he laid down right beside her and shut his eyes, a smile on his lipless mouth. She smiled too as she laid down, facing away from him.

Flint, who had come back to the camp after washing their bowls, saw that Tom had moved. Looking around in vague alarm, she saw their two forms in close proximity, and cocked her head.

Hmm.

"RISE AND SHINE, BOYS AND GIRLS!"

Dominique shouted in alarm and bolted upright, nearly smacking her own head into Flint's. The robot cackled with glee and helped the half asleep girl to her feet.

She swayed once, but managed to keep her balance. "What's going on?" she muttered. To her surprise, all of their camp had been packed away; the robot was nearly snorting in her impatience to continue.

"We've got to keep going! We've gotta get to that tree before Keller and Orphius know where we're headed! What did you think, I was gonna let you guys sleep in?"

"It would be nice," Sadiki grumbled, pushing himself up. He yawned once and shook his head.

From beside the girl, Tom sat up, blinking rapidly.

"How is it morning?" he asked groggily. Dominique arched an eyebrow and offered a hand to help him up. He took it quickly and leapt up, grinning.

"Come on," Flint growled. "I'm gonna need help carrying this lump."

The robot was hefting Shayla's dead weight. *Someone* had to carry her. Dominique swore she heard a spring creaking somewhere in Flint's back.

"I'm up," the skeleton croaked. He looked around. "Where's Sadiki?"

"Don't ask me," Flint snapped. "I'm not the one in charge of the little bugger."

"No," a sarcastic voice came. "I'm in charge of myself, thank you very much."

Dominique rolled her eyes as the Marauder came up to them, waddling in his silver cloak. His enormous green eyes looked at her unblinkingly.

"Girl, I have a question for you," he said solemnly. His tone caught her off guard; she nodded in surprise.

"Where are you from?"

She stiffened, but answered honestly. "From Earth," There was really no point in lying. "Why do you ask?"

"Because you seem different from other Earth-born beings I've known. I noticed it the first time we met."

"Wow, you're that observant?" Tom snapped sarcastically.

"It's just her eyes," Sadiki murmured. "I've never heard of a creature from Earth having naturally violet eyes."

He dropped it after that. Dominique's brow was furrowed with worry and nerves as she watched the creature begin to follow Flint, who was blazing a trail ahead of them. Glancing toward Tom, she frowned.

"What was that all about?"

Her friend didn't answer. He kept staring at the creature, hands clenched into fists.

After their brief exchange, the going for that day was steady and silent. Shayla woke up about halfway through their trek, complaining loudly about the sore neck she had from being carried by Flint (The robot then smacked her on the head after hearing that remark).

It was another hour before Dominique finally spoke.

"So...where are we now?" she asked, looking around. "I didn't think there would be forests here."

They were walking at the edge of one of the densest forests she had ever seen in her life. Green light filtered down through the leaves, making everything it touched appear unusually colored and mottled. In its murky depths, Dominique could hear the calls of strange animals.

"The Restana woods," Tom explained. "One of the more dangerous parts of Yumurango. Even *I* don't know what's in there."

"They're bordered by the mountains on their far side," Flint said, gesturing to a few vague shapes on the horizon. "We had to go around the woods; no one that's gone in has ever come out."

She shrugged apologetically. "But now that we're on the other side, it should be pretty easy to reach this so called 'silver' tree."

"Let's see..." Shayla said, tapping Tom on the shoulder. She gestured to his hand for the map. Grudgingly, he handed it to her.

"We're here," the shape shifter said, pointing to a particular point on the map. Dominique looked over her shoulder to see.

"And that's where the stupid thing should be."

The shape shifter pointed to another point, and Dominique groaned. They were almost there, but it still looked like another full day's walk from their current location.

"Oh joy," Sadiki grumbled, seeming to share her feeling. Tom reluctantly had to agree with him as well—they were all pretty tired.

"I could fly us the rest of the way," Shayla pointed out. "We're far enough away from any region that Keller or Orphius patrol."

"Works for me," Flint said eagerly.

Nodding once, Shayla motioned for all of them to step back; they did so, and instantly she began to change.

After her shift to dragon form, they all began to clamber up onto her back, some more awkwardly than others. Dominique and Tom had to half push, half pull Sadiki into a sitting position, while Flint just leapt gracefully on.

"Let's go!" Dominique called. Shayla nodded regally and leapt into the air. The girl hung onto a spike for dear life as they accelerated into the sky.

Dominique hunched low over the dragon's back, looking at the ground, now far below them. The green sea of the forest was a sharp contrast to the blankness of the plains. It struck her as odd, seeing such a change.

She glanced behind her; Tom was looking down at the ground too, but with more of a nervous gaze. She supposed it was because he couldn't fly. But he was sure brave even to get up on a dragon's back.

Hmm. As she looked at him, she thought about all he had done for her, even though they had met only a week ago. The amazing criminal mastermind, also her friend. It was sort of funny.

"Hey!" she called. He looked up, his hollow eyes wide.

"How're you holding up?"

"Oh, I'm just fine," he answered in a high voice, gripping the spike in front of him even tighter. "Just remind me not to look at the ground."

He curled into a smaller position and stared fixedly at one of Shayla's scales, muttering something to himself. Grinning, Dominique swiveled her head to look at Flint, who was inspecting her rifle. The robot felt the gaze and looked up, her eyes flashing in a brief smile before she returned her attention to her weapon.

There was something about today...something that was missing. It had been over a week since she arrived in Yumurango, and it was weird to think about what people were doing back home. She thought that the Junior Prom might be today, and she would have been going. June fifteenth...

Wait a minute. She glanced toward Tom again. He was still staring at Shayla's scale.

"Hey Tom!" she called. He looked up nervously.

"Yeah?"

"Happy birthday!"

He stared at her for a moment, and then grinned widely.

"You know, I had almost forgotten about it," he said.

"You're twenty four now, right?"

"Right you are. So that makes for...seven years difference between us."

Dominique narrowed her eyes. "Well, how old do you think Flint is? You don't see her going around calculating the differences between her own age and ours!"

"Because I don't remember it," the robot added sullenly. "I don't know how long I've been asleep."

They fell silent at her remark, but Dominique jumped back. "Well, what do you want for your birthday?" she asked her friend. He shrugged, suddenly looking away.

"Nothing that you can buy," he said.

"Okay...what? For the war to end? Some chick you like?"

"What's a chick?" he asked. Dominique smacked her forehead.

"A *girl.*"

Tom grew very still, and he stared at her for a long moment. Then, he cleared his throat and looked toward the ground again. "Maybe," he admitted.

"Ooh!" Flint said, jumping up. "Do tell us the dirty details."

From behind them, Sadiki snorted. "Are you talking about Jerina?" he sneered. Tom gave him a glare.

The Marauder laughed. "That's priceless. You know that sorceress hasn't been in touch with the Red Shield ever since she went undercover to work for Orphius at least a year ago. I've never seen Moony here languish over someone for so long."

"Oh, shut up!" Tom snapped. "I'm over Jerina. She was a pompous pain in the-"

"Now now, don't go using foul language in front of the ladies," Flint scolded.

"None of you count. You're a robot, Shayla's a dragon, and Dominique's a girl," Tom grumbled.

"Hey!" his friend protested. "I can be a lady when I want to be!"

"Sure you can, and I could be king of the world," Tom teased. He looked away again, and Dominique caught a spasm of something strange in his black eyes.

"Are you okay?" she asked. He nodded once.

"Just a little tired. Traveling, you know?"

Dominique did know what he meant; she felt as if she could fall asleep there on the dragon's back. The only thing keeping her from doing so was the knowledge she'd fall a few hundred feet, probably to her death. Better to avoid that.

Something appeared in the corner of her eye, and she turned her head lazily. Two black dots were on the horizon; she frowned, straining her eyes.

"What are those?" she asked, pointing. Shayla turned her large head around to look, narrowing her icy blue eyes.

A growl emanated from her; Dominique barely had time to grab the spike in front of her before the dragon dove down, suddenly accelerating.

"What's going on?" she asked. Shayla's only response was another growl.

"Hold on!" Flint shouted. Behind her, Dominique could hear Tom alternating between cursing and praying. She didn't dare to glance back, though she couldn't help but worry. What if he went tumbling down? He might be killed on impact.

Shayla roared again. Now, everyone could clearly see that the two quickly approaching black specks were turning out to be dragons. Their red eyes eyed the white dragon gloatingly as they flew closer, roaring challenges.

"Oh my God!"

The dragons pulled alongside Shayla, one on each side of her. Dominique jerked her head around, scoping out the riders. One of them had a thin, gaunt man perched atop of it, and the other...

"Umm...GUYS?" Dominique said in a hoarse whisper.

"What?" Flint shouted over the slipstream.

"THAT'S KELLER!"

She screamed the last sentence. There he was, in all his armored glory, hunched low in a jockey-like position, giving the dragon more maneuverability. An advantage that Shayla, with her four passengers, didn't have.

"This is so not fair," Dominique growled. "Okay, Flint! You and I have to get off! Sadiki and Tom, you guys help defend Shayla, got it?"

Tom looked at her with a grim expression on his face, but nodded. She gave him a hurried smile before she hesitantly began to stand up, taking a deep breath.

"Now!"

She leapt; her power enveloped her mind as she struggled to focus on staying aloft. Keller swiveled in his seat to watch the girl. What was she doing?

Flint did a dive bomb and activated the rockets at her feet, propelling her into the air. Tom, meanwhile, began to spin a protective web of yellow fire around Shayla.

"Come on!" Dominique shouted to the robot. "We've got to take him out first!"

She pointed to Keller, who had guessed what they were up to. Shouting an order to the other rider, he turned the dragon around and sped toward Flint.

Dominique flew straight at him, readying her power. It wouldn't be a very strong attack, since she was already using so much energy on flying, but perhaps it would be enough to knock him off his mount-

Before she had a chance to attack, the dragon whipped its head around and snapped at her. She gave a small scream of surprise as her powers failed temporarily. Like a stone, she fell through the air.

"Come on," she hissed to herself, screwing her eyes shut. "Come on!"

There! She had control again. Cursing herself for being so weak, she zipped after the three flapping creatures. This wasn't going to be easy...

"What's taking your report so long?" Orphius snapped into a small orb, on which he had bestowed a communication spell. Another similarly bewitched orb was held by Gupper, who seemed nervous.

"Master, we have some activity over the forest, umm...looks like three dragons. Two are Keller's, but the third one is white."

The man's violet eyes flicked up, and he arched a nonexistent eyebrow. "Is it the shape shifter?" he demanded. Behind him, he motioned impatiently for a Rhinox to come forward; one of the largest quickly obeyed, giving an odd, snuffling noise.

"Yes sir, I believe it is." The spy's voice was filled with tangible excitement. Orphius felt himself grinning.

"How long will it take for you to get here?" Gupper asked. The man laughed.

"A matter of seconds. Watch and learn."

In a flurry of motion, Orphius mounted the Rhinox and began to mutter something under his breath. The beast beneath him stirred uneasily as a feeling of power washed through it, and suddenly-

They were in the air, directly over the dragons' duel. The Rhinox gave a squawk of surprise as it hurriedly beat its wings. Orphius slumped forward, gathering his strength. The spell he'd used wasn't easy, and it had taken a lot of energy...

"Take that!" Flint screamed, and slammed a kick into the dragon's throat. The worm coughed once, and began to descend at an unpleasantly fast rate.

"Nice going!" Tom shouted from Shayla. "Why can't you do the same thing to Keller?"

It was true; although Flint had taken out the gaunt man and his mount, the larger danger of Keller remained. Growling in frustration, she turned to see Dominique striving to catch up to them.

"Come on, girl." She muttered. Shayla's wing beats were beginning to slow. She was tiring rapidly.

Sadiki, who had been awfully quiet until then, suddenly glanced upward.

"Heads up!" he shouted, pointing. Flint looked-

And barely avoided a swipe from a Rhinox's claws. With a shout of surprise, she lashed back and maneuvered herself further away, looking uneasily between the Rhinox and dragon.

"Okay," she said. "This is ridiculous. Where did *he* come from?"

She pointed with disbelief at Orphius, who had a homicidal gaze locked on Keller. His brother turned on the dragon and gave him an equally poisonous look.

"Hey!" a voice called out. "I've got an idea!"

The fighters turned to see Dominique come racing up, her eyes bright white as she cruised between them.

"TAKE YOUR DOMESTIC ARGUMENTS SOMEWHERE ELSE!" she screamed.

"Dominique! Do you know where you were born?" Orphius shouted to her. She turned her head slowly.

"I don't think that's any of your business!" she snapped. Readying her energy, she prepared to strike-

"Although I despise agreeing with this blood traitor, we both know the truth!" Keller interrupted. She glared at them both.

"What the hell are you saying?" she spat. Keller shook his head.

"Dominique, you're our-"

"Shut it, Keller!" Tom shouted.

The skeleton stood upright on Shayla's back, and he looked livid. "I think you're gonna have to fight me, not her!"

"Shut up, Horter!" the man snapped back. "I'll deal with *you* in good time. Right now, I'm a little-"

Tom dropped the protective web shielding Shayla and fired a stream of intense yellow energy at him. Keller's dragon dropped altitude to avoid the blast...but that was when Orphius made a move.

The Rhinox whisked to the side, and Dominique felt someone grab her in midair. Screaming in indignation, she concentrated as hard as she could on whoever had a hold of her-

And was rewarded with a shout of pain from Orphius. The man dropped back, clutching his arm.

"How dare you touch me?" she screamed. "You're an evil, twisted man, the same goes for your entire family-!"

"So it goes for you as well?" Orphius gasped, gritting his teeth against the pain. She stared at him.

"I don't know what you mean."

"Oh, I think you do-"

"Take this!"

From out of nowhere, Flint had rocketed up and slammed the Rhinox in the face. The creature gave a roar of pain as it reared back, blood spewing from its nose. Orphius swore as he began to lose altitude.

"No!"

He outstretched his hand toward Keller, in a last, desperate attempt, and fired black energy at him. Dominique watched in horror. That power was so similar to her own-

Keller retaliated, and she was even more horrified to see that it was the same type of energy, the kind that *she* had!

"Oh my God," she whispered.

The two energies collided, and suddenly, all hell seemed to break loose.

A shockwave emanated from the meeting point of the two energy streams, giving Dominique the odd sensation of being pushed in mid-air, and then, a roiling white light released from the center of the energy collision, spreading out to reach all of them...

The next thing she knew, she was hurtling through the air at an incalculable speed, as the green of the forest flashed by blurrily beneath her, until, dropping enough altitude, she hit a tree.

She went spinning to the ground.

And everything was dark.

13

Memories...and a Cave

Dominique was ninety percent sure she was dreaming. For one thing, she had never been here before; a beautiful room surrounded her, gilded with purple and gold. She looked around in mild confusion, wondering how she had come to be here in the first place.

A pillow cushioned her head. Turning slowly, she saw that it was purple as well. She frowned as she sat up...why was she in a bed?

"Hello?" she called. The room's ambiance projected a feeling of protection, something she hadn't experienced for a long while. Nervous, she got up and walked to an adjoining room.

It was a bathroom. Dominique shuddered at the feeling of cold stone on her bare feet as she padded in, trying to be quiet. She didn't want to disturb anyone, if another should be in close vicinity, especially if they were somehow sinister.

Although...anyone with a house like this couldn't be entirely evil. The window at the far side of the enormous bathroom was open. Dominique went over to it, appreciating that it was sunny and warm outside.

Looking out, she suddenly had the strangest sense of déjà vu. There was a long, straight drive, which led to a gate at the edge of the property. The mountains loomed close by.

The structure of the building, or at least, what she could see, was familiar to her. Flying buttresses...she even saw a variety of beautiful gardens spanning the grounds, and she gasped. Was this...?

Someone moved behind her; she whirled with a startled gasp, and suddenly slid down the wall, trying to convince herself she wasn't going crazy.

Another 'her' was in the room, assessing her reflection critically in the mirror. Another Dominique. What was going on?

"Umm...h-hello?" she asked. The girl didn't hear her. She looked *just* like her, except appeared younger. Perhaps...

"Twelve years old," Dominique murmured, staring at the image of herself. The girl had riding breeches on, and a tank top. She seemed to be getting ready to go riding.

From outside the window, someone shouted her name. Dominique looked out the window in alarm, while the other, younger version of herself rolled her eyes.

"I'm *coming!*" she shouted in an exasperated tone. "Geeze, I have to tell him to get a life someday. Just because he's inheriting daddy's stuff..."

Finally finished at the mirror, the other girl began to sprint off, and it took Dominique only a split second to decide to follow her. There was something just there, locked in the recesses of her mind, banging to be free. She needed to see this.

Her other self was running through an absolutely enormous hallway, then padding down a huge flight of stairs...just how big was this mansion? Dominique looked around in wonder at the tapestries that adorned the walls.

"Dominique!" the voice called again. "Where are you? You're taking too long!"

The young Dominique stopped and looked around. "Hold on a second, would you? I've got to tell mom something!"

"HURRY UP!"

Ahead of them, a door creaked open, and a young man stuck his face through the opening. His eyebrows, over violet eyes, were raised expectantly. His black hair, streaked with one band of purple in the front, flopped into his face. Irritably, he blew on it so it flew out of his eyes.

"Orphius, you're really not very patient, are you?" the young Dominique snapped.

The present Dominique almost had a stroke. This kid? Orphius? What had happened to him? How had he become what...?

She stopped thinking, trying to let it all sink in. Okay, obviously something weird was going on here...

"Are you four leaving?"

The voice came from behind them. From the doorway, Orphius grinned and scratched his head.

"Well, we would be, but *someone* here is too slow for her own good," he said, glaring at the young Dominique. She stuck her tongue out at him and turned around.

"Just wanted to say goodbye, mommy!" she said.

Dominique whirled, her heart in her throat. The woman coming toward them had black hair, and beautiful blue eyes. She wore the most loving expression on her face as she looked at the two children.

"Well, you have fun," she said. The young Dominique ran toward her and gave her a quick hug. The woman laughed.

Dominique wracked her brain, trying to determine who this woman was. It was all in her head, but somehow, she couldn't remember...wait a minute.

Trianna. The reigning Shadow's wife. She looked around, watching for him to appear, but he didn't. Her younger self waved and finally ran out the door, accompanied by Orphius's snipes.

"We could've been halfway there by now. Keller's throwing a fit; I hope you packed something to eat..."

Although Dominique wanted desperately to stay with Trianna, she had to find out what this was leading up to. Turning, she ran after the other Dominique and the young Orphius.

Outside, there were two other people waiting. One was about the young Dominique's age, and had a mischievous grin and a wink waiting for her. The other one was by far the oldest. He was astride a magnificent horse, waiting calmly for them to approach.

"Come on, you two," a familiar baritone voice rang out, though being lighter in his youth. "We haven't got all day."

"I've been telling her that, Keller! Sheesh..." Orphius complained as he mounted his horse. "She might think that we have no responsibilities, the way she acts."

"Oh yes, because going riding all day is *so* important," the young Dominique sneered. "Let's just go."

"Right you are, then," Keller said. "Hey Kivar, you want to take point?"

He gestured to the younger boy, who put his nose in the air and directed his small horse to trot up to the front. "If you insist, brother."

Orphius and Keller exchanged an amused look. Before they could go, however, Keller looked up beyond his siblings.

"There's father!" Dominique shouted, following his gaze. She waved ecstatically, seeing two men walking across the grounds.

The present Dominique jerked her head around. One of the men she recognized instantly; Val, without an eye patch. His hat, however, still adorned his head. The other was a thin, pale man with a shock of purple hair and vibrant purple eyes. He grinned and waved back, but appeared to be in deep discussion.

"He's been busy with Val a lot lately," Keller muttered. "I still don't trust him, you know."

"Oh please," the young Dominique responded. "Just because he's the one who gets to know all of daddy's plans. You're jealous."

"Alright, that's enough," Orphius snapped. "Kivar, *go.*"

And with that, the four of them spurred their horses into a full fledged run, and Dominique watched all of them ride away, carefree and laughing.

It all came rushing back to her then. Kneeling on the ground, her eyes widened as she remembered everything, before and during the fire...

The scene around her changed. Screams she had never again wanted to hear came to her ears, accompanied by the sound of flame consuming wood. She whirled around, seeing the mansion in flames.

"Get out!" Trianna's voice came from the house. "Dominique! Go!"

Dominique saw herself come crashing out of the house; she had been thrown through a window by Orphius, who was attempting to rush back and grab their mother-

There was a crash of falling timber inside, with a cry of pain coming from him. Dominique saw herself black out, and screamed.

Still screaming, Dominique jerked her head up, wildly looking around. Everything she saw was leafy and green. Where was she? In the forest somewhere?

She began to cry, hauling herself to a tree, grabbing its bark with such force it snapped off in her fingers. What did it matter? Her entire family was burned, except for her two brothers, who hated each other for some unknown reason. They had been the best of friends until the fire...what had happened?

Dominique shook her head and buried her face in her hands. She couldn't believe what she had nearly done to them. Almost killed them! Shakily, she took a breath and looked up, trying not to hyperventilate.

First things first; she needed to calm down. Taking slow, steady breaths, she finally got to a point where she wasn't breathing as if she had just finished a marathon.

Next, she needed to get moving. Yumurango was a dangerous place, trusting her friends' advice; she knew she had to get out of the forest as soon as she could. But the question was...where exactly was she?

For all she knew, she could be at the very edge of the woods, or in the very heart. The words that Tom had spoken before their separation were still clear in her mind. Even he didn't know what was in here.

Well, the sooner she started to try and find her way out, the better. Dominique just hoped she wouldn't run into anything...unfriendly.

As she began to wander, her mind ran through all her recently recovered memories. Her father was the Shadow named Singe. He had married Trianna, and they had four children together. First Keller, then Orphius, then Kivar...she was the youngest. They all had violet eyes. She shook her head. How could she have been so blind to the now obvious clues indicating her to be a Shadow? Maybe living on Earth for so long had closed her mind, preventing her from seeing the magic around her.

Oh, God. Orphius and Keller were at war. They were killing innocent people to get at each other's throats. Dominique suddenly remembered her vow to kill both of them for what they were doing to Yumurango...not the sort of thing a sister was supposed to do.

But what was she going to do? There was a reason that they were fighting, she just didn't know what their reason was. With her memories returned, she knew her brothers well enough to know that they wouldn't fight without a good cause.

Ethan said the fighting had started five years ago. That was also when the fire had occurred. Had something happened at that time to push them to hostilities? She wasn't sure.

"Okay," she said, to calm herself down. Drawing her sword, she began to hack away some bushes blocking her path. It helped to maintain her sanity...a little.

She wondered where Tom and the others were. As soon as she found them, she would have to tell them what she remembered. Because, if they were looking for something that would kill the Shadows, that sort of included *her* now. Not only did she not want to die, but the thought of anything happening to her brothers was nearly unbearable.

God, this was a change of mind. Shaking her head in bemusement, Dominique took another step into the forest.

Something called, but it sounded like a mournful bird. Dominique froze, looking around for something to show itself. It had sounded very, VERY close.

Nothing. Maybe she had just imagined the noise. She wasn't really surprised, seeing how creepy it was in this forest. The gloom and tricks of light playing out on the leaves seemed ready-made to cause hallucinations. Still, she became warier after that, glancing suspiciously at every plant.

A rustling noise to her right made her shriek, and she brought her sword to bear. It glinted in the dim light that filtered through the trees as she readied her powers to stop anything intent on harming her.

Still nothing. Moving slowly, Dominique gripped the sword tighter. Now that she knew she was a Shadow; the sword seemed to be a connection to who she really was. Glancing around worriedly, she continued on her way.

Just as she was about to take a short break, something behind her hissed. Screaming, she bolted, adrenaline running through her system. Behind her, plants were smashed as her pursuer chased her...and it was something big.

Glancing back, Dominique thought she caught a glimpse of a many jointed leg, and tried not to imagine what was chasing her. Suddenly, she tripped and fell, sliding over the ground. Her sword slid a few feet away from her, just out of arm's reach-

A terrible hiss from above made her scream and she jerked her head up...and her eyes widened. Her face turned a pale white, stark against the green foliage around her.

An enormous spider, easily three times as big as her, towered above her. Behind the hairy mandibles it sported, its teeth dripped with venom, and she was close enough to see the stinger at the end of its abdomen.

"Oh my God," she squeaked. Not like this...not at the hands (well, legs) of a giant spider...

Then, it lunged at her. Barely avoiding the bite, she used her powers to slam energy into its face as she grabbed her sword. Her hands were shaking so badly that the blade quivered in her grasp as she began to slowly back away from the creature. Her posture warned the thing to keep its distance.

Not that it was working. The spider took a few cautious steps forward, eyeing her hungrily. Her throat worked, but no sound came out. All her life she'd been afraid of spiders...

It twitched; she screamed.

And then, it leapt at her again. She slashed at the creature with her sword. It fell back, gibbering like an evil monkey as it hissed at her again.

"Don't even think about it," she choked out. Her voice was all wrong; too dry, and no volume. So much for the brave effect.

Just as the thing was about to lunge at her again, a small tremor emanated through the ground. Ignoring the distraction, Dominique focused on the spider, afraid to let her guard down.

Feeling the tremor, the spider hesitated, testing the ground with one of its many segmented legs. It tapped it a few times, then decided it was nothing...it came at Dominique again.

"Stay away from me!" she screamed.

She fell down backward. Her frightened mind had only a limited time to grasp the concept that she had fallen through a hole in the ground. The next thing she knew, she was sliding downward over loose gravel.

An angry chattering drew her ear, and she was horrified to see the spider leap down the crevasse toward her, sliding ever closer. Dominique drew her legs close to her chest in an attempt to reduce resistance and increase her speed as she plummeted into darkness.

All of a sudden, the easy decline turned into a sharp drop; Dominique screamed as she fell a few feet. She landed on her knees, hard. Wincing in pain, she screamed again as something vast and hairy flew over her head and impacted on something not too far away.

They had landed in a cave. Unfortunately, the hole through which she had fallen was now completely blocked with large rocks, mangled roots, and dirt disturbed by the rather large spider that had followed her. To her surprise, Dominique could see. Some kind of eerie light source kept her from the blindness of the darkness, although the sun couldn't reach down here. Slowly, she got up and watched the spider carefully. A stalagmite had halted its progress quite abruptly. It looked like the creature was unconscious.

Dominique bolted toward the mysterious light source, which cast the surrounding environment in a blue white glow. Sprinting down a narrow tunnel, she reappeared in an adjoining cavern.

This part of the cave was easily bigger than any mansion (the Shadow's included) she'd ever been to. The eerie glow originated from the very center of it. Frowning, Dominique looked back toward the original cavern she had landed in; now only darkness beckoned.

Hell. It wasn't like she was in any rush. Turning back toward the light, she began her trek toward it. The going was hazardous; several times, she slipped and fell on loose stones as she clambered over them, earning her several cuts on her knees and hands.

As she finally made the last few strides toward it, however, Dominique paused. Instead of a magic light, as she had expected, the light was coming from some sort of...sword.

It was embedded in a rock, and as she got closer, felt waves of heat that repelled her immediately. Blinking from its brilliance, she tried to study it more closely. The thing looked like two parallel blades originating from a common hilt. However, the entire thing was made of some blue, luminescent material.

As she dared to inch closer, she tripped over something. Cursing, she thought to give the offending rock a good kick as she spun to glare at it.

Then, she realized that it wasn't a rock at all. Giving a shout of surprise, she backpedaled on her hands, crawling away as fast as she could.

Whatever was on the floor, it didn't look very friendly. Its mouth was open in a silent snarl; sharp teeth lined its reptilian mouth as it stared motionlessly at the cave's ceiling. It reminded Dominique of a dinosaur, or lizard, with its leathery skin and slit yellow eyes, except for the fact it didn't have a tail...and it was wearing armor.

The armor suit was silver, with a few white accents. To its right, she could even see a helmet that was obviously designed for a reptilian head. Cautiously, she crept closer. From what she could surmise, the expression on its face appeared, well...surprised.

As she got closer to it, she felt how cold it was near it, and shivered as she hesitantly touched its arm. There was obviously some sort of spell around it, freezing it, perhaps for eternity...

But then there was that sword, which gave off so much heat. Dominique looked at the two, an idea coming to mind. Then, she shook her head.

Of course she wouldn't do it. Waking this creature up might be the worst idea she'd ever had. Who knew what it could do to her? One gnash of those teeth, or one swipe of those claws, and she'd be mincemeat.

Turning away, she decided to leave it be. Whoever had cast that spell in the first place probably had a good reason to do so. Maybe the creature had attacked them.

A scraping sound resonated throughout the cave; instinctively, Dominique crouched down by the strange, frozen creature and stared at the opening of the original cavern with rapt attention. Was it just her, or was there a leg sticking out of the passage?

Oh, God. She wasn't hallucinating. The spider was coming for her, again! In desperation, she looked around for another way out...nothing.

Swearing, Dominique looked again at the reptilian creature. If anything, she'd rather be killed quickly by this thing than eaten alive slowly by a spider.

"Alright," she muttered to the still form. "You'd better be quick about it!"

With that, she turned to the sword embedded in the rock, and reached her hand toward it. The heat quickly blistered her skin; she cried out in pain, but kept reaching out. Determination *not* to be eaten strengthened her resolve.

There...she had it. As she had grabbed the weapon, she jerked it back toward the frozen creature, and saw, with a mix of trepidation and relief, that the frozen lizard-like creature on the ground began to thaw.

The spider, on the other hand, was wasting no time pushing through the narrow passage. It was almost all the way through to her cavern. Dominique could see its nasty teeth bared as it focused each of its eight eyes on her. Almost crying in desperation, she held the sword even closer to the creature...its legs appeared free now.

As she kept the sword's heat close to it, the spell began to recede from the entire body. Even as the girl watched, the creature's eyes closed, and its face went limp. It sprawled onto its side, beginning to breathe again. Slowly, stiffly, one of its arms twitched.

By now, the spider was fully in the cavern. Moving toward them, it began to navigate the rock field surrounding them. Dominique screamed.

"Wake up!" she shouted, putting down the blade and shaking the creature by its shoulders. "Damn it, wake up!"

But it was the spider's menacing hiss that finally did the trick. Slowly, the brown lids slid open, and the yellow eyes focused on Dominique's face.

"Who are you?" it asked. The voice was deep; a male.

"We're in trouble!" Dominique shrieked.

The spider hissed again. Jerking his head to the side, the reptile's eyes narrowed. Dominique clambered off of him as he grabbed his sword and stood up.

"Stay back," he ordered, holding out a four fingered hand toward Dominique. She nodded enthusiastically and readied her own sword, just in case.

The heat emanating from his weapon seemed to not affect the creature; he held it up in front of his face, waiting for the spider to get closer. When it finally did, he raised it upright, and suddenly-

He lunged forward, the sword going straight for the spider's head. Dominique screamed as she saw the spider's teeth gnash. He was going to be killed!

But somehow, the creature whipped himself around and ended up *on top* of the monster. Surprised, the spider screeched, attempting to scrape him off using a leg, but he was having none of that. In a swift, clean motion, the creature brought the sword down into the spider's head.

It gave a sharp wail that seemed to cut through Dominique's head; giving a groan, she dropped her sword and pressed her hands to her ears, trying not to hear. Finally, the dying call faded away, and the creature leapt down from the corpse.

Fear crept into Dominique. What was he going to do now? But as she watched, he came over and regarded her shrewdly.

"Are you alright?" he asked. "It looks as though you've handled my sword; something humans aren't supposed to do."

Dominique just gaped. "Th-thank you!" she gasped. "You saved my life!"

"And I'm assuming you saved mine," he said. "How long have I been frozen in that spell? I have to find someone and kill him."

"Uhh...I don't know, I sort of found you lying on the floor here-"

"Hmm," the creature said. Crossing over, he found his helmet on the floor and donned it. Dominique gulped.

"Umm...what exactly are you?" she asked.

He looked at her in surprise. "What?" he asked. "You mean you don't know?" She just shook her head.

"Why, I'm an Adamean," he said. "My name is Yakimi."

14

Separate Paths

"Oh, this is just PERFECT!" Tom shouted. "Just brilliant! It's not everyday you get LOST IN THE FOREST!"

Swearing angrily, he kicked a rotten log until it caved in, then sat down on the ground, shaking his head. What the hell had happened? The last thing he remembered was Orphius and Keller going at it. Then, there had been that white light, and now...now he was lost. He didn't like it.

Getting up, he made sure his cello hadn't been harmed by his own violence and set off again at a furious pace, hoping to come across anything that wanted to pick a fight with him right now. He would have *welcomed* it. Anything but this sea of endless green!

He was *so* going to kill both of those men when he got out of here. They would have to answer to the full wrath of Tom Horter. There was no getting out of it. Once they got to that stupid tree, this would all be over. Shadows dead, war done...*end of story.*

All he wanted to do now was find somebody, anybody, so he could know that at least one of his friends had survived the explosion-

Suddenly, a shot rang out through the woods. It whizzed right by Tom's head, who snapped his head around to follow its path into a tree.

Yet another shot landed right between his legs. Yelping, he ducked behind a tree.

"Alright!" he shouted. "Whoever's out there, why don't you calm down? I don't want anyone to get hurt!"

"Tom?" a metallic voice asked.

Tom paused, and looked suspiciously around the tree trunk. "Flint?"

"Oops," the robot said, holstering her weapon.

He gaped at her. "OOPS? You almost killed me!"

"Well, if you haven't noticed, there are a lot of bushes in here! I couldn't see!"

"And if you haven't noticed, there aren't usually many six foot tall skeletons walking around! Come on!"

"Oh, shut up," Flint growled. "Any sign of anyone else?"

"No," he said. His angry posture deflated. "But I think we've got a better chance of finding them from the air, don't you?"

"Probably," Flint agreed. She leapt into the air and let her boosters do the rest of the work. Then, she flitted forward, grabbed his arms, and shot straight up.

Tom screamed as they cleared the tree tops, looking down at the ground in absolute terror.

"I think I prefer riding the dragon!" he shrieked. Flint just laughed and began to comb the woods, searching for anyone.

But the vastness of the forest was problematic. Even if their friends were still alive, it would take days, if not weeks, to find them with a proper search. Tom couldn't bear the thought of any evil befalling them. Although perhaps with the exception of Sadiki...

"Hey, that might be something!" Flint said, releasing one of his arms and pointing. He shouted and grabbed onto her other arm.

"Don't do that!" he snapped.

"Alright, alright..."

But as she spoke, she brought out her gun and aimed it toward an object on the ground. No sense in being unprepared...

What she had thought was Shayla's crashed bulk, however, turned out to be the sinuous Rhinox. Sighing in frustration, she made sure the thing was dead (it had broken its neck on a tree) before putting her rifle away.

"So much for that," Tom said. She nodded grimly.

"Yeah, but there's always-AUGH!"

Suddenly, she began to lose altitude, as though she had been shunted downwards by a large hand. In fear, she saw that her feet were encased with black energy.

"Oh no..." she said. "Tom! I'm gonna drop you. There's no sense in both of us getting captured!"

"You're not going through anything alone," Tom stated grimly, latching onto her metal arms with a vice-like grip. Even as she tried to shake him off, he held tightly.

"I just hope you don't regret this! HANG ON!"

And then, they were both slammed into the ground. Tom shouted in pain as something cracked in his arm. Flint, seemingly unharmed, scrambled to her feet and looked all around.

"Who did that?" she hissed. "It was one of the two-"

A surge of energy blasted her. The robot was again knocked over and slammed into a tree. Okay. This was not fun.

Tom, on the other hand, was suddenly enveloped in black energy. Flint, attempting to rise, suddenly found herself streaming toward him, flying through the air-

And slamming right into Tom. He was knocked out instantly, and even Flint, who was tougher than most, felt her systems begin to shut down.

As her world grew smaller and smaller, she saw someone come over and stand over them. She groped for her gun, but someone kicked her arm back, away from the weapon.

Her final sight was that of Orphius's violet eyes.

CRACK!

Another tree fell. Underneath it, one of the enormous spiders was squished. Giving a roar of satisfaction, Shayla whirled around and slashed another hairy beast with her claws.

She had stumbled onto an entire colony of these freaking things. They had swarmed all over her, but so far, she had been able to fend them off.

Using her fiery breath, she scorched several that tried to skitter up her leg. Giving a dragonish grin, she whipped her tail around and watched the rest of them retreat into the murky forest. It was starting to get dark, and who knew what other creatures came out at night in this forest?

Not willing to chance it, she decided to sleep as a dragon. Although she couldn't fly out of the woods-her fragile wings would likely be damaged by the dense web of tree branches-she felt safer on the ground as an enormous, fire breathing lizard. Sniffing the air carefully, she curled into a defensive ball and watched the moving branches unblinkingly.

It didn't come as much of a surprise to her when something broke out of the bushes and moved toward her. Hissing, she reared her head back and evaluated the threat. Her finned ears stuck straight out as she prepared to kill whatever it was-

Oh. She lowered her head and flattened her ears. It was just Sadiki. The Marauder came over with a dignified air, but then collapsed at her head. The dragon huffed once, but reluctantly placed him inside her protective, scaly circle and continued her watch. Keller and Orphius were still out there, among other possible threats.

It was going to be a long night.

"So let me get this straight," Dominique said, eyeing her new companion warily. "You were put under a spell by another Adamean?"

"Yes," Yakimi said mildly. "There are three clans in the Adameans, and our clan was at war with another. My companion was a member of the opposing clan. I thought he was my friend, however..."

He trailed off, his yellow eyes bitter. "Well, we know how that one turned out, don't we?"

They moved off together, seeking an exit from the cave's confinement. The cave turned out to be much larger than either of them could have imagined. In the darkness of the cave, the glow of Yakimi's sword provided the sole light source, enabling them to safely move about.

After a few hours of wandering through various passages and dead ends, Yakimi finally found another, unblocked exit from the cave. Not that it made that much of a difference. It was now completely dark, and the only light came from the moon that filtered down through the tree branches and from Yakimi's sword. Looking at him, the girl was once again struck by how strange he seemed, even among other Yumurangonians she had seen.

"I've never heard of an Adamean before," Dominique said curiously. Yakimi huffed.

"Then you're obviously not from around here. By the way," he said, eyeing her. "You wouldn't happen to be a Shadow, would you?"

She sighed. "Yes, I am."

"Your family has grown in stature," the Adamean said with a reptilian smile. "The new leader is a man named Saren, correct?"

Dominique looked at him blankly. Now that she remembered her family and her life, she knew who Yakimi was referring to...and how deeply confused he was.

"Umm...Yakimi," she said slowly. "Saren was my great, great grandfather."

The Adamean blinked once, a frown tugging at his mouth. "But, if that's the case, then I've been asleep for-"

"For over a hundred years," Dominique finished.

He stopped walking. His yellow eyes kept staring at her, as though wondering whether she was going to call the joke off. She gulped and shrugged, not knowing what to say.

"Well," he finally choked out. "That's, umm..."

Then, he simply sat beneath the nearest tree and stared straight ahead. Dominique watched him, slightly worried.

"I think I should take a look at your arm," he said. The girl shook her head stubbornly, trying to ignore the pain. Yakimi snorted.

"Come on, those blisters can't feel too good."

With that truth stated, Dominique rolled her sleeve up and thrust her arm out in his direction, trying not to act childish. The Adamean studied the wound for a minute before he got up, beginning to comb the forest.

"Let's see..." he muttered to himself. "It usually grows on trees, but I don't know if these are the right kind-aha!"

He plucked a few strands of a vine from a tree and walked back toward Dominique. The girl watched him warily as he began to wind the plants around her arm. To her surprise, the throbbing sensation abated.

"There," he said, obviously satisfied. "If you keep those on your arm for the night, then it should be good as new by morning."

"Thanks," she said, taken aback. He smiled, but then his face lapsed back into despair.

"Where are they? I couldn't be the only Adamean left alive!" he whispered. "If there are others, what happened to everyone? Not all of us could have been frozen under a spell like me!"

"The forest is a big place," she said. "Maybe they're just hiding in here or somewhere else."

"Yes," Yakimi said bitterly. "For a hundred years, so everyone else in Yumurango has forgotten them? I know my people; it would never happen."

Dominique sat down beneath a tree and patted the spot next to her. Slowly, the Adamean came and joined her.

"I think we've got enough to sleep on," she said.

"Agreed," Yakimi said with a nod.

"Hold on," the girl suddenly snapped, bolting upright. "What if one of those spiders comes back?"

Yakimi laughed. "With an Adamean escort, you'll be hard pressed to find a Hupareech brave enough to challenge you."

"A what?"

"A Hupareech. They do have names."

"Well they don't deserve one," the girl said. Her eyes began to slide shut. Yakimi blinked once.

"Oh, and Dominique?"

"Hmm?"

"Thank you for freeing me."

"Yeah, no problem."

She patted him on the shoulder and sank down into a horizontal position. Her head began to spin with all the things she had learned that day. Remembering her life as a Shadow, the battles she and her friends had fought, their separation and the discovery of Yakimi-

But before she knew it, she was asleep.

Sleep, however, was the last thing on Tom Horter's mind as he finally began to gain consciousness. His blurry vision came into focus slowly, and he wasn't surprised to find himself tied up.

Groaning, he swiveled his head and looked at his bonds; manacles on his ankles and wrists that were chained to a wall. Flint was tied in the same manner. She also wore metal boxes containing her feet and hands.

She was already conscious. Tom saw her look in his direction and expel a sigh of relief.

"Gee, I was afraid you weren't going to wake up," she said. "Do you know where we are?"

Grimly, Tom nodded. They were in a dank, moldy dungeon, where the only light emanated from a crack in the entrance door. Even then, it was weak torchlight. He gulped.

"Orphius was the one who got us, I take it," he muttered tensely. "This is one of his dungeons."

"How do you know?"

"Because Keller is more of a military man. He'd have us locked up in a bunker somewhere, awaiting execution by firing squad. Orphius has more...traditional tastes."

"Oh goody," the robot said dryly. "I'm hoping that the traditional method is better for the victims?"

"Guess again."

"Great."

Tom felt the locks around his wrists, slowly fingering them with a bony digit. "You know, I may be able to pick these," he said. "Let me see if I can just-"

He moved too quickly, however, and his head began to spin. He groaned as he shook it. "I think I got hit a little harder than I thought," he said.

"Are you okay?"

"I'm fine, I'm fine," he said irritably, waving her off. "Don't worry about me. Just hold on while I get these undone."

With that, he used his slim pinky to start picking the lock, hoping to unclasp his wrist manacles. Just as he was about to release the first lock, the door swung open.

He immediately stopped what he was doing, and fixed a stony glare on Orphius as the man swept into the room and placed a suspicious looking bag on a rusting table at the far end of the dungeon. Whistling a tune to himself, he began to take out old-looking tools, one by one.

Tom gulped. None of those things looked friendly.

Flint, however, seemed unfazed. As a robot, she could easily ignore pain, and wasn't as affected by it as organic creatures were. Orphius would be at a loss to torture her. The only real concern she had was for Tom. Even as she watched, the skeleton's face appeared to be turning a pale green.

"So," Orphius said evenly, turning around to face them. Hate shown in his violet eyes; Flint was sure the same was reflected in theirs.

"So what?" Tom snarled.

"So, where's Red Shield?"

The two of them exchanged glances. "I haven't been to headquarters for over a year," Tom said smugly. "They change the locations every time. I still haven't gotten the memo where the next one-"

Without warning, a surge of black energy flowed over and slammed into him, constricting his throat. Tom gagged as his air flow was cut off, and he began to lose consciousness-

The energy flow ceased. Gasping for oxygen, the skeleton slumped forward, giving a baleful glare in Orphius's direction.

The man had what looked like the top curve of a scythe in his hand. Coming over, he crouched down next to Tom and slowly, but surely, drew a line across the skeleton's forehead using the razor sharp implement. Tom gritted his teeth and didn't scream at the pain.

"I'll ask you again," Orphius said evenly. "Where is Red Shield?"

"You know what I'm starting to hate, just a little bit?" Shayla growled. "THIS FOREST!"

"Well, complaining about it isn't going to be at all useful," Sadiki snapped. The shape shifter pointed at him threateningly.

"Mark my words, one of these days-"

"Yes, yes, one of these days you'll just up and kill me," the Marauder said mockingly. "But I've got news for you."

Without warning, he whirled around and stared directly into Shayla's ice blue eyes, the green in Sadiki's eyes sparkling with malice; she gave an instinctual growl.

"I am a Marauder," he hissed. "That means that, even when I'm in my bound form, you could never hope to kill me. The only ones who could even think about doing so are-"

"The Shadows, and Val," Shayla said, crouching down to be at his level. "But I've got one more thing to add to your plate, pal,"

She lunged forward and grabbed the front of his robes, hauling him aloft and standing to full height, until she was holding him at eye level. "The Shadows may not be as far away as you think."

Suddenly, she chucked him away. Sadiki gave a yell, shocked as he flew through the trees, cursing her with every second-

Until someone else caught him. Slowly, very slowly, the Marauder turned his head to look. A small squeak escaped him.

Keller looked angry. *Very* angry. The Shadow's hand seemed barely in restraint from snapping the creature's neck, and Sadiki appeared highly aware of this fact.

"Kill *her*! I didn't want to be with them since the very beginning! It was her fault that we we're all in this mess to begin with-"

"Shut up," Shayla snarled. Her eyes, however, didn't leave Keller. With an abrupt movement, he hurled Sadiki away into the trees, and he stood very still, rigid as a spear made of onyx. Slowly, she moved to the right.

Only his head turned to follow her movement. The shape shifter growled and suddenly morphed into a dragon. Trees snapped as she expanded to make room for her bulk.

"Oh good," Keller said with a harsh laugh. "I was *hoping* you'd do that."

When Dominique began to wake up, she felt like she was moving. Confused, she opened her eyes to stare out at the forest, expecting a wind to be blowing.

"WHOA!" she shouted.

She was draped over something, staring down at the forest floor, which was several feet below her. The rocking sensation came from Yakimi's movement. She was slung over Yakimi's shoulder.

At her cry, however, he laughed. "Awake?" he questioned, letting her down and setting her upright. Dominique blinked up at him.

"Do me a favor," she said. *"Don't carry me."*

The Adamean just laughed.

She glared at him. "Where are we?"

"I know this forest," Yakimi said. "We've been hiking toward the western edge for about two hours now."

"I was asleep on your shoulder for two hours?" Dominique asked, rubbing her eyes. He nodded, amusement showing in his yellow eyes.

"You seem to be in a better mood today," she groused.

"Well, it's my people's...well, now, apparently my own, creed," he said. "What's happened has happened. Plus, I'll see them all again eventually."

The girl smiled. "What's happened has happened..."

She thought back to her own life. With all its many depressing events, she was glad she finally had something, even if it was an extinct race's motto, that helped make sense of it all. Finally, she looked up at him.

"So you know where we're going?"

Before he could nod, however, the Adamean stopped and perked up. He seemed to be listening to something.

"What?" Dominique asked.

"It's a dragon," he said, blinking in surprise. "But this forest isn't big enough. Why would a dragon-?"

"Shayla!" the girl gasped. "Where is it?"

"Follow me."

With that, he sprang away; cutting through the bush as if it were nonexistent. Dominique tried, at first, to run with him, but it was obvious that he was too fast for her. In frustration, she leapt into the air and concentrated on her levitation, maneuvering through the trees.

Sounds of combat reached her ears; a roar echoed through the forest, along with the sound of snapping trees. There was a shout of surprise, and Dominique recognized it instantly; Keller.

"Oh God," she said, hanging her head. What was she supposed to do in this situation?

Perhaps it would be easiest to pretend not to remember either of her brothers. Yes, that would make it easier on all of the family. Gritting her teeth, she plunged forward-

And slammed directly into Yakimi's frozen back. Yelping, she held a finger up to her nose-it was bleeding.

"What's the big idea?" she asked in a nasally tone, pinching her nose shut.

Then, she realized he had black energy nailing him to the forest floor. Summoning up her own energy, she began to contradict her brother's magic, knowing he was behind it.

Magic was just as much a mental exercise as a physical one. You had to *believe* you could win, and Dominique was feeling very confident at the moment. She sensed her brother's magic begin to give way; she pressed harder, adamant.

Finally, Yakimi was freed. He stumbled forward, looking at her with concern.

"Your nose is bleeding,"

"Yeah, I know, it'll heal," she snapped. Then, she cupped her hands around her mouth. "SHAYLA!"

Yakimi mirrored her. "Umm...SHAYLA?" he called, glancing at her. "Since when do dragons have names?"

"She's not a real dragon, she's a-"

A huge, white bulk trotting through the forest broke her off, and she was relieved to see that her friend was alright, albeit bleeding from a gash on her foreleg. She looked around apprehensively for her brother, but Keller was nowhere to be seen.

"Shayla!" she shouted in happiness, running forward. The dragon drew herself up regally and gave a roar of triumph.

Behind Dominique, Yakimi stood, absolutely dumbstruck.

"She's beautiful," he murmured.

When the dragon began to shrink, his eyes widened even further.

Dominique, on the other hand, waited impatiently for Shayla to finish before she threw her arms around her friend. The woman laughed and returned the gesture.

"Well then," she said, tossing her long hair back. "Where have you been?"

"Oh, umm, Shayla?" Dominique said, motioning to her new friend. He came forward shyly. "This is Yakimi. He's an-"

"HOLY CRAP! AN ADAMEAN!"

Shayla goggled at him, and Dominique was surprised to see a red tinge appear over his leathery skin. Raising an eyebrow, she cleared her throat.

"Umm...yes," he said. "If I may introduce myself properly, my name is Yakimi."

"Shayla," the shape shifter said, offering a hand. Yakimi stared at it for a moment, and then smiled and got the message. He met her gaze, and they shook.

"Okay," Dominique said. "Who were you fighting?"

"Well, Keller was there, but that little turd Sadiki started fighting alongside him!" the shape shifter growled. "I knew we couldn't trust him from the start. But Keller took off with a black dragon that basically appeared out of nowhere, and-"

"Who gave you that wound?" Yakimi asked, staring at her scaly arm. She glanced at it.

"Oh, umm...Keller, I think. He had a gun with him, but his shots only grazed me."

"Then I will make sure he is killed," Yakimi snarled. Shayla blinked once, and then, arched an eyebrow.

"Is this one of those stupid male things? I'm not your property, pal. I can get damaged and do whatever the hell I want."

"And, umm," Dominique interjected nervously. "About destroying Keller..."

She began to tell of the revelation she'd had after they'd been separated. At first, the shape shifter was smiling, obviously thinking it was a joke, but then, her eyes widened.

"You're serious?" she murmured. "You're...you're a..."

"A Shadow. Yeah." Dominique said.

"But, but...that thing under the silver tree, that's gonna end the war, that'll kill you too!"

"I...I know," Dominique murmured. "There's nothing I can do about it now, though."

She sighed. "We'll just have to deal with it...somehow. Especially with this thing with the tree."

"What's this tree?" Yakimi asked. Shayla looked at him, irritated, and quickly began to explain. When she finished, and they were all on the same page, she looked toward Dominique again.

"What do we do?"

"How should I know?" Dominique wailed. "If Sadiki's still working for Val, then he could already have that stupid thing and might be carrying it back to Red Shield to...wait a minute..."

"Well, we'll just have to get there before him and tell Val what's going on," Dominique said. "He used to work with my father. I remember him."

"So he'll be on your side!" Shayla said, smiling brilliantly. "But, then...why did Tom have such a hard time convincing him to let you stay at headquarters?"

"I don't know," the girl said grimly. "Maybe we should get to the tree first, and hide whatever the object is somewhere. On the other hand, if Sadiki already found it, we'll be wasting our time looking for the tree," Dominique realized.

"That's true," Shayla said. "If Sadiki has the...whatever, then Val gets it from him and uses it, you're dead. We can't risk that. I won't risk that. We head to Red Shield and get to Val first."

She pinned them both with cool looks. "Any questions?"

No one said anything.

"Good, but here's another issue," the shape shifter added. "What happens if we meet up with Keller or Orphius again? What will you do?"

Dominique's stomach lurched; she looked back at her friend's eyes unblinkingly, and finally, she sighed.

"They've killed innocent people in their blind rage," she said. "If I have to fight, then I'll side with you guys."

Shayla smiled. "Thank you," she said. "We need a Shadow on our side."

"Yeah, well..." the girl didn't finish.

"So," Shayla said briskly, turning to Yakimi. He blinked once. "You know your way around here, right?"

"Yes..."

"Then show us to the edge of the forest nearest the mountains! We've got our destination. We've got an appointment with Val, and we need to get to it!"

"Yes ma'am!"

Yakimi turned and began to walk off purposefully, but then stopped, and turned around.

"This way," he said. Shayla and Dominique exchanged glances.

"Are you *sure* he knows what he's doing?" the shape shifter asked.

"Umm...no."

15

The Tower

"Hey look," Tom said with a grin. "It echoes. ECHOOO!"

Sure enough, his voice came bouncing back. Flint twisted in her bonds enough to glare at him.

"Tom, are you alright?"

"I think so."

"Good. Then do me a favor and shut up."

Tom grinned once, but then, coughed. "When do you think he's coming back?" he asked weakly. Flint's yellow eyes dimmed.

"I dunno. But when he does, I'm gonna-"

"Don't do anything stupid," Tom said suddenly. He drew himself up. "I'm the one he's really after, not you."

"But I wanna hurt him!" Flint whined. "Not only do I hate him, I hate being tied up! Two bad things, see? It wants to make me hurt him *more.*"

"Just take deep, calming breaths," Tom said. "I've heard they work."

"I don't breathe."

"You *know* what I mean."

He looked ahead at the dungeon wall, watching a small trickle of water run down the stony side and puddle on the floor. "I wonder what the others are doing," he muttered.

"Don't you mean, what *Dominique* is doing?" Flint sneered. He looked at her sharply; it made his head spin.

When his world had righted again, he cleared his throat. "What do you mean?" he asked.

"Oh, I think you know."

If Tom was human, he would have been bright red. Instead, however, he looked away and stared at the wall.

"I must be crazy," he muttered. "I mean, she's probably one of the most important people in Yumurango for many years, what's she gonna want-"

He broke off. "What's she gonna want with me?"

"Well," Flint started. "I don't know much about love, being a robot and all...it is love, right? Or just a crush that might change-"

"I don't think so," Tom cut her off.

"So, if we get out of here, you should just tell her how you feel."

Tom balked. "Look, Flint, it's not really that simple-"

The door opened. He shut up immediately and looked defiantly at Orphius, who had just entered. Like last time, he went over to the crappy table and started to rifle through his torture instruments. The scratch on Tom's forehead started to throb as he remembered the abuse from yesterday.

His forehead wasn't the only thing; pain lanced up his entire right arm, and a bone in his foot had been broken when Orphius had trodden on it as he'd exited. Talking to Flint was a distraction from the pain, and talking about Dominique helped...

"Well, hello again," he said to Orphius. "Had a rough night?"

Their captor did seem haggard; dark circles made his eyes appear to sink into his face. He ignored the quip.

"After all, with the rest of our friends about to close in on the silver tree and kill both you and your brother-"

"WHAT?"

Orphius had whirled, his eyes wide. "No one knows where that is. How did you-?"

"Wouldn't you like to know?" Tom hissed.

But by now, Orphius had lapsed into thought, his violet eyes staring straight ahead. The knife he was holding in his hands wobbled dangerously as his grip loosened.

Who knew about the secret, aside from his family? Neither he nor Keller would tell, to protect themselves, Dominique didn't remember, and everyone else in his family was dead...

It didn't make sense. Who else could have known?

Suddenly, he sucked in a breath. The knife dropped from his fingers, clattering to the floor.

"Val," he spat.

Without another glance at his two prisoners, he swept out the door. Tom and Flint exchanged glances.

"Well...*damn,*" Flint said. "How does he know who Val is?"

"I don't know," the skeleton said, glaring at the door. "But it can't be good."

"Green, green, green," Shayla growled, shoving plants aside as she marched. "I'm gonna make something nice and *red* when we get outta here!"

Her little rant seemed to fascinate Yakimi; he kept glancing over at her out of the corner of his eye, and Dominique stifled a grin.

They had been walking for several hours. Here in the forest, the afternoon sun hardly reached the forest floor, but there was enough light to go by. Since they were kept cool, they were able to maintain a reasonably fast pace.

"So," Shayla said, interrupting the peace again. She turned toward Dominique. "I'm bored. Tell me about your boyfriends back on Earth."

The girl arched an eyebrow. "Excuse me?"

"Oh, come on, little Miss Shadow," the shape shifter said, her mouth dropping open. "You didn't have a boyfriend?"

"Well...no," Dominique said, blushing. "I did like this one guy, but now..."

She trailed off, staring into space. "Now I like someone else."

"Oh yeah? And who would that be?"

Dominique didn't say anything. She just cleared her throat and looked at the floor. Her cheeks flamed red. "No one you'd know," she said, though her voice was high. Shayla glared.

"How stupid do you think I am? Spill!"

When the girl wouldn't say anything, Shayla resorted to threats.

"You know, I could just assume it's who I'm thinking it is, and tell him without letting you know," she said darkly. Dominique lifted her head.

"Well, since he's not here right now, you'd find that a little hard-"

"Aha!" Shayla said, pointing. "You've narrowed it down. This proves that it isn't Yakimi."

She gestured toward the Adamean, who sighed and shook his head. "Leave me out of this."

"Alright," Shayla said. "Well, since you don't like guys from Earth, how many guys do you know here? It's true that since I met up with you and Tom, after you guys had been traveling together for a while, you could've met other boys, but...somehow, I doubt it."

She turned around, her eyes glittering mischievously. "I think there's only one candidate," she said, and began to prance off in the other direction.

"I missed that," Yakimi admitted. "Umm...who is it?"

"Wouldn't you like to know," Dominique muttered. He grinned.

"Okay, if you're so interested in my love life, then what about yours? After all, the way you gawked at her when she changed back from a dragon-"

His hand was over her mouth before she could finish her sentence, and she laughed as he pulled her away.

"Told you!"

"Told him what?" Shayla asked, rejoining them. Yakimi muttered something under his breath and kicked the dirt with his booted foot.

Suddenly, he froze. His nostrils widened, and he sniffed the air. "Ah," he said. "We're here."

He began to run, leaving the two females in the dust. Angrily, they exchanged glances and began to pursue him. Dominique was flying before she knew it; there was light up ahead!

"YES!" she screamed, as they broke through the trees. The Sistern range loomed up ahead of them, cold and forbidding. Shayla was only a second behind, and the instant she hit clear air, she morphed into a dragon and soared up into the sky, bugling.

Yakimi skidded to a halt, watching the two of them circle each other in midair. In wonder, he sat down and sighed.

These had to be the most incredible women he'd ever met.

When they'd (finally) come back down, Dominique and Shayla were already talking about making camp, and set about doing so.

"We have problems," the shape shifter announced as they stoked the fire. "Sadiki's out there, looking for the thing that will kill you, your brothers, and this stupid war. He may already have it. We don't know where Tom and Flint are-for all we know, we ditched them in there,"

She jerked her thumb back at the forest, and Dominique winced.

"I don't know, but I have the feeling they're somewhere else," she said. "Flint can fly, and maybe she landed by Tom and scooped him up..."

Her voice trailed off hopelessly. "Oh, who am I kidding?" she wailed. "For all we know, they could've been eaten! Tom could have been chewed up by some enormous dog! YAKIMI!"

The Adamean jumped as she whirled on him. "There aren't giant dogs in the forest, are there?"

"N-no, n-not that I know of," he stammered, looking at her nervously. She growled angrily. "I mean, you'd think we'd have some sort of way of communicating, wouldn't we?" she asked. "I mean, it's all very well to talk when we're together, but did anyone think of *long distance?* NO! I don't even think there are phones here!"

"What's a phone?" Shayla asked.

"Exactly my point!"

"Well," Yakimi interjected. "I'm not sure about a...phone, but I may be able to help in this endeavor."

He crouched down, and traced one of his nimble fingers along the dirt's surface, concentrating hard on something. Dominique and Shayla squatted down beside him.

"What are you doing?" the girl asked.

"This is standard Adamean knowledge," he said, with a hint of pride. "We know how to call up the images of the ones we wish to see. Now, what are their names?"

"Just say Tom Horter," Dominique said.

"Right," Yakimi said. Looking back to his drawing, he stated clearly to it.

"Tom Horter!"

The result was instantaneous. The inscriptions he had written began to glow with a soft light, which grew brighter and brighter as they spanned outward to create a rectangular shape. As soon as they joined, an image was conjured up, bordered by glowing streaks.

Dominique almost cried with relief; Tom was alive, and not in the forest!

"Thank God," she muttered, expelling a huge sigh of relief.

"Don't do that just yet," Shayla said grimly.

The girl frowned. "Why not?"

"Look."

Shifting back to the image, Dominique's spirits fell. He was tied up...that was a problem. As the image broadened, she could see Flint next to him in similar bondage. She gulped. There were two people who could be responsible for this...she didn't want to know-

Orphius, of course. He was the only one who would use dungeons like that. Keller, she knew, was more modernized, and would probably have them locked in a barrack somewhere.

"Damn it," she hissed. "We've got to do something."

"And let me guess, we can't hurt Orphius in the process," Shayla growled. The agonized look Dominique expressed confirmed it.

"I'll eat him if he gets too close," the shape shifter said sulkily, folding her arms over her chest. "I will."

"Yes, and wouldn't that be a lovely sight," Yakimi muttered. He waved his arms across the image once, and it vanished. "I assume you know where they are?"

"Orphius's tower; it's the only place secure enough," Dominique said with a nod. "He'll never expect an outright attack on it."

Shayla snorted. "Yeah, because it's suicide!"

"So we'll go in covertly," Dominique said, an idea forming in her mind. "It won't be easy, you know...but I think I have a plan."

The cart slowly rolled its way up the dusty road, pulled by two Shartans and crewed by four brown cloaked figures. Their faces were hidden hoods, protecting them from the scorching sun. The servants of Orphius who weren't soldiers worked out in the fields all day, providing food for the army. In this particular case, they were carting ridiculously heavy loads of a plant called Yama, which grew in the plains.

All the plants were stored in crates. Or at least, they were *supposed* to be. The actual vegetables had been removed, and in their place...

"Damn!" Dominique swore as her head bumped against the lid of the box. "Why can't Orphius be smart enough to pave his roads? Grrr!"

"He's *your* brother. Tell him at the next family reunion," Shayla snarled. "God, how can you be related to these freaks?"

"They didn't used to be this bad. Something must have happened during the fire,"

"Excuse me, ladies," Yakimi's voice came from a third crate. "But can you both shut up? I'm a little claustrophobic, and all the tension in the air isn't making things better!"

With that, he took deep, calming breaths, trying to forget he was in a tight, dark, enclosed space. Dominique rolled her eyes.

"Why would a guy who's been in a cave for over a hundred years be claustrophobic?" she snapped.

"Well, I was asleep, okay? And Adameans like being able to *move,* thank you very much!"

"Alright already," Shayla snarled. "It's not like it's easy for a dragon either."

They all shut up after that, though Dominique was sorely tempted to complain about all the bumps on the head she continued to receive. The bumpy cart maintained its bumpy process until finally, it came to a halt.

"Now remember," the girl whispered. "Wait to break out until we're sure they've moved the crates into the basement. We don't want to get caught."

"Really? I thought that was the whole point," Shayla sniped sarcastically.

"Shh!"

The servants had come, and began to unload the crates; Dominique heard a few grunts of complaint as Yakimi's was handled. She supposed, in his armor, an Adamean could weigh a lot...

"Take those down," a gruff voice instructed. Dominique narrowed her eyes and held back the urge to break out of the box and throttle whoever was giving orders.

Finally, she was set down. A few thumps next to her signaled the others being placed beside her, and she gulped. Okay, phase one of the plan was complete. Now for phase two.

As soon as the footsteps of their transporters receded, Dominique heard someone crash out of their box. Her eyes snapped wide open, and she (quietly) opened the lid on hers.

Yakimi was breathing hard; his yellow eyes wide and fearful as he glanced in her direction, and she sighed.

"Calm. Down."

Shayla popped her head up. "Geeze, it's alright big guy," she said, clambering out and putting her hands on Yakimi's shoulders. "Look at me."

He did; she gave him a penetrating gaze, blue meeting yellow. "You're not going to die. The box is open." she said. "But if you don't stop making so much noise, then we all just might *really* die."

That shut him up.

"Good boy," Shayla said, offering him an arm. He took it to help clamber shakily out. As he stood, he cleared his throat and tried to maintain some dignity.

"Where are your friends?" he proclaimed, reaching for his sword. Dominique grinned and pointed up a stairway.

"If I remember, Orphius had started making plans for a tower like this even before our parents died. He always said it was his dream to rule over Yumurango from a tower. Keller would always disagree and say-"

She broke off noting the disgusted look on Shayla's face. "Well, let's just say that I might know where to go."

With that, she took off at a run. "The dungeons would probably be toward the top, to make break outs- and ins- harder."

"Oh goodie," Shayla snarled. "That makes me feel *loads* better."

"Shut up and run!"

"HORTER!"

Tom and Flint both jumped as Orphius came storming into the room, crossed over to Tom, and towered over him threateningly.

"Where is Red Shield?" he shouted. The skeleton blinked.

"Umm...have the last twenty six hours been any indication that *I'm not going to tell you?"*

"Alright," Orphius said, turning away. "You leave me no choice. This was supposed to be relatively easy on you, but no, you chose the hard way..."

Suddenly, he whirled and outstretched his hand at the skeleton, who was jerked into the air by the black energy that suddenly surrounded him. Orphius concentrated for an instant—the skeleton's arm snapped in half.

Tom screamed. Desperately, Flint took her gloves off and began to saw through her bonds, something she should have done ages ago.

"Tell me!" Orphius demanded. "Or I'll break another one!"

The skeleton gritted his teeth and said nothing. Orphius concentrated again.

This time, nearly half of Tom's rib cage snapped. He screamed bloody murder, feeling the agony that coursed through him with every slight movement.

"Horter, where is Red Shield?"

"TAKE THIS!"

Flint leapt up and slammed a kick into Orphius's head. The man dropped back, losing his concentration on Tom. The thief fell to the floor, gasping weakly. He used his good arm to gingerly sit up and prop himself against the wall. His whole world seemed to be tinted red with pain.

"AAAAAAH!"

He kept up a steady pace of screaming in agony as Flint walked in a slow circle, keeping Orphius in her sites. She was pissed off. He had gone too far this time, hurting Tom like that.

"Son of a bitch!" she snarled, and threw herself at him. An angry cannonball of metal and fire (from her feet) slammed into him at full force and introduced him to the wall, hard.

Orphius created a shield around himself just in time, and bounced back, unharmed.

"Little robot," he said, his voice filled with dark anticipation. "You have no idea what I'm going to do to you now."

"Did you guys hear that?" Dominique asked, looking up the spiraling flight of stairs. "That scream?"

Shayla nodded grimly. "Let's get up there faster, shall we?"

The girl agreed by leaping into the air and rocketing upward. Shayla began to change, but suddenly turned to Yakimi.

"Grab a hold of my tail when I'm finished," she told him, and then resumed her shift. When she was done, the Adamean latched onto one of the spikes on her tail and gave a shout of alarm as he was suddenly whisked upward.

Above them, Dominique strained herself to go even faster. Tom was in trouble...she had to find him...

Another scream guided her. Whisking to the right, she flew down a hall, and then up another, narrower flight of stairs. A door was ajar, and she flew into the room.

She took in the situation with a glance. Tom was propped up against the wall, seeming to be too injured to even move. Flint was being pushed up against the wall by Orphius, who had glommed his dark energy over her.

Without thinking, Dominique drew her fist back and slammed it into her brother's face. His whole body was thrown backward, and she turned to Flint.

"Take him and go! Quick! Shayla and Yakimi-"

"Who?"

"JUST GO!"

The robot ran over to Tom quickly, and was careful as she eased him up. He shouted in pain as Flint carried him away, and looked back at Dominique.

"I'll be right there!" she promised. Then, she turned to look at her brother.

Orphius had composed himself again, though his lip was bleeding. Wiping it once, he stared at her unblinkingly.

"Dominique," he said formally. "I know you don't remember me, but I am-"

"I remember," the girl said, her voice thick. She cursed herself as her lip began to tremble. "When I was unconscious, everything just...came back."

He stared at her. "Then you remember me? That I'm your brother?"

She nodded. "But what I don't understand," she said. "Is why you and Keller are killing *innocent people* to get at each other? Why?"

Her eyes were wet now, and she began to sob. Orphius took a cautious step closer, but she shook her head.

"You two were best friends, the last time I checked!" she said. "What happened? Was it something that happened during the fire?"

"Keller started the fire!" Orphius proclaimed. "And he blamed me for it!"

"And I'm sure that, if I asked him, he'd say the same thing but the other way around," Dominique snapped. She shook her head in despair. "Red Shield is trying to find the tree," she whispered. "You two have got to stop."

"I'm sorry, but we're already in too deep," Orphius said in an agonized voice. "There's no going back for us now."

"There's always a choice!" Dominique choked out. "Look, what's happened has happened, alright? Kivar, Mom, and Dad are all dead! That's just the way w-we have to live now!"

She was blubbering, she knew, but she had to get this message across. "I still love you both," she said. "But if you won't stop fighting...I'll be there to stop it myself."

Her eyes had become hard, and steely. "There will be three Shadows fighting each other, instead of just two. I hope you guys can live with that."

"No, Dominique, don't say that-"

"Orphius," she interrupted. "I have to go take care of my friends...THE ONES YOU TORTURED!"

With that, she whipped around, still crying, and ran from the room. Her brother stood in the dungeon, dumbstruck. His sister had just declared war on her two brothers. Maybe this was a family tradition forming.

"Oh, God...what have I done?"

16

Revelations

"I can't believe he did this to you," Dominique said in a hollow voice, inspecting Tom's arm carefully. He gritted his teeth and tried not to cry out. "I should have gotten there sooner. I should have just knocked him down the stairs when I had the chance."

"There's a question," Flint said, giving her a measured stare. "Why didn't you?"

Both Shayla and Yakimi winced, and they gave her a look. The robot huffed.

"What?"

"I'll tell you guys later," Dominique murmured. "Right now, can we concentrate on him?"

Tom raised his head, starting to sit up. "You know, I'm really feeling much better. I think I could-OW!"

He looked sharply at Dominique. She had smacked his injured leg. "What was that for?"

"For being stupid. Lie back down."

Sighing, the skeleton did as he was told, and Dominique patted his head.

"Good boy."

Flint ducked her head, smiling to herself. Then, she looked up and pinned Yakimi with a sharp gaze.

"So," she said. "What the hell are you?"

As the Adamean began to explain things, Dominique half listened as she concentrating on focusing some of her energy to hold Tom's broken ribs in place. She wrapped them securely with bandages they had stolen from a supply drawer. Right now, they were in a small house—Shayla had recently eaten the soldiers who had occupied it. Her purple eyes were underlined with dark circles, and her mouth was little more than a thin line.

"You look tired," Tom observed. She glanced up at him.

"Do I?"

"Mmm hmm. I think you need a nap."

She shrugged. "Can't argue with that. But I wouldn't be able to sleep anyway, with you like this."

He bit his lip. "I don't know what that means."

Her eyebrows rose. "Well, usually it means that you're my friend, and I'm worried about you."

"Ah," he said, taking on a politely disinterested tone. She smiled.

"I'm just so glad that you're okay. That everyone's okay," she added hastily. He smiled back at her.

"There," she said with satisfaction. "All better. Does it feel better? Now your bones are set properly and won't be able to move while they heal."

"That's good," Tom said, sitting up cautiously. He seemed pleasantly surprised when they didn't twinge with pain. "Thank you."

Dominique smiled. "I think I'm gonna take you up on that nap offer. You guys can hold down the fort, right?"

Shayla nodded enthusiastically. Holding up her hand, she made her face look solemn. "We shall murder all who approach."

Yakimi jumped. "We will?"

"Sarcasm, my friend. Sarcasm."

"You do that," Dominique said. "Oh, and by the way...*tell* them."

She gave Shayla a loaded look, and then tromped up the stairs.

"Well, that's just typical," Shayla groused. "Leave me to do all the hard work for ya."

"Actually, I know as well," Yakimi added.

"You don't count."

"What's going on?" Flint demanded. Tom leaned forward, interested.

"Well, the thing is, Dominique's sort of a..."

From the stairwell, the girl could hear the heavy sigh emitted by Tom. He didn't seem *too* shocked. But then again, she had been unusual from the very beginning, hadn't she?

"But I already *knew* that," Flint complained. "It took this long for you all to catch up with me?"

Dominique slouched as she climbed upstairs, feeling awful. But she really did need sleep, so she would only have time to feel sorry for herself for just a few more moments...

As she passed the bathroom, she glanced in. Something curled in her stomach, and suddenly lurching, she moaned as a wave of nausea hit her. It probably had something to do with stress, but for now, all she knew was that she wanted that toilet.

Leaning over, she gagged, trying not to watch as the contents of her stomach splashed into the water. God, she just wanted everything to resolve itself without her...

Downstairs, four people perked up as they heard the sounds of retching from the bathroom. Tom frowned and got to his feet, running to Dominique's aid.

As Yakimi and Shayla made to follow, Flint grabbed their arms.

"Let him go," she said. She looked at Shayla pointedly, and the shape shifter grinned, raising her arms in surrender.

"Don't worry, I get it."

"What?" Yakimi asked.

"Listen, pal, I don't know if you've noticed..."

Tom looked into the bathroom hesitantly, and saw the girl hanging over the toilet, hair falling into her face. He cleared his throat; she was turning her head in his direction when she gagged again.

"Hello," he said, kneeling beside her. She coughed once and wiped her mouth on a tissue.

"Hi," she croaked.

"Can you tell me what's wrong?"

"Well, didn't Shayla tell you?"

"All she told us was that you're a Shadow," Tom murmured. Dominique groaned and blew her nose. She was starting to cry.

"But you know what? It doesn't matter," the skeleton said. "You're still my friend, no matter what family you belong to."

She looked up at him, her eyes doubtful. "So what, you're not afraid I'm gonna kill you all in your sleep?" she snapped sarcastically. He arched a bony brow; she sighed.

"Sorry, I guess I'm just a little..."

"Worried? Stressed? Overwhelmed? Believe me, there are plenty of words to describe the feeling. Come on, let's go to bed-"

He broke off suddenly, and began to babble. "Well, what I meant was *you* go to bed. *I'm* going to sleep downstairs."

Dominique grinned. Her eyes really did feel like lead. Staring at him, she yawned once and staggered upright, beginning to wander from the bathroom.

"Umm...do you know where to go?" Tom asked, coming up behind her. He took her by the shoulders, steering her in the right direction. Dominique felt shivers race up her spine as he finally set her down on the bed.

"Thanks," she mumbled, already trying to get under the covers. He stared at her.

Suddenly, she sat up. By the glazed look in her eyes, Tom could tell she was half asleep already. "Tom?" she asked.

"Hmm?"

"What happens when you love your enemies? Are you still allowed to kill them? Orphius and Keller are my *family.*"

Tom didn't answer. All he did was reach over and take her hand in his.

She stared at him for a long moment, and he smiled.

"Thanks," she said. He nodded.

Sometimes, all a person needed was a quiet moment to think.

After the girl had fallen asleep, the skeleton got up silently and rejoined the crowd downstairs. Shayla and Flint were quietly bickering about something, while Yakimi focused on inspecting his sword for any potential problems.

"Is she out?" Flint asked, suddenly abandoning the conversation with Shayla. The shape shifter gave her a glare, but looked toward Tom with interest for his answer. He nodded.

"Okay," Shayla said. "What do we do?"

"Do?" Tom asked. "We don't *do* anything."

"Well, we've gotta do *something,"* the shape shifter snapped. "We can't just ignore this, Tom. She's a Shadow, but in order to keep our world from being destroyed..."

She took a breath. "I've been thinking," she muttered. "At first, I was all for stopping Val from using the power source, so we could save her, but look around you!"

With her eyes wide and incredulous, she gestured outside. "Half of this entire town's been run out by the men who were in this house! Keller and Orphius are making people's lives miserable!"

Her blue eyes were pained. "We've gotta find the Shadow's power. We have to destroy it-"

"NO!" Tom shouted. The woman jumped back, startled.

"We're not going to kill them?"

"If you kill them using that, then Dominique dies too," Tom snarled. "Can you live with that? WELL?"

Shayla's eyes turned hard and steely.

"Tom Horter, I don't think you understand how many people have-"

He froze suddenly, and Shayla stopped talking immediately.

"Well," she sputtered. "What I meant was, in this area your judgment may be a little clouded-"

"You don't think I know how many people have died?" he asked quietly. "Believe me when I say this, shape shifter. I do."

With that, he whirled around and stalked off in the opposite direction. Flint and Yakimi exchanged alarmed glances.

"I DON'T THINK YOU DO!" Shayla shouted after him. "I'M THE *ONLY* SHAPE SHIFTER LEFT!"

A moment of silence followed her screaming, and finally, Yakimi spoke quietly.

"Well," the Adamean said. "I suppose that didn't go as planned."

"Shut up," Shayla snarled as she sat down.

"Tom!" Flint called, getting to her feet. "Hey, Tom!"

She ran to follow him. Yakimi stood up as well, and Shayla stammered in frustration and rage.

"My God, what's the big deal? I *know* what we have to do!"

"Shayla," Yakimi said quietly. "Dominique freed me from a one hundred year long sleep. I cannot allow her to die."

His yellow eyes flicked to her. "Perhaps you should think about what the girl has done for you."

With that, he turned and nimbly trotted after Flint, who had followed Tom into the other room.

At the sound of the Adamean's entry, Tom turned his head marginally in his direction, but kept staring out the window, framing a small town. He saw several of Keller's men tormenting an old woman; he looked away.

"There must be another way to stop this war," he said.

"Of course there is," Flint said briskly. "We just haven't been looking in the right places."

"Like what?" Yakimi asked. "Shayla, Dominique and I were headed toward a place...Red Shield?"

"Really?" Flint laughed. "Well then, I think it's time we paid someone a little visit."

Tom looked around, his bony brows raised.

"Who?"

"Val."

Reyzar flew straight and true over Yumurango, his wings beating tirelessly in a steady pattern. People that saw a dragon knew to be wary, but this one in particular had an ill feeling to it. They fled with additional urgency from his black form, without knowing the reason.

Keller sat in a jockey-like position, his armor protecting him from the biting wind and cold of the high altitude. He glanced down at the people below him. Focusing his thoughts, he pondered...

Such helpless fools. But what was he to do? Orphius was close to being crushed, and his sister had reappeared. He had to keep this war alive, just long enough to end his brother's life.

Then, perhaps, Yumurango would be at peace.

He straightened on the dragon's back. "Let's land down there," he instructed, pointing to one of the larger buildings that marred the horizon. They were over the capitol city. It would be neutral ground.

Citizens were surprised to see the dragon land in their city, but were even more surprised when they saw who was riding it.

People shrank back in fear as he moved through the crowd. He barely noticed. There were archives he had to check. What had those fools been doing so far out in the forest? No one went there without a reason. Not unless they wanted to die an early death...now, he didn't know about most of that group, but his sister wasn't that stupid.

Reyzar skulked along behind him, hissing at anyone who came close. His red eyes were narrowed in distaste at being on the ground for so long.

His owner understood. Giving his mount a nod of reassurance, he stepped into the capitol's library.

Inside, all was quiet. Keller subconsciously relaxed in the presence of the familiar surroundings. He had been here many times with his family. His father had enjoyed many visits with the governor...was he still governor, even now? If so, was he coping with all this chaos?

Enough, he chided severely. He just needed to get in and get what he needed. His armored boots clanked loudly as he strode through the halls.

He paused as he passed the book stacks, checking to determine the subject category in each area. Government...nope, no way was there gonna be anything in there of use to him. History...maybe. Perhaps there was something about the forest in those stacks.

As he began to skim books, he saw a few that mentioned his family's name. Vaguely interested, he picked one up and browsed through it.

The beginnings of his line, with the finding of Yumurangonian magic. Blah...his family's history...blah...

Wait a minute. Keller stopped suddenly, and looked toward the end. There was a very large section about him and Orphius. None of it good.

Sighing, he put it back and suddenly sensed a presence to his right. Turning slowly, he was surprised to see a little boy staring at him.

The boy, of course, was petrified with fear. Keller studied him for a moment, then decided to ignore him. Returning to the books, his hand twitched toward one. *Yumurango's Forest; Cursed?*

Scanning it quickly, he found many unfounded rumors in the book. Gigantic spiders, Adameans, constructs that could take the form of wind or water...but not what he was looking for. He needed to find out about the magic in the forest.

A commotion drew his gaze. He caught a glimpse of a teenage boy pulling a teenage girl behind a stack, his hand over her mouth. Keller stiffened, and without delay, he stalked over.

He could hear the sounds of the girl struggling, screaming through the boy's hand and trying to kick and bite. But she was small, and it just seemed to amuse him.

"Don't be like that, baby," he cooed in a horrible way. "There's no one here to help. Might as well enjoy this..."

Keller circled behind them, so the boy wouldn't be able to see him. The teenager whipped the girl around, so she was facing him.

"Don't tell me you've been dropping me all these hints for nothing."

The girl began to respond, but quieted as her gaze was drawn to Keller appearing over the boy's shoulder. The man pressed a finger to his helmet, where his mouth would be. She got the message.

"Well," the youth continued. "Either way, I'm gonna have what I want, so you just-"

That was when he felt the tap on his shoulder. He whirled, a cover story forming on his lips.

"My girlfriend here got frightened of a book. I was trying to calm her down and-" he stopped, gawking.

Keller straightened to his impressive seven foot height, and stared disdainfully down at the boy. With a slight twitch of his head, he indicated for him to let the girl go.

He did, instantly. The girl ran off, screaming, leaving the boy to stare in terror at the general. The man leaned down just enough so they were eye to eye.

"Bad move, kid," he growled.

That broke the spell; the boy ran off, whimpering as he went. Laughing quietly to himself, Keller strode back to the stacks he had left and began to paw through books again.

"Mister?"

Slowly, the man moved his head. The scared little boy was still there. He seemed less scared than perplexed.

"Hmm?" he asked, vaguely interested.

"If you're evil, then why did you help that girl?"

The child was obviously confused. "My mommy says that you're evil, but if you save people, doesn't that make you good?"

Keller looked away. "Life is complicated, kid."

"Okay. But mister?"

"What?"

"Your armor is cool."

With that, the kid turned and walked back to his mom. Keller watched as the woman jerked her head up, a nameless fear moving through her. She grabbed the boy's arm and they left. Fast.

Ooookay. Keller thought. His day was rapidly becoming weird.

"Excuse me, may I help you find anything?"

Keller turned, and the woman who had addressed him turned a startling shade of white. "Oh, I'm sorry, umm...that is, I-"

"Yes, actually," he said. She winced at the sound of his voice. "I need to find a book that explains what types of magic are said to be in the forest."

"Th-the forest? Why?" she asked.

He leveled her with a look.

"I mean, uh, yes sir, I'll get it to you."

"Thank you."

She went off, and Keller continued to find rubbish about imps and Marauders in the book he was reading. Good God, was there anything-?

"Here you are."

He took the book from her and began to turn through the pages immediately. Some ancient spells were said to exist there. But experience with magic, and his father, had proved those to be false.

A memory came back, powerful and unbidden. Keller had been walking through the mansion's grounds with Singe, during what seemed a lifetime ago. He still remembered how brightly the sun seemed to shine back then.

"All the stuff you read in books these days are rubbish," Singe said snobbily. Keller arched an eyebrow.

"Oh really? And why is that?"

"Because no one but our family knows the first thing about powerful magic. You'd think that they'd have learned that by now."

Keller laughed. "But father, we give the Taraban library a piece of our private collection each year."

"I know, but they don't know what to make of it."

"If you say so."

"I say so. But just remember, there are a few things that will never be recorded in a book. You know one."

Keller snapped back into reality. Of course! The forest! That was where his family was said to have stored the source of their power. Every book in the history of Yumurango had said so. There had even been maps constructed eons ago to show the way for any Shadow...

Without bothering to hold it back, Keller began to laugh out loud. Those fools thought they were finding the silver tree in the forest. He snapped the book shut and continued to crack up.

A few people looked up in alarm, and then stared with astonishment as they recognized him. Keller again hardly even noticed.

The source of the Shadow's power was in something silver, all right, but his ancestors had been cleverer than that. They had put it inside something that would be able to defend itself, without knowing what was inside it.

As his hilarity ended, he cleared his throat and put the book back, still chortling occasionally.

"Thank you," he said to the librarian. She looked at him coldly.

"Did you find everything?"

"Oh yes, I believe I did."

A few minutes later, Taraban citizens looked up in astonishment as the dragon took off again, a triumphant Keller on his back. Reyzar thrummed happily at his master's good mood. The man gave him a pat.

He knew what he had to do now. Get to the power source, and hide it so no one would ever find it again. As far as he knew, he was the only one who knew its true location. Unless...

Unless his father had shared his most trusted secret with his advisor, Val. Keller stiffened suddenly, and looked toward the mountains. He was there somewhere, hunkering down with Red Shield. The traitor.

His sister was Val's ally, and that meant her friends were as well. That was bad. That meant the source would be near him! If he knew...

Suddenly, he swore. "Head for the mountains!" he shouted. Immediately, Reyzar whipped around, confused at the sudden mood change. The dragon, however, *was* Berra's son. He narrowed his red eyes and flew on as fast as he could.

If Dominique and her friends got there first, it could mean the end for the entire Shadow line...along with all of Yumurango's magic.

"Come on!" Flint sniped, patting Shayla's side. "Can't you go any faster?"

A growl was her only response. Laughing to herself, Flint turned around to look at Dominique. The girl seemed pale. Not that she wasn't always fair, but there was a piqued tone about her face.

"What's the matter?" she asked. Dominique looked up.

"Hmm? Oh, nothing. I'm just not feeling too well, I guess."

From his seat behind her, Tom cleared his throat. "What's wrong?"

"I'm fine," she said firmly. "There's nothing to worry about."

The skeleton huffed unhappily, but let it go. Yakimi, on the other hand, frowned.

"When we land, let me take a look at you. I know a few spells that might be able to help."

"Thanks," Dominique muttered. Tom crossed his arms against the cold air and muttered something under his breath.

"So," Flint called back. "Anyone want to take bets Sadiki's gone back to Val with nothing, groveling for forgiveness?"

"I say five bucks," Tom said instantly. "I've known that sniveling weasel for way longer than any of you."

"I see you and raise you ten," Flint shot back.

"I'm confused," Yakimi added.

Dominique grinned.

Abruptly, they began to angle downwards. Every rider grabbed onto their respective spike and held on with all their might. White, swirling fog enveloped them as they aimed for the mountain top. No one could see where they were headed-

A sudden jolt announced Shayla's landing. Dominique gave a startled squeak as she was suddenly flung forward into Flint. The robot, caught off balance, yelped as they both slid off the dragon's side.

"Whoa!"

"Dominique!" Tom shouted. He couldn't see her; the fog was too thick. "Are you okay?"

"Fine," she called back meekly.

"Oh yeah, don't worry about *me!* I didn't fall or anything!" Flint shouted.

Tom and Yakimi dismounted, just as Shayla started to shrink back into human form. They groped through the fog, trying to find each other.

"Okay," Dominique said. "Whose hand have I got a hold of?"

"Mine," Shayla rang. Flint stuck close, her yellow eyes a beacon.

"Boys! We're over here!"

There were sounds of shuffling, and a curse from Tom as Yakimi's armored elbow slammed into his chest. "Watch it!"

"Sorry, I can't see..."

The skeleton stumbled forward, of course, slammed into someone. Whoever it was yelped and fell back; by sheer reflex, he grabbed them and held them up.

When he realized it was Dominique, he hastily released her and cleared his throat, looking away. She brushed herself off and looked around at their assembled group.

"Okay," she said. "Flint, can you find the *right* entrance this time? Tom, you help her."

"Yes ma'am!" the robot said sarcastically, saluting her.

With that, the robot began to lead the way. Dominique fell into place behind her, beside Tom. Shayla and Yakimi brought up the rear.

"Let's see," he murmured. "The problem is, I have no idea where we are with this fog around...hmm..."

"We should probably hurry up," Yakimi interjected nervously. "So we don't freeze to death."

Shayla laughed. "Buddy, have you forgotten what I can turn into? I can make enough heat for all of us."

"Alright, alright, I just don't like the cold."

"What? Adameans don't hang out in the mountains often?" Dominique teased.

"*No,* we don't."

She snickered.

"Ah ha!" Flint said. "Is this something?"

Tom squinted through the fog. There was some kind of door built into the hillside, and he nodded.

"I think this is it."

"You *think?* Listen, pal, the last time you *thought* it was the right way, we ended up-"

"Flint? Shut up. Move."

He shoved by her and knocked on the door twice. There was a hollow, reverberating sound, going deep into the mountain. Dominique swallowed. She could hardly wait to get into a normal bed again.

"Come on," she grumbled. No one had answered.

All of a sudden, a flower sprang up from the snow bank beside them; Dominique jumped away with a yelp, straight into Tom. He held her protectively for a moment, and then laughed.

"There's the camera. Kinda cute."

Dominique looked closer. Indeed, the flower's center was a camera. She waved to it and motioned toward the door.

It sucked back into the ground, and then the door opened. Flint shuffled in first, followed by the rest of them.

"Well then," Tom said, as the door shut behind them. "Let's go."

This particular tunnel was nicer than the last one they'd gone through. The way was illuminated, for one. Red Shield operatives were also stumbling into the main hallway from other side ones, giving their group nods and grunts of acknowledgment. Dominique nodded back to a few.

She glanced back at her friends. Everyone had been here before except Yakimi, and he seemed skittish. His yellow eyes glanced uneasily from side to side. Once, when someone up ahead shouted, he jumped about three feet in the air.

Dominique gave him a pat, and he smiled at the effort.

"I've never been in a cave this small before," he grumbled, looking up at the ceiling. She smiled.

"It'll be okay. The longest we'll be here is probably a couple of days."

"If you say so."

Suddenly, he stopped. The girl stopped with him and frowned. "What is it?"

"Listen, as an Adamean, I have an honor to uphold. I owe you my life, so..."

He knelt down , and removed his helmet. The rest of their friends had stopped by now, too, and were staring at him curiously.

"I pledge my life to be of service to you," he said. The solemn look in his eyes made Dominique feel as though she was the one being bound into service, not him. "I shall stay by your side for as long as I live, and will never disobey an order."

"Yakimi, you don't have to-"

The seriousness in his face, however, made her rethink her words.

"Okay," Dominique said. "I'm not sure what this means, but, uh..."

"Perhaps later, you'll see what I mean." He said with a smile.

She nodded, and then, without seeming to know why, she stepped forward and hugged him tightly. He hefted her up onto his shoulders, and she shrieked with delight.

Dominique looked down at the rest of her friends. Flint looked amused. Shayla looked confused. And Tom looked angry.

She looked at him. The skeleton had his arms crossed, and he was glaring at Yakimi. Why? What had he done?

The Adamean, apparently, didn't notice. He walked on, with Dominique holding onto his helmeted head for support. She actually just felt grateful. Now she knew that one of her friends wouldn't be leaving her anytime soon.

Someone cleared their throat; Dominique saw that Tom was tapping Yakimi on the shoulder. Immediately, the Adamean let her down and smiled at the skeleton.

"She's all yours," he said, giving them a strange glance as he left to rejoin Flint and Shayla.

"Can I talk to you for a moment?" Tom asked, pulling Dominique gently to the side of the tunnel. It was almost empty now. He had to whisper to keep his voice from echoing.

"What is it?" she asked.

He sighed. "Listen, Dominique, we've been through a lot together."

She nodded. "Yeah,"

"And, when you experience life and death situations with someone, it doesn't just go away."

Dominique arched an eyebrow. "I'm confused."

Tom gulped. "Look, I guess what I'm trying to say is-SADIKI!"

"Sadiki?"

But the skeleton brushed by her and headed straight for something behind her. She whirled around, and saw the short, hooded figure running away from them. Before he got far, Flint and Shayla leapt out from in front of him, giving him icy glares.

When Yakimi set eyes on him, his brown skin blanched. "A Marauder," he murmured, utterly horrified. Sadiki's green eyes narrowed.

"An Adamean? How is that your people are still alive?"

"Wouldn't you like to know," Dominique sneered, coming up behind him. He grimaced as she crouched down by him.

"I need to speak to Val," she said sweetly. "Right. Now."

The Marauder glared at her, but muttered darkly under his breath and began to lead the way down a side passage. Glancing smugly at her friends, Dominique began to follow them. Tom came up right next to her, and she took comfort in his presence.

Sadiki led them through the twisting, curving tunnels with practiced ease. People who they met along the way stared at Dominique in disbelief. At least now she knew why.

Soon, they entered more familiar territory. Dominique recognized the carvings on the wall as they walked down a hall, and then, saw the door with the Shadow's crest on it.

"That came from my home," she complained. "The door was on my father's study. Val always used to-"

"Ah," Sadiki said knowingly. "So you've finally come to terms with who you are."

"No thanks to you," Dominique snarled. "Open the door."

He bowed mockingly, and did as he was told. Dominique stepped through, but when Tom tried to follow her, Sadiki stepped between them.

"She goes alone," he instructed.

Without another thought, the girl whisked to the large desk in the room and slammed her fists on the wood. The man jumped, obviously surprised by her aggression.

"So," she hissed. "Trying to get me killed, are we?"

"Come on," Keller hissed. "Almost there."

Reyzar coughed once, but didn't respond. He simply kept flying until, at last, he began to descend. Cold mountain air blew around the pair of them as the dragon landed. Keller slid off, giving him a grateful pat.

"Don't worry," he said. "I won't be long."

After all, how long could it take him to get in, kill Val, and kidnap his sister?

Probably not too long.

"Listen," Val said soothingly. "Dominique, I knew you when you were twelve years old, and I know you'd never-"

"Never *what,* Val?" she said, then continued in a threatening tone. "Think carefully before you answer me."

The man stared at her with his good eye, his response held in the back of his throat. Dominique straightened, her Shadow heritage coming through. She was used to being obeyed, not being made to run about like a rat while trying to find the key to her own destruction.

He seemed to sense her anger. "Just calm down," he said placating. "Do you want any tea? You must be cold from your journey-"

"Save me your pleasantries!" Dominique commanded. "I've had just about enough of you. You and your entire organization!"

"What would you have me do? Let your brothers tear this world apart?"

"Do you even know *why* they're fighting?" Dominique asked suddenly. "You knew them, Val; you could have calmed each of them down-"

"The time of the Shadows is over," the man suddenly proclaimed, standing up. "The magic of Yumurango must be handed down to others."

"Others," she said. Her eyebrows slanted downwards. "You mean, like you? You son of a-"

"Enough!" Val barked. She shut up, more out of surprise than obedience.

"You're meddling in affairs that you don't have the slightest clue about, little girl. I don't know how you survived that fire. You were supposed to be *dead,* along with your entire family-"

"YOU!" she screamed. "YOU STARTED THAT FIRE!"

Before she could react to what she had just learned, someone opened the door behind them.

"Val!" Sadiki squeaked excitedly. "You won't believe this; we've had the power source all along!"

"What do you mean?" the man asked, his eye widening. "That's impossible. I would have known-"

"What do you think has been giving that robot free will?"

"Huh?" Dominique asked.

He ignored her. "You mean..."

"Yes, sir. It's *in the machine."*

"Oh my God," the girl said. "FLINT! YOU'VE GOTTA-"

Something slammed into the back of her head, and she fell forward onto the cold stone floor. Her mind was spiraling into darkness, but still she groped for the door.

"Flint..." she gasped. "Run for it!"

A second blow finished the job, and she collapsed, unconscious.

17

The Future

She was floating.

That was the first thing that came to Dominique's confused mind. Opening her eyes, she looked around. Mist surrounded her, swirling as she moved her hand slowly up to her head.

"Augh," she muttered. Her head throbbed horribly.

"Lie ssstill," a sliding voice came to her. "You've had a nasssty knock on the head. You are lucky it did not caussse permanent damage."

"Who's there?" the girl snapped. She was still mad after the Val encounter, and was ready to pick a fight.

There was the sound of laughter, from two beings. Dominique looked around to each side, appalled.

"What are you? Where am I?" she snarled.

"You are nowhere," another hissing voice said. This voice seemed lighter, more delicate. "You are between worldsss,"

"What do you mean? Which worlds?"

"Yumurango and Earth," the first, and darker, voice said. "You mussst decide where to go on."

"What kind of a question is that?" Dominique snapped. "Let me back! I need to warn my friends-"

"That you have been betrayed? That Val wasss the caussse of everything?"

"Well...yeah. Hey, how did you know-?"

Quite suddenly, Dominique stopped. A pair of yellow eyes had snapped open in the darkness surrounding her. They were familiar.

It was the same creature that had been by the portal, trying to warn her back from Yumurango. Instantly, she tried to pitch to her feet, but since she was apparently floating in midair, the maneuver didn't work well.

"We are the portal guardiansss," the creature said. "Charged with the duty to protect Yumurango from interlopersss, of which you are a dangerousss one."

"Hey, I belong in Yumurango!"

"Do you?" the second voice chimed in. "Are you sssure?"

"Okay, let me see you!" Dominique commanded.

"Asss you wisssh,"

Suddenly, the girl saw a figure come sliding out of the darkness, suddenly illuminated by a ghostly light.

It resembled a very large, bloated snake, but was propped up by two stubby looking forearms. Its triangular head was adorned with two enormous, luminescent eyes. The scales that adorned its body were sand-like in color.

"I am Poz," the creature said. "My mate isss Duna."

He nodded to the right, and Dominique saw a second, slighter version of the creature come sliding up. She glanced between both of them.

"So...we're in the portal?"

"You could sssay that," Duna said. "You sssee, we have been charged with your sssafety asss well. A lassst wisssh wasss made by your father, that hisss children be ssspared-"

"From Val," Dominique hissed.

Poz nodded. "We have managed to keep our promissse ssso far, but thingsss have become desssperate."

"Because of Flint."

"Yesss," Duna growled. "We were not aware that your father had moved the Ssshadows' sssource. Thisss was never meant to be. It wasss foolisssh of him."

"Don't talk about him that way," the girl snapped. Duna gave her a reproachful gaze.

"I'm sssimply ssstating factsss," she said huffily. Poz glared.

"Lisssten, in order to keep our promissse to your father, the bessst coursse of action to keep you alive would be to sssend you back to Earth."

"No."

He raised a stubby arm. Dominique couldn't help but notice the claws on the ends of his fingers appeared very sharp. "Let me finisssh, pleassse,"

She shut up.

"Your brothersss are already in danger. If you are on Earth at the time when the sssource isss dessstroyed, you will be ssspared. You are cut off from magic in the other world, so the absssence of it would not affect you."

"And what about my brothers?" Dominique asked.

"We would move them with you, but their original home hasss a ssstronger hold on them than it doesss you. If they were transssported to the other world, they would die of ssshock, mossst likely."

"So either way, they die?" Dominique cried in frustration.

"No, not all hope is lossst. It isss jussst that you, at leassst, ssshould be sssafe."

"Well, I'm sorry," the girl snapped. "But I won't abandon my family, or my friends."

Poz sighed. "My dear, you are making a missstake."

"Sue me."

"Wait," Duna pleaded. "Let usss ssshow you what you are going back to. The future, if you will."

"Fine."

Instantly, Dominique felt a rushing sensation, and suddenly, she was standing on the Yumurango plains, blinking rapidly. Poz and Duna flanked her on either side.

"Follow me," Duna announced, and scuttled off through the grass. Poz flicked after her, and the girl tried to keep up.

As they topped a hill, Dominique's ears suddenly picked up the sound of machinery.

"What is this?" she asked.

"Jussst look," Duna said grimly, from the top. The girl found herself running the rest of the way, and she gasped.

The towers of Implitic rose up above them, as usual, but there was something wrong. Instead of the lights shining from magic within them, they looked like fire. Dominique looked down toward the ground level in desperation.

People shuffled along in rags, darting from one shadow to another. Some seemed utterly terrified as they looked up at the towers. Why?

"I'm gonna go look around," she informed the two...things. They gave her solemn looks, and nodded.

"You will sssee," Poz said regretfully.

She ignored him.

As she flew overhead, people screamed in terror and ran for cover. Dominique looked around, trying to find something familiar among the burned out houses and buildings around her. It looked like a scene from hell.

Wait a minute. She stopped suddenly, and looked sharply to her left. A glint of armor had appeared on the edges of the town. Could it be?

"Yakimi!" she called, zipping over before she knew what she was doing. Sure enough, it was him. His reptilian face was hidden in the shadow of the building he crouched behind.

"Yakimi?"

He jumped suddenly, and turned toward her. She inhaled sharply.

His face was scarred on one side, three thick welts that looked like scratches dragged down the left side of it. The eye they ran through was a whitish shade; she realized he was blind in that eye.

"Oh my God," she said.

"Dominique?" he asked, looking at her in disbelief. "But...that's impossible! You're...you're..."

"I'm right here," the girl said. "Listen, how long has it been since we went to Red Shield that last time? I've been sort of...delayed."

"What?" he asked. "Umm, I don't know how to tell you this, but...it's been ten years."

The girl looked at him oddly for a moment. "Okay," she said. "Well, Poz and Duna did say that this was the future,"

"Who?"

"Don't ask," she said. "Listen, where are the others?"

"Others?" he asked.

"Yeah," she said, giving him an odd look. "You know, Tom, Shayla, and Flint? Come on!"

"Oh. Them." His yellow eyes took on a distant gaze. "That was so long ago."

"What do you mean? Haven't they been with you all this time?"

"No," he said somberly. "Tom and Shayla were killed in the initial attack on the city."

Dominique looked at him oddly for a minute. "That can't be true," she said.

"Yes. When Val and his weapon came through, they killed everyone in their way. Shayla fought, and Tom was finally overwhelmed when his magic gave out. I don't remember details. I've seen too many battles."

"But," Dominique said desperately. "What about Flint?"

A cold look came into Yakimi's eyes. "The robot you remember no longer exists," he stated without emotion. "When the power source was removed from her systems, she became something horrible."

"I don't know what you-?"

"Well," a voice said from behind them. "Look at this. The general for the entire rebellion, at my feet?"

Yakimi whirled, his hands going immediately to his sword, and Dominique readied her powers and hovered in the air. What she saw, however, made her lose control; she fell with a soft thump on the ground.

It was that woman from before, Vilondra. Dominique suddenly recalled her existence in Red Shield, but what was on her belt...

Tom's head. On her belt. Dominique stared at it, openmouthed. The eye sockets were blank and empty, as though he was just staring off into space.

"This family inherited the magic," he murmured. "Val was their ally, so they let him live."

"The Collins?" Dominique asked. Vilondra's green eyes flashed.

"Who are you?" she demanded. "I have no use for a little girl. Leave if you want to live."

The way she said it infuriated Dominique. Rising into the air again, she found that her powers, as of yet, weren't gone.

"You're nothing but a copycat," she hissed. "*I've* got the real magic."

Vilondra looked at her hard, trying to place her somewhere. Suddenly, her eyes widened.

"What? How did you...? YOU'RE DEAD!" she finally spat. "You disappeared! No one knew-"

Dominique slammed her with a blast of dark energy, and the woman shrieked. "This is impossible!"

The girl flew at her again, and again, making sure that she would be dead before she left this God forsaken place-

Suddenly, someone rocketed past her, making her lose focus. It was so fast, looking like a silver bullet-

Wait a minute. Silver?

Dominique looked, and to her horror, saw Flint rocketing back toward her, in an apparent hurry.

"Flint!" she screamed.

The robot didn't hear her. Without warning, though, she turned in midair and brought out her rifle in one smooth motion. Dominique jumped as the gun fired-

A hole appeared in Yakimi's head. Purple blood began to trickle slowly from the wound. His yellow eyes were wide in shock; as though he hadn't quite registered the fact he'd been shot.

"Yakimi!" Dominique called desperately, flying down to him. He looked at her for a moment, and then, his yellow eyes lost their focus.

"NO!"

Dominique looked up at Flint, who was aiming the rifle at her now. Vilondra was cackling with glee, laughing at the girl who was about to be killed.

Rage filled Dominique, and she leapt at the woman, determined to bring her down before she could be.

And quite suddenly, she wasn't there anymore. A now familiar dark, misty place floated in front of her eyes, and she screamed.

"NO!"

"We told you," Duna said solemnly, appearing out of nowhere. "That isss the way thingsss are meant to be. You mussst go to Earth, where you will be able to live out your entire life."

"What was I doing? Huh?" Dominique snarled. "When my friends were dying, what was I doing on Earth?"

Poz and Duna exchanged glances. "You were getting married," he said simply. "At that time."

Dominique shook her head. "But to who?"

"A man named Alan. That isss all we know."

Her head flew up. "Alan?"

The idea seemed faintly ridiculous to her. He was a high school crush, nothing more. There were people in Yumurango she cared about far more deeply than him.

"If I stay," she said. "Will the future be different?"

"Perhapsss," Poz allowed. "But thisss isss the mossst likely courssse. You sssee, even as they were being attacked, Keller and Orphiusss ssstill refusssed to sssee the truth, and were killed before they even realized what wasss happening."

"I can tell them," Dominique said desperately. "I can't abandon them. I CAN'T!"

"Ssso be it," Duna said wearily. "May we be forgiven for what we are about to do."

She turned to Poz, who closed his eyes for a brief instant-

18

Escape

"Contacts moving to block D8; move to engage." Dominique's first contact with the real world was the sound of a cool, female voice. The announcement repeated as she sat up shakily.

"What's going on?" she muttered to herself. Contacts?

She looked around. It was dark, like the last place she had been, but instead of swirling mists around her, she smelled mildew and heard dripping not too far away. Straining her eyes, she stood up and began to feel her way around. Cold, damp stone met her fingers as she crawled, and she painted a mental image of the cell around her.

"Classy," she muttered.

"Look out!"

The shout came from nearby; Dominique whirled, and heard the voice reverberate throughout the stone around her. Where had it come from?

She was obviously close to the action; gunfire and shouts drew her ear, and a familiar roar. Shayla!

"Ha," she hissed. "I knew Val wouldn't get away with this."

Farther off, another roar broke out. This one *wasn't* familiar. Dominique frowned. Another dragon? But that could only mean one other person!

"Run for it!"

"Crap, we've gotta move!"

"GO GO GO!"

People ran in every direction in a panic. Keller drew his gun and slammed bullets into their backs, watching them fall. His gaze was drawn to the direction where the other dragon's roar had come from. Reyzar was behind him, guarding his back, so that meant...

They were already here. Swearing, the man holstered his gun and began to sprint in the direction of the roar. The walls around him shook dangerously. He hoped they wouldn't cave in during the battle.

"Oh my God!" someone shouted. "How the hell did *he* find us?"

Keller didn't bother to respond. After the fighting inside the structure had started, it hadn't been too hard to find the location of the Red Shield base. There was no doubt who had started the fight, either.

Someone flashed by him. The yellow sheen of bone was no surprise. Keller reached out with his power and nabbed his quarry.

"Whoa!" Tom squawked in alarm as he was frozen. As he floated into the air, he sighed. "Dominique, don't let me fall,"

"Sorry, Horter. Wrong Shadow."

Tom stiffened suddenly, and his hate filled gaze turned toward Keller. "So," he said. "You finally found this place."

"Luckily for you," Keller said.

Then, of all things, he released him. Tom watched him warily. "Why are you helping me?" he asked.

"Not *you,*" Keller corrected. Tom snorted.

"Figures. Well, if it means anything, I don't know where Dominique is either."

"That's not the most pressing matter. What matters is the source. I need to find it quickly-"

"Well, then let's go. Do you know where it is?"

"Inside something," he said vaguely.

Tom gave him a nasty look. "If you want help, you'll have to be a little more helpful yourself."

"I don't play well with others."

"So I've seen," the thief sneered. "Especially with your own family."

Keller ignored him. "We have to meet up with your friends," he said swiftly.

"Shayla and Flint should be over-"

"AUGH!"

There was a sudden commotion to their right. Flint came sailing through the air, and slammed into the general. Springing to her feet lightly, she waved to Tom.

"Hey, just thought I'd let you know that we have problems over there."

"Just thought I'd let you know you just flew into Keller."

"Ha ha...wait, what?"

An angry exclamation made her jump, and she yelped as Keller slowly stood up, trying to keep his temper in check.

"Hello," he said through gritted teeth.

"Oops."

"Alright," Tom intervened. "Apparently, the hulking metal case here knows where the Shadows' source of power is. Care to enlighten us?"

"Inside *her,*" Keller said, pointing to Flint. They both froze.

"Umm...you're kidding me, right?" the robot said. "How could it be inside me? That doesn't make any sense!"

"No scientist can create free will in a machine," Keller snapped. "It's the magic inside of you that's been doing that. We need to get you out of here, before Val realizes what's happened."

"Oh, I think he knows," Tom said.

Their conversation was interrupted by gunfire from down the hallway. Tom swore as bullets streaked toward him, and he braced himself for an impact-

A dark wall appeared in front of him, repelling the gun's fire. Keller waited patiently for the attackers to run out of ammo before he released the shield.

"You know," Tom started. "Your sister could learn something from you."

"Let's go!" Flint said impatiently. "We've gotta grab Dominique and get out of here! I know where she is!"

"You do? How?" Tom asked, as they sprang to follow her.

"It's a robot thing. You wouldn't understand."

Keller snorted. "She's using her link to the Shadows to find her. It's not brain surgery, Horter."

"Shut up!" Tom snapped.

"Right!" Flint said, skidding around a corner. Keller leapt to follow, mirrored by Tom.

The two of them exchanged glances as they began to sprint down the hall. Keller pulled ahead; Tom increased his speed.

"This is pointless, Horter," Keller said as the sprinting quickly turned into a race.

"I know, but we'll see how you feel when you lose to me."

Flint, however, was outpacing both of them easily. She was already turning another corner, when she suddenly stopped.

"She should be right here," she said, perplexed.

Dominique kept listening, waiting for someone to find her. The cell around her wasn't a place where she wanted to die.

"Come on!" she bellowed. "I'm right here!"

"Whoa!" Flint yelped. "Did you hear that?"

"Where is she?" Keller snapped, looking around. Tom gritted his teeth and peered closely at the wall.

"Hold on," he said. "Look at this."

In the wall, there was a hidden panel, almost invisible through the thick layer of dirt masking its gray color. It looked just like any other section of the stone wall. But the smoothing of the rock from repeated use over time gave it away. When the skeleton touched it, it sparked and electric arcs jumped out. Flint yelped.

"Alright," Tom said uncertainly. "This has to be overridden, but I'm not sure how-"

Suddenly, Keller's fist descended on the panel. The wires and knobs began to smoke, and a secret wall began to open up.

"Well," Tom said. "That works."

The light was sudden, and blinding. Dominique gritted her teeth and narrowed her eyes to slits. After complete darkness, even the dim cave lights made her eyes water.

"Dominique!" Tom's familiar voice rang out. She grinned widely and threw herself at him. He squeezed her tightly, and she felt as though she never wanted to leave his arms again.

That is, until someone else spoke. "Get your hands off her!"

The girl's eyes were rapidly adjusting. She pulled back in shock. "Keller?"

Her brother stood stock still, somewhat nervous. She knew he was thinking back to previous encounters, but then, she smiled.

"I remember! It's okay!"

She looked at him. He looked at her. Then, at the same time they both laughed and embraced. Dominique tried to get her arms all the way around him, but his armor was too large.

"Listen," she said, pulling back and displaying an intense look. He reflexively stiffened, and they parted, ready for action. "I know who started the fire. It wasn't Orphius."

Keller laughed. "Wouldn't we all like that?"

"No, Keller. It was Val!"

"Val?" Tom thundered. "Why would Val do that? He never even knew the Shadows!"

"Yes he did," Dominique and Keller said in unison.

"He was our father's advisor," the girl added. "Listen, he wants all the power for himself. That's why he tried to kill our family in the first place!"

"But, we managed to survive the flames," Keller said.

"I know *I* did," Dominique said bitterly. "And I suppose that you and Orphius did because you're both so strong."

"Umm," Flint interjected nervously. "As touching as this conversation is, I think we've gotta go. I'm sensing something coming this way. Something bad."

"Sadiki?"

"Yeah. He's still bound, but there's something...different."

"Come on," Keller said, beginning to pull Dominique away. She grabbed hold of Tom's hand, dragging him with them.

"Watch the robot carefully," the general ordered. "If Val gets a hold of her, we're screwed."

"I see you haven't lost your ability to charm people with words," Dominique muttered. He shot her a look; she smiled.

"God, it's good to see you again."

"GO!" Tom snapped.

"Where's Shayla? And Yakimi?" Dominique asked.

"I don't know. The last time I saw them, Shayla was just about to take a bite out of Vilondra."

"Good," the girl said smugly.

That said, the walls around them began to collapse. Dominique and Keller created shields above the group as they continued moving away from the cell that had held Dominique.

"Go right!" Flint shouted above the sound of crashing rubble. The girl managed to nod, and shoved Keller down the side tunnel. Tom went to follow, but all of a sudden, he stumbled.

Flint walked past him without knowing it, and he swore. "Guys! Wait!"

But the sound of sliding rocks drowned out his voice. As he scrambled to his feet, a large falling boulder pinned his foot. He howled in agony; the bones had been crushed.

"No!" he shouted, still trying to reach out. He had to be there for her, be there to protect her-

Another rock slammed into his leg. Stars appeared before his eyes, and he tried to ignore the pain as he attempted to wriggle out of the death trap he was in.

More rocks were piling up around him, and soon, he couldn't see anything else. Apprehensive and in pain, he looked up and saw a large rock at the top of the wall begin to wobble dangerously.

"Fall the other way," he pleaded. "Come on..."

But the rock, or the world, was against him. The boulder fell straight toward him, and he swore as it fell toward his head-

He was still thinking of Dominique as his world went black.

"Look out!" Flint snapped, shoving Dominique out of the way of a falling rock. The girl looked gratefully at her friend.

"Thanks."

"No problem. Keller, COME ON! Don't you know where you're going?"

"Oh, forgive me. I seem to have misplaced the mental map I have of a place I've never been to!" Keller roared back.

"YAAAH!"

The cry came from above them. Dominique grinned. She knew that battle shout.

"Yakimi!" she cried. "Down here!"

A tunnel above them had evidently collapsed. Yakimi slid down a broken piece of the smooth floor and rolled to his feet.

"Dominique, are you alright?"

"I'm fine. Oh, umm...Yakimi, Keller, Keller, Yakimi."

The two of them exchanged frosty glances, but otherwise, said nothing. Dominique was proud that they, at least, could control their outward emotions.

"On your left," the Adamean said. Keller turned and fired; a creature resembling a living tree was shot down while preparing to shoot at them.

"Don't look now, but we've got company," Flint warned. "Keller, I hope he's with you."

Dominique turned. A black dragon was hunkered down, breathing fire at anyone who ventured near. The entire Red Shield army seemed to be in flames before the dragon saw them.

A roar tore from his maw, but Keller simply held up his hand. Dominique could hear him talking to the dragon using some form of mental communication; she looked at her friends, who obviously didn't know what was going on.

"It's okay," she said. "Keller's telling Reyzar that we're friends."

"Reyzar?"

"That thing has a name?"

Keller turned back to them. "He wants us to know that the other dragon is heading here. In a most unorthodox manner."

"What does that mean?" Dominique asked.

"I'm not sure, but I think it might mean-"

Suddenly, the wall facing them began to rumble threateningly, and the group looked up in alarm. "Umm..."

"DODGE!" Flint shouted.

She leapt. Dominique was shoved out of the way by Yakimi. Keller began to jump, but a white wall of scales pinned him against the wall as Shayla leapt out of the stone, roaring her fury.

Looking around, the dragon's gaze alighted on her friends, and she grinned.

"Shayla! Move!"

"Get off me, you idiotic worm!" Keller roared. The dragon growled, offended, as she moved aside.

When she realized who she had been squishing, however, her slit eyes widened, and she roared again, her gnashing teeth getting closer to him-

"STOP!" Dominique screamed.

Shayla froze with her mouth inches from Keller's face. The man hadn't moved. Dominique felt a sudden surge of pride that she was related to him. He could bravely face death without flinching.

"Back. Off." She snapped. Shayla reared back reluctantly.

"We've gotta go!" Flint shouted. "Val and Sadiki are headed this way!"

"I'll kill him," Dominique yelled.

"No, we've gotta go. Now!"

Shayla roared a command to the girl; she clambered on, followed by Flint and Yakimi.

"Keller!" she shouted. "Get on!"

Her brother, however, was sprinting for Reyzar. The dragon was in a bit of a tough spot. People wielding magic had cornered him, and were firing various colored energy bolts at his dark scales. Keller headed straight for them.

Dominique understood. Reyzar was Berra's son. Berra had been their pet growing up. She must have been the only thing that had kept Keller going for so long. Now that all he had was her son, he wasn't going to let him go.

Keller smashed his armored fist into two faces at once, and swung up onto Reyzar's back. The dragon roared in triumph, spitting flame at their other offenders-

Another hole was made in the wall. A shower of rubble rained down on the two black figures, and Dominique stiffened on Shayla's back.

Sadiki. The Marauder, though small, looked insanely dangerous as he stared at the dragon. Reyzar shifted once, and Keller started to laugh.

"What the hell is that? I didn't know Val would stoop so low as to use midgets-"

A green bolt fired from Sadiki's hand. Time seemed to slow as it flew toward Keller. The general cocked his head arrogantly, and went to dodge the bolt-

It swerved to follow his movement, and the energy crackled through his body. He went rigid, as stiff as a board...and then went limp.

"KELLER!" Dominique screamed.

Reyzar bugled questioningly and turned around, looking at his rider. When he saw him slumped over, the dragon roared and bared his teeth protectively, shielding him from further attack.

"Over here!" Dominique shouted.

To her surprise, Reyzar turned. His red eyes were narrowed, as though he couldn't quite believe his own flapped ears. She repeated her command, and he, obeying, came over to Dominique.

"Follow us! Shayla, GO!"

The white dragon turned, quick as an eel, and darted up the tunnel. Reyzar followed them, black on white. The girl felt tears streaming down her face; she didn't care.

Light came to their faces, and they all gave sighs of relief as they leapt into the air, finally free. Shayla and Reyzar both roared in triumph and Dominique looked at her brother. He was still slumped over, smoking slightly. She hoped it was just his armor.

But there was something missing. Something that would have made this moment even sweeter. She cocked her head, looking at her friends. What could it be...?

Suddenly, she screamed.

"Oh my God!"

"What?" Flint asked. "What's wrong?"

"TOM!"

"Huh?"

"He's not here! Where is he?"

Yakimi's yellow eyes narrowed. "Did you lose him back there?"

"That cave-in!" Flint snarled. "Damn it, I *knew* I'd seen something under that rock!"

"Tom...." Dominique wailed.

"It's okay," Yakimi said. "He's a soldier. He'll be able to face whatever's in store for him."

"Yeah. He won't talk." Flint said grimly. "I've seen it first hand."

"Shayla," Dominique said grimly. "Land."

The dragon swiveled her head around questioningly.

"Just do it! I've gotta see if Keller's alright."

With that, she descended. Reyzar followed them as Dominique instructed him to do so. Both dragon and girl were still surprised at their ability to communicate.

As the girl went to approach the black dragon, however, he snarled menacingly and bared his teeth. She gave him a cold look.

"My brother is on your back, probably injured," she hissed. "If you don't let me get to him *right now...*"

The dragon shuffled uneasily, and finally allowed her to come closer.

It took a combination of strength and her powers to get Keller onto the ground safely, where the girl immediately took to finding a way to pop his helmet off. His armor was still smoking.

"Please," she begged. "Don't die on me now."

"Would that be such a bad thing?" Shayla asked dryly.

"SHUT UP!" Dominique screamed. The shape shifter narrowed her eyes, but remained silent.

"Come on, come on..."

At last, she found some kind of seal, and a latch. Yanking the latch open, she tore the helmet off of her brother's head, and saw his face for the first time in five years.

It was familiar, to say the least. His skin was pale, since he wore his armor all the time. His dark hair was cut extremely short, but his features had retained their good looks.

For now, his face was peaceful. Dominique wondered what it looked like when he was awake.

Well, they were about to find out...

"Keller," she said, shaking him. She checked his pulse hurriedly. Good, it was still strong. "Come on, you big lump. Wake up!"

She shook him again, harder.

"I could shake him," Yakimi offered.

Flint snickered.

Suddenly, the general woke up screaming.

Dominique, who had been exchanging a smile with the robot at the image of the Adamean shaking her brother awake, jumped back in shock.

"What the...?"

Keller began to writhe on the ground, shouting in agony. His sister pinned one of his sides down, but wasn't strong enough to hold him for long. Calmly, Yakimi pushed her out of the way and nailed both of the general's arms to his sides; Flint took his legs.

"What's wrong?" Dominique demanded. She wiped the sweat on his brow away with her sleeve. His violet eyes, darker than the rest of the siblings', looked up at her.

"I need...spell," he choked out. Another scream ensued.

"Okay, okay, where's the spell?" the girl asked. "It's okay, just relax-"

His shout cut her off. He gritted his teeth and forced out just one more word.

"Orphius."

Then, he collapsed again, unconscious. Dominique gulped, and looked at each of her friends.

"I hope you all didn't just hear what I heard," she said.

"Actually, I think I did," Shayla said dryly. "Oh fun; let's go drag your two brothers together. That'll end up great."

"Avoiding Orphius's troops," Yakimi added. "It wasn't easy the last time, either."

"We've got no choice!" Dominique snapped. "Orphius has a spell, and if we're going to save Keller..." she trailed off, looking at all of them.

"Unless you guys *don't* want to save him," she said. A haunted look came into her eyes. "Oh God, I'm surrounded by-"

"By what? People who've been oppressed by this man for half a decade?" Shayla snarled. "He's the one who first went after all the shape shifters to recruit them! And if they didn't join, he killed them! I'M THE ONLY ONE LEFT, I-"

"Enough!" Yakimi barked. The shape shifter's jaw clamped shut. None of them had ever heard the Adamean shout so loudly.

He took a deep breath. "It would seem that our friend on the ground here has made his share of mistakes," he said. "But it all began during the fire, correct? The one which Val started?"

"Yes," Dominique said stiffly, glaring at Shayla. The woman stared right back, defiant.

"And for five years, this war has torn Yumurango, or at least this side, apart."

"Alright! We already know this!" Shayla exploded. "Tell us something we don't know!"

"If you'd let me finish, then I will." The Adamean hissed. His voice was ice cold. She stepped away from him, blinking.

"Anyway," he continued. "Haven't you all fought? Haven't you all killed? I know I have. What makes him so different?"

He gestured to Keller. "Right now, we have him at our mercy. If you had your way, Shayla, you would crush him into bits where he lay."

"Correct,"

"But Dominique," he said, looking toward her. "You would save him?"

"He's her brother, of course she would!" Shayla snapped.

"SHUT UP!" Yakimi roared.

Without even looking at her, he pressed on. "I believe it's very noble for Dominique to believe this is for the best. I will go with her."

"I'm in," Flint chimed.

They all turned to look at Shayla. The shape shifter was bristling, indignant at being silenced by the Adamean so many times.

"I..." she sputtered. "I...I WILL NEVER HELP KELLER OUT, YOU HEAR ME? NEVER!"

Silence ensued, and Dominique felt her stomach drop. She'd thought she could trust Shayla. She'd thought that she was her friend.

"But," the shape shifter amended. "I will help my friends."

Dominique smiled, and Shayla's mouth quirked in a friendly gesture.

With that display of committed friendship, Dominique hurled herself forward and gave the shape shifter a hug. Shayla's blue eyes widened, and she smiled as she returned the embrace.

"I'm sorry," the girl said. "I know how much you hate him, it's just that..."

"Hey, if I were you, I'd be doing the exact same thing right now," the woman said, patting Dominique's back. Then, she snapped away.

"But, if we're gonna get this over with; we have to do it *now,* before I change my mind!"

With that, she began to change. Dominique managed to drag Keller out of the way before the dragon's tail nearly transformed on top of him.

"Reyzar," the girl called as she put Keller's helmet back on. "I need you to go back to the other dragons, and tell them what's happening!"

The black dragon balked. He garbled something to her, and she got the message; he was young, and no one would listen.

"Alright then..." she said. She looked around, and then, took off Keller's helmet again. "Here. Bring this with you."

As she held it aloft, the dragon took it delicately with two of his claws and leapt away, with a last roar. Dominique understood, and nodded solemnly.

Take care of him.

Well, she would.

19

Best Laid Plans

"Something's wrong," Dominique said grimly, looking toward Orphius's towers. "There's something *very* wrong. Where is everybody?"

Everyone was scanning the area, trying to spot at least one soldier. There was a wall that encircled the tower with a radius of five miles in all directions. Usually, the compound was so full of soldiers and assorted creatures that it was hardly possible to move from one point to another.

Now, there was no one. Tents were pitched, fires were stoked, but there were still no people. It was as if they had simply disappeared en masse.

"What's going on out there?" Yakimi murmured, staring out over the plains.

"I guess we'll have to ask him," Flint said sarcastically, pointing toward the tower. Shayla growled, and began to ascend to the tower top, which appeared to offer a perfect landing spot for a dragon. Nice and flat.

"Umm...Shayla, we'll have to land at the base of it," Dominique instructed. "The top is a spike. You can't see it because of the magic around it. It was one of his ideas of a joke."

"Your family is weird," Flint commented as they landed. The girl gave her a dry glance.

"Well, it's true!"

"I'll carry him," Yakimi said. He hefted Keller over his shoulder, staggered, but stayed upright.

"You're sure you're okay?" Dominique asked, concerned for her friend. He nodded once, stiffly.

"But I suggest we get going. I don't know how long I can carry him. This armor is very dense. I wonder what-?"

"We'll save the science lesson for later," Shayla interrupted. "Come on. Let's go swaggering in like the fools we are."

With that, Flint slammed a kick into the metal door at the base of the tower. Yelping, she jumped back, holding her foot and cursing.

"Ow! What the hell? That always works!"

"I think I may know how," Dominique said. She raised her hand, and allowed some of her energy to flow into the door.

Like a charm, the enormous doors began to pull outward, and they stumbled backward to avoid being shunted aside. When the door movement halted, the group moved in.

It was eerily quiet in the tower. Each of their footfalls echoed loudly throughout the structure.

The interior of the tower projected an ominous feeling. Black was the main theme, with ancient silver decorations set everywhere. Dominique looked around warily.

"Hey!" she said. "I recognize that. That's my coin tin from my bedroom!"

She jumped forward and looked at it closely. "I wonder if I've still got my old coin collection in there. Man, I've got so many earth coins to add in my old jean pockets-"

As she spoke, she had leaned forward and grabbed the tin from a mantelpiece. When she touched it, an ear piercing alarm wailed through the entire tower. Swearing, she whirled around. All of her friends did too.

Nothing. Not even a single shout. The tower was apparently deserted.

"Okay," Flint said evenly. "There's something wrong. Why is no one here?"

Yakimi lurched over to a table and set Keller down on it, stretching his back. "Ouch," he muttered.

"You okay?" Shayla asked.

He glanced at her. "Fine."

Dominique looked between the two of them, watching as they began to bicker quietly. It reminded her of how she had used to be with...with...

All of a sudden, her thoughts turned to Tom. The skeleton was still at Red Shield. He had been buried in that rock slide and they had all just kept running-

She didn't want to think about it. Not now. In an effort to distract herself, she headed toward an orb which was flanked by two ancient looking statues. She reached her palm out toward it, and the orb began to glow. A picture was displayed in its depths.

A hysterical reporter was shouting from the orb's surface. The human female's face was terrified. Behind her, fire crackled and numerous explosions sounded.

"Orphius and Keller's armies have met on the plains, not too far away from the town of Spirana!" the woman shouted over the noise. "I don't know about everyone else, but it seems to me this is the battle to end the war. Sightings of Orphius and Keller themselves are pouring in, and-"

She was cut off, most abruptly, as a Rhinox's roar drowned her words out. She screamed, and the communication orb she had been holding smashed onto the ground, clearly abandoned. The feed flickered once, and went black.

Dominique's jaw dropped, and she turned the orb off with another outstretching of her palm. Her power deactivated it.

"Damn it!" she suddenly screamed. Flint yelped and ended up tripping over a step. She smashed a vase on her way down.

"What?" Shayla and Yakimi both demanded.

"They're fighting!" Dominique hissed. "Right now! That's where his army is!"

"You're telling me," Shayla said. "That Orphius's entire army is out there; waging war on Keller's?"

Dominique shrugged helplessly.

Flint looked at her for a long while. "Okay then, people? We've got problems."

"Listen," the girl said. "It's possible there may be a healing spell in Orphius's library. I should search there. That's the only thing I can think of right now. Then, maybe we can get him to the battle and force my two *stupid* brothers to talk to one another..."

Her voice trailed off. "God, this is lame, isn't it?"

"Yeah," Flint said. "But right now, it's the best we've got."

They went to work quickly; Dominique, who had been shown plans of the tower incessantly since her childhood, knew exactly where to look.

"It should be over here somewhere..." she muttered. They had climbed about three stories, then turned down a short corridor. Doors lined each side of the passage, but Dominique strode knowingly up to one and pushed it open.

"Ha," she said with satisfaction.

Inside, books upon books were stacked in piles of disarray. She rolled her eyes as she tried to find a particular order to them.

"He's still a slob," she muttered to herself. Shayla kicked a pile over.

"Hey, check it out," Flint said. "I think I can narrow these down."

Her yellow eyes started to flicker, and, to everyone's surprise, turned a cool purple hue. Her eyes took in the library inventory, and then, she pointed.

"That one."

"Erm...what one?" Yakimi asked, looking doubtfully at the shelf of books she was pointing toward. With absolute confidence, the robot picked one up and handed it to Dominique.

"This one's about Marauders and their magic."

"Have I mentioned I love you?" Dominique asked, snatching the book out of her friend's hands. She began to flip through the pages, muttering under her breath as she read of Sadiki's deeds.

"Actually, no." Flint said. "Although, I think there should have been someone else you said that to before today."

Her yellow eyes betrayed no emotion, but Dominique could tell that the robot was disappointed. The grip she had on the book tightened.

Jerking thoughts of Tom out of her head, Dominique went back to the book. Information on Marauders...what spells they knew...horror stories of what happened to people who tried to stand against them...

Wait! Reversing the effects. Frantically, the girl flipped the pages, looking for any spell that was similar to what Sadiki had used on Keller.

"Okay, I've got it," she said. "Yakimi, bring Keller over here."

The Adamean had set the general on the ground, but obediently went to retrieve him and brought him closer. Dominique knelt down on the ground beside him.

"I don't know if I'll be able to do this," she said. "It says here that only a mature spellcaster would be able to manage it. I don't know if I am. Orphius would be, but he's not exactly *here* right now."

"Try it," Flint said. "If worse comes to worse, I think I'll be able to help."

"How?"

"Just do it!"

Taking a deep breath, Dominique focused on the spell and began to concentrate on the specific words. The words had to form mentally in the mind, and then be allowed to pass through the body of the spellcaster and into the body being saved. It was very important to keep a high degree of focus.

Her brows furrowed. The magic was there, but it wasn't spreading through her body like it was supposed to. She focused harder, gritting her teeth at the effort.

There! She could feel it working through her veins, moving to her head. Once it got to her brain, the magic would feed its way into Keller. All she had to do was keep concentrating...

Sweat beaded on her brow, and she felt someone wipe it away. Meaningless. All meaningless. All that mattered was the spell.

It had reached her brain. Dominique felt her strength ebbing. But now that the spell had her, it should do its work. If it was strong enough, however, it could kill her...

"Her face is turning white!" Shayla snapped. "Do something!"

Dominique's mind failed to comprehend anything spoken after that. Flurries of unintelligible voices reached her ears, and suddenly, a cold hand clamped onto her shoulder-

A burst of power, more powerful than anything she had ever experienced, flooded into her mind. Dominique's eyes snapped open, and she turned her head in disbelief.

Flint was kneeling beside her, allowing power to be channeled through herself to Dominique, and then Keller. Her yellow eyes were focused on the general's prone form.

Wind, generated by the magic in the room, began to blow in Dominique's face. Shutting her eyes again, she helped the robot finish the spell. A blue glow crept across Keller's body, and then-

It was over. Dominique and Flint dropped back. Though the girl was panting, the robot seemed unfazed.

"Good job," she said. The girl looked at her in awe.

"I didn't know that you were so powerful," she said.

"Well, I do have that source thing in me, don't I?" Flint asked. "I guess it's a good thing I don't know how to use it."

"Only through others, huh?"

"Where are we?"

Everyone looked toward Keller; his eyes were open, and he was looking up at them incredulously. Dominique grinned.

"You're okay!"

"Just fine. Where are we?"

He sat up, and suddenly, his eyes widened. "Orphius's tower!" he hissed. Old hate sprang in his eyes, and he leapt to his feet.

"Hey, we talked about this, remember? Val started the fire. Not Orphius," Dominique said, standing as well. She crossed her arms and stared her brother down.

It was almost comical, a seven foot tall man locked in a staring contest with a girl who was barely five and a half feet tall. Yakimi finally intervened.

"I hate to interrupt this 'dual of wits', but we do have a battle to stop," he said. "Keller, Orphius has taken his army and moved against yours. Without their commander, they won't stand a chance."

"What are we supposed to do?" Dominique demanded. "Even if Keller arrived in time, the battle's just gonna go on for a longer time!"

"Hold up," Shayla suddenly said. "Yakimi, can you do your magic thing? Let's see where everyone is."

"That's fine," he said, kneeling down on the floor. Dominique went by him, and he began to inscribe his peoples' language onto the stone.

Finally, there was a square drawn of a glowing line, and he spoke clearly into it.

"Orphius Shadow."

There was a ripple in the stone floor, and suddenly, Orphius appeared. He was garbed in battle armor, leaning low over the back of a Rhinox. He was overhead, engaged with a flying creature which seemed quite insistent on destroying him. Twisting on his mount's back, he let loose a black ray of energy—the creature squawked in surprise as its wing was immobilized.

Yakimi let the image fade. "The battle's already begun."

"Try Tom," Dominique blurted suddenly. Yakimi gave her a glance, and did as he was told.

Everyone (except Keller) leaned forward eagerly, wanting to know their friend's fate. Suddenly, Tom's head filled the screen.

"He's alive!" Dominique screeched. Her friend was walking unsteadily over the plains, followed by...

"Oh dear," Flint said. "That's Val, isn't it? And Sadiki."

Sure enough, the man and his evil little companion were right behind Tom. He was being held at gun point, she was sure. And behind them...

"Oh my God," Dominique said. "Look!"

Yakimi broadened the image, which displayed a sea of people, all dressed in black uniforms, trudging behind their leaders. Red Shield had been emptied.

"Damn it!" Keller barked. "None of us will stand a chance with three armies competing! Whose suicidal idea is this?"

"It's what Val wants," Flint snarled. "To weaken his enemies by spreading their armies' forces more thinly, picking them off opportunistically, and then crushing them when their strength has diminished!"

Everyone looked at her oddly.

"Wow," Shayla said. "I guess *that* explains everything."

"There's only one chance," Dominique said. "Keller! You and Orphius *have* to get your armies to stand together!"

Her brother looked at her oddly. "Are you kidding?"

"It's the only way we've got! Red Shield is full of people who are willing to do whatever it takes to end your stupid war. Do you think they're going to stop now?"

She fixed another laser stare on him. "You know the truth. Now go and use it!"

Keller stiffened, but then, he sighed and nodded. "Alright. I'll get there as fast as I can. Where did Reyzar go?"

"He's doing something important. You're hitching a ride with us," Dominique said. "Let's go, guys."

Shayla flew at breakneck speed, her ears flat against the sides of her head and her wings straining. Her riders crouched low over her scales to give her optimal flying capability. Dominique kept her gaze grimly fixated on the rising smoke they flew toward.

The battle had begun in a town, or what had *used* to be the town of Spirana. Now, nothing remained save for ashes and smoking, blackened ruins. Any people once living there were either dead or had run away.

"This is bad," Flint muttered. "*So* bad."

Below them, the armies clashed. The sound of swords pinging and guns firing nearly deafened the girl, even far above it all. Screams of dying men seemed to affect her terribly; she blanched.

"This is much worse than anything Adameans ever did," Yakimi muttered. Keller gave him a look.

"This is war. Even if it's a futile one."

"Okay, guys, be on the lookout for Orphius. The last time we saw him was on the back of a Rhinox," Dominique instructed.

Easier said than done. The air around them was becoming increasingly populated by Rhinox as they flew into the midst of the battle. Dominique felt a twinge of apprehension; where were the dragons?

Keller seemed to share the thought. His eyes strained for any sign of the scaled creatures. Finding nothing, he looked toward Dominique questioningly.

"Where did you say Reyzar was?"

"I told him to tell the dragons our plan to unite the two armies. He has your helmet, if you're wondering. It was for proof."

The man shook his head. "Dragons aren't easily persuaded. Especially by one as young as Reyzar. Of course, he is Berra's son."

He fell silent, and Dominique sighed. "Listen, about Berra..."

"It's alright."

But the stone cold face greeting her was anything but alright. Still, now wasn't the time to dwell on that.

"Is that him?" Yakimi asked suddenly, pointing. Shayla swiveled in mid-air to locate the Rhinox he directed her toward.

"No," Keller said. "He doesn't ride like that. That rider's too sloppy."

Shayla abandoned her chase. A few Rhinox, however, had noticed her presence, and had decided to become unfriendly.

The dragon dove; three Rhinox followed her, snarling and baring their teeth. Keller swiveled in his seat, palms outstretched-

"No! If they're gonna be on our side, we'll need all we can get!" Dominique shouted. He withdrew his energy back into his body, and turned around.

"There!" her brother shouted.

Dominique looked to the right. Sure enough, one of the largest Rhinox she had ever seen was heading straight for them, and on its back...

"Orphius!" she shouted, waving her arms. A flicker of surprise ran through the man's pallid face, and he drew his mount up.

"What are you doing here? This is dangerous! You shouldn't be-"

He broke off suddenly, as he saw Keller. His purple eyes glittered dangerously. "So," he said through gritted teeth. "You've decided to believe *him.*"

"No!" Dominique said, shaking her head. "It's not that. I know you didn't start the fire, Orphius!"

"See? That's what I've been telling you all along!"

"But," she said. "Keller didn't either."

Silence fell on them. Orphius's eyes narrowed.

"What do you mean?"

"She means it wasn't you, or me!" Keller suddenly barked. "It was Val!"

"Val? That man who used to work for father?"

Everyone was nodding.

"And what's worse," Flint added. "He's got his entire Red Shield army headed this way to take you both out. And probably to steal me, while he's at it."

She shrugged. "If I've got the source inside me."

"Wait, *you're* holding the source of our power?" Orphius snapped, gawking at her. The robot crossed her arms.

"Yes, okay? And if Val gets a hold of me, then goodbye Yumurango!"

Shayla gave a snarl; her wings were beginning to tire from staying aloft for so long. The Rhinox carrying Orphius was panting as well.

"We'll land behind my army's lines!" Keller instructed.

"I don't think so! We'll land among *my* men, thank you very much!" Orphius snapped. Dominique rolled her eyes.

"Why should I trust you? You've tried to kill me for the last five years, for no reason!"

"I can say the same thing about you!"

"ALRIGHT, JUST SHUT UP!" Dominique roared. "SHAYLA, LAND IN THE MIDDLE! ORPHIUS, FOLLOW US!"

Shayla dropped like a stone, followed by the Rhinox. Dominique noticed, with some amusement, that her brothers remained silent.

"Heads up," Yakimi warned. "I can see Red Shield approaching."

"Oh, joy," Flint muttered.

As they landed, Shayla roared at anyone in their way. Soldiers went scrambling for their lives, appalled at the sight of the enormous dragon.

They slid off her back. Shayla remained in dragon form to fend off any interruptions to their conversation.

"You two, decide on how to make this work!" Dominique ordered, and she began to ascend into the sky above the battle. "We're gonna take the fight to Red Shield!"

Her brothers either didn't hear, or didn't listen. They were staring at one another, not quite sure what to say. But she had to go, she couldn't stay to help.

"Good luck!" she called to them. Then, she rocketed off. Shayla took off, and Flint carried Yakimi. A black energy bubble appeared around them to ward off any attackers.

Dominique turned to her destination. At the edge of the battle, she landed, then scrambled up a low hill to survey the incoming forces.

It was like a tide of black sand that had come to life. There were so many of them. At the head, she could make out Val and Sadiki, and also...Tom.

She bit her lip. What hurt the most was that the majority of these people, like her, were only fighting for what they believed in. Red Shield was purely volunteer. They thought they were fighting for the good guys. Dominique directed the group to move down the hill, positioning themselves to block Val's advancing army.

"If anyone survives this, there's gonna be some stories," Flint said, taking a deep breath. Yakimi snarled softly and fingered his blade.

Shayla, from the rear, spread her wings and roared a challenge; from within Red Shield's ranks, there were a few smaller answering roars, but none matched hers. The hair of Dominique's neck prickled as the dragon's hot breath washed over her.

Val's army stopped about a dozen yards away. Dominique stood bravely, sword in hand. Her eyes tracked Val as he swaggered closer, dragging Tom along with him. The skeleton didn't flinch.

"Little Shadow, you're in my way," he said.

"So I'm aware," she said coldly. "You're going to die today."

"Am I? Well, at least one of your friends is..."

Suddenly, he held a gun up to Tom's head. Dominique wailed inwardly. He wouldn't! He couldn't!

"Stay calm," Yakimi muttered to her. She managed to keep her racing heart and mind under control.

"You think that'll stop us?" Flint proclaimed proudly. "I've got this source, or whatever. Nothing you have even compares!"

A dangerous glint had appeared in Val's eye. His gaze flicked to Sadiki; the Marauder was smiling, evilly.

"He won't take the collar off," Flint said confidently. "Sadiki would kill him as soon as he did."

"Maybe," Dominique said doubtfully. Shayla snarled deeply.

"Leave this place, and Horter lives," Val said. He clicked the weapon off of safety; Tom's face betrayed no emotion.

"You have five seconds," the man said. His finger began to tighten on the trigger.

"One,"

Yakimi gritted his teeth and tightened his grip on his sword.

"Two,"

Flint steadied her aim directly on Val's forehead. Her sniper rifle was in the hands of a master. There was no way she would miss.

"Three...can you hear me?"

Shayla roared again, flexing her talons and beginning to tighten her muscles, preparing to spring into the air.

"Four...this is your last chance!"

Dominique's throat gulped. She looked toward Tom, and shook her head. He looked right back her, and suddenly, his mouth moved.

"I love you!"

The words left his mouth just as Val began to say, "Five".

But before he could finish, everything around them suddenly went black. Dominique's eyes widened, and she looked toward the only light source available; Yakimi's sword.

"What's going on?" Flint growled. She raised her rifle, moving it slowly around, looking through the night-vision scope for a target.

In the gloom, there was a shout of surprise from Val; Dominique shrieked as something slammed into her, but it felt familiar...

"Tom?" she asked.

"Wait a minute...am I dead?"

His familiar voice caressed her ears, and she gripped him tighter. Like a switch, the lights came back over the battle. But instead of five people facing the army, there were now seven.

Orphius and Keller stood in front of Dominique, their arms crossed.

"Out of the blackness and into the frying pan, Val. No one messes with our sister," Orphius snarled.

"Especially not a rotten piece of filth, like you," Keller said, nodding to Val. The man sputtered.

"How...why...what are you...? But..."

"Oops, sorry," Flint said conversationally. "I guess we forgot to tell you that they know *all* about the fire now."

"You have three very pissed off Shadows to contend with, I think," Tom said. He looked toward Dominique. She smiled at him.

"Let's do this," she said.

"Yes," he agreed. "Let's."

And with that, they ran forward to meet the enemy.

20

Battle

Dominique swung her sword like a madwoman, nearly cleaving a man in half. Her brow was furrowed as she swung around and neatly gored another incoming soldier through the chest.

"Behind you!" she shouted to Flint.

The robot whirled and leapt, digging her fingers into the unlucky woman's throat. Gagging on her own blood, she collapsed.

"Okay," Flint said. "I've officially decided something; fighting in battles is *not* fun."

"LOOK OUT!" someone screamed. Both girl and robot dove out of the way. An enormous Shartan had just collapsed.

Dominique concentrated, and suddenly, half a dozen people simply keeled over, lifeless. Sickened by what she could do, the girl forced herself to her feet and picked her way over corpses, toward more enemies.

They were easy to spot; the black uniforms always gave them away, and the girl was well aware that she too was wearing one. More than once, she'd had to stop a friendly-fire attack on herself.

Finally, she ditched the black top, abandoning it for the neutral white shirt underneath it. She gave a sigh of relief. Now she wouldn't have to worry about-

"YAAAH!"

Something leapt over her head, screeching a battle cry. Dominique watched as Yakimi literally flew into a knot of enemies, decimating them. His sword was the most effective weapon on the battlefield. No one could get near him long enough to even begin an attack before the blistering heat descended upon them.

His yellow eyes looked toward her; she smiled hurriedly and whirled around to parry a blow from another swordsman. Rolling to her feet, she circled him warily, watching his every move.

Finally, he lunged; she rolled underneath him and struck a mortal blow into his stomach. Howling in agony, he went down.

In the last half an hour, Dominique had forgotten to feel sorry for her victims. There were just too many of them. Even with Orphius and Keller's forces on their side, it was still taking a long time to push Red Shield back.

But they were falling back. Slowly but surely, the enemy was being pushed away. Dominique pushed a strand of hair out of her sweaty face and pressed forward.

Someone touched her arm; she yelped and raised her sword, but stopped as she recognized Keller. The general was using his powers and a stolen axe considerably well. Anyone who saw him coming ran away as fast as they could.

"Are you alright?" he asked, suddenly whirling and stabbing a nasty, slimy looking thing through the chest. Dominique nodded. Blood of different colors ran down her shirt, forming a disturbing tyedye pattern.

"I think we've got them," Keller said with a boyish grin. "Just a few hundred feet, and they'll have to give it up. There's not enough room for them to maneuver up toward the canyon-"

Screams, louder than the usual battle sounds, stopped him. Dominique turned to see an entire platoon of men, *their* men, go flying.

"What the hell?" Keller asked tightly.

An earth shattering roar blasted the battlefield. Dominique screamed and covered her ears. It was as loud as Shayla's, but had a metallic edge that caused the air to reverberate painfully inside of her head. A hot, acrid smell washed over the armies, and they turned to look.

Dominique saw something taking form, a spiraling, twisting column of energy, rearing high above the heads of the other species. Soldiers caught in its wake burned to crisps as it grew.

"Damn it all," Keller murmured. "The Marauder!"

A column of white flame suddenly rose up, and a gaping mouth could be seen at the very top of it. There was another ear-piercing shriek, and it looked down...straight at Keller and Dominique.

"Sadiki?" the girl asked in disbelief. Sure enough, two green eyes decorated the sides of the flaming column, near the mouth. They stared at her.

"*That's* a Marauder?" the girl squeaked. "*That* thing? HOLY-"

"RUN!"

Keller pulled her away quickly, and the two Shadows began to sprint away as fast as they could. People screamed and began to race with them, until the mob became a panicked stampede.

In the throng, Dominique glimpsed a familiar figure.

"Tom!" she called. He turned, and reached his hand out toward her.

She took it.

Keller swore. "Turn! TURN!"

All three of them switched direction in a heartbeat. Dominique rose above the crowd, accompanied by her brother. They each grabbed one of the skeleton's arms and lifted him away.

Sadiki gave a low, evil cackle, and began to rise into the air in pursuit of them.

"Tom!" Dominique shouted. "We're gonna drop you!"

"What? No!"

The skeleton's voice was shrill with terror.

"Flint will catch you!"

Sure enough, the robot was keeping pace below them, providing a safety net from the ground below.

"This is gonna hurt," he whined.

"Now!" Dominique hissed to Keller.

They let him go.

He gave a scream as he began to hurtle to the ground, his life flashing before his eyes. He was gonna die, he was gonna die-

"And where do you think you're going?" Flint asked teasingly, grabbing him out of his freefall.

"Flint! Sadiki's-"

"I'M NOT BLIND!"

All of a sudden, she tossed him away, and Tom gave another high pitched squeal as he flew through the air—straight into something warm and scaly.

"Shayla, I don't think I've ever been happier to see you," he said, latching his arms around her in a death grip. She gave a cough of laughter.

A wave of heat passed over them; Tom looked fearfully behind them, but saw that Sadiki was still in pursuit of the Shadows. His eyes glimpsed another figure flying upward to join them; Orphius.

"So," he said grimly. "It's come down to that. Three Shadows and a Marauder. God, what is our world coming to?"

"You're asking us?" Flint queried, rocketing along beside them. In a skillful move of acrobatics, she flipped onto Shayla's back.

"Whatever," he muttered.

"Seriously, you're asking *us?* You're a living skeleton. I'm a robot with the Shadow's source of power inside me. Shayla's the only shape shifter left alive. Yakimi's the only Adamean. And Dominique..."

She gestured helplessly. "Shadow!"

Tom looked toward the girl. She was squaring to face the Marauder, alongside her two brothers. He shook his head.

"By the way, I'm proud of you for telling her," Flint said. "It might not have been the best *time,* but-"

"Flint! Shut up! You're not my relationship coach!"

She shut up.

Suddenly, she looked down. "Look! Yakimi!"

Tom followed her gaze, and his eyes widened. The Adamean was backed against the remains of an old stone building, slicing away at the group of enemies overwhelming him. But that wasn't the main problem.

The main problem was Val, coming up behind him. Even as they watched, the man kicked Yakimi from behind, causing him to stumble forward. When the creature attempted to raise his sword, three other soldiers rushed in and contained him.

His roars of outrage were audible in the distance. Flint screamed in fury and leapt down, followed closely by Shayla...

"It seems," Val whispered to the Adamean. "That your race is about to become extinct, again."

With that, he drew a gun and leveled it at Yakimi's forehead. Even with three captors holding tight, the Adamean drew himself up proudly, nailing Val with an unwavering gaze.

"You may defeat me," he snarled. "But my friends will keep fighting."

"After my Marauder finishes with them, that won't be the case."

"DIE!"

Something crashed down onto Val's back. The man howled with pain as he went down. His hat was knocked from his head, and he grimaced as he looked up.

Flint planted a foot on his head. "Actually, I have to agree with Yakimi on this point."

Tom and Shayla destroyed the soldiers restraining the Adamean. Yakimi stood shakily, and retrieved his sword from the mass of death.

Val glared at them. "You have no idea what you're doing," he said. His voice had a hysterical edge to it. "You really don't."

"Hmm, let's think about this for a minute..." Flint said.

But before she could finish her thought, Yakimi lunged forward, and cut off the man's head.

Everyone was silent as they watched the head go rolling. Yakimi looked at them defiantly.

"I didn't want to think," he said.

Shayla sniffed him suspiciously for any injuries, and he shook his head.

"I'm fine."

"Guys! Look!"

Flint was pointing up to the sky. Tom was the first to turn around, and swore darkly as he saw the Shadows had stopped running, and were flying back toward the Marauder.

"They're gonna die!" he whispered in a panicked voice.

"No," Yakimi said. "Dominique is strong. And since those two are part of her family, they are strong as well."

"I hope you're right," Flint muttered.

Dominique watched as the column of white fire came toward them, ever closer. Keller and Orphius were on either side of her, their hands clenched into lethal fists.

"Is this how it ends?" Orphius asked quietly. Both of them turned toward him.

"What do you mean?" Dominique asked.

"No, it's just that...I never expected to die alongside *either* of you."

Keller snorted with laughter. "Me, as well."

"Hey, I don't plan on dying right now," Dominique piped up. "There's no way! I'm only seventeen! I mean, I know you guys are already old, but-"

"Hey!"

"Little shrimp."

"Shut up!"

Nervous laughter followed their jokes, and they looked again toward Sadiki. The Marauder had stopped, and was looking toward them as well.

"At this time," Dominique said. "There's only one thing I can say to him. You guys ready?"

Orphius and Keller exchanged glances. Then, they nodded.

"BRING IT!" Dominique screamed.

Sadiki roared again, and barreled directly toward them.

"On the count of three!" Keller barked. "Then we'll hit him with everything we've got!"

"One," Orphius hissed.

"Two," Keller added.

Dominique took a deep breath.

"THREE!"

All of them moved in perfect unison. Their arms spread out, their fingertips barely touching each others.

Energy spread throughout their bodies, merging their minds together for one instant. In that instant, they had no secrets from the others. It was as if they were one entity, reaching out beyond the boundaries of their physical forms-

But as abruptly as it began, it stopped, and Dominique once again found herself in her own body, hurtling power out in a fast and furious way.

She yelled in defiance to the Marauder; Sadiki's white energy reared and clashed with the dark energy. Keller and Orphius added their shouts, and the black roared back.

In the darkness that surrounded them, Dominique noticed something startling; her brothers' eyes were red, and glowing. Hers must have been doing the same. What was going on?

As their eyes changed, though, so did their power. The black energy level rose above and beyond what should have been possible for them, and then-

The Marauder vanished.

Temporarily weakened, Dominique dropped her arms in relief, staring in astonishment at the now empty space. Orphius and Keller grinned and looked toward each other.

But then, something snapped inside of them. Dominique blinked as a wave of dizziness came over her. Her brothers seemed to feel it, too.

"What's happening?" she asked. "I feel-"

Her eyes shut, her confused mind still trying to grasp what was happening. The last thing she felt was her body falling through space.

Oh well. She thought dreamily. *At least we beat that little turd.*

The first thing Dominique became aware of were hands grabbing her.

She frowned in her semi-conscious state, trying to remember what had happened. Sadiki had been chasing them, and then all of a sudden...

Her eyes flew open. A hideous creature was grinning down at her. With a yelp of shock, she slammed a punch into its face.

"OW!"

She leapt to her feet and watched in fear as Red Shield soldiers began to close in on her. To her right, she saw the prone forms of her two brothers. Kicking them, she swore angrily.

"Wake up!"

Orphius stirred, and Keller moaned. She kicked them again, harder.

"WAKE UP, YOU IDIOTS!"

That did the trick.

"Why are you kicking me?" Orphius demanded. "After defeating a Marauder, I would think that-"

"Get up!"

With a quick glance around, Orphius swore and leapt up, preparing to use his powers. Keller shook his head blearily.

"What's going o-WHOA!"

He stood up as though he'd been electrocuted. The Shadows stiffened as rifles were aimed in their direction.

"They must have regrouped," Orphius hissed.

"This battle is over," one person declared. "With your deaths, we will ensure that Yumurango is peacefully ruled from now on."

Dominique stiffened. She knew that voice! She knew who it was!

"Come out where I can see you, *Vilondra,*" she sneered.

There was a parting in the ranks, and soon, the woman appeared. Her green eyes flashed with triumph as she surveyed the Shadows.

"The most powerful people in Yumurango, all here at my feet," she said. Dominique cringed at the memory of the alternate world she had seen.

"What do I do? Hmm..."

There had to be a way out of this. The girl's eyes quickly canvassed her surroundings, searching for her friends. Where were they? They wouldn't abandon her!

"Dominique," Orphius hissed. "This would be a very good time for your tiresome friends to come through, guns blazing."

"Tell me about it," she muttered back.

Vilondra's upper lip curled in a contemptuous sneer. "I hope you three don't mind, but once you're all gone, the power in the source will be transferred to *my* family. Your line is over!"

"The Collins," Keller said. Even now, he was intimidating as he straightened himself and pinned her with a defiant glare.

"Correct," Vilondra said icily. "Men!"

The weapons were clicked off safety. Dominique bit her lip and tried not to let her fear show. After expending so much energy and magic defeating Sadiki, she and her brothers all knew that their magic needed time to regenerate. There was no way it could help them right now.

Slowly, surely, she found each of her brothers' hands and held them. They squeezed back lightly. Glancing behind her, she saw that they had joined hands with each other, as well.

"Does this mean you two have made up?" she whispered.

"I think so," Keller muttered. "A little late, though."

"See you two on the other side," Orphius said.

With that, Dominique squeezed her eyes shut, waiting for the rain of lead that would kill her instantly-

It never came. What did come, however, was completely unexpected.

A roar. A *dragon's* roar.

Dominique looked upward. Although the sun shone brightly in the Yumurango sky, darkness began to cover the small force that remained of Red Shield. There was a moment of hushed silence, and then the screaming began.

Black dragons. Hundreds of them! The girl grinned like an idiot as their leathery hides and red, glowing eyes came into view. She laughed hysterically and turned to Keller.

"Have I ever mentioned I love dragons?"

"Good grief," Orphius said. His purple eyes were wide with shock.

The flock descended upon the army, tearing apart anybody they managed to snag with their razor sharp talons or six inch teeth.

Around the Shadows, the men who had once been so intent on killing them screamed and ran for cover, only to be picked off, one by one. Dominique thought she saw Vilondra get carried off, screaming, but she couldn't be sure.

In the midst of the chaos, two dragons in the horde particularly caught their attention. One was white. Dominique's heart leapt out of her chest. Shayla was alright! And all her friends rode with her on her back!

The other dragon was black. A little on the small side, but in his claws...

In his claws was Keller's helmet. Reyzar gave a triumphant roar as he spiraled down and handed the helmet to his master.

Keller stroked his nose, and laughed. "Good boy," he said.

Shayla landed beside the black dragon. In an instant, she was transforming, while familiar figures rolled off her back.

Before she even knew what she was doing, Dominique was running for one of the new arrivals in particular. The lanky one, the skeletal one...

Tom turned around and watched her coming toward him. He smiled and outstretched his arms, beckoning to an embrace-

She slammed into him, and before she knew it, his lips were on hers.

How do you kiss a skeleton? Well, Dominique didn't really know, but as of right now, she didn't *care.* All she did was kiss him back, absolutely sure that this was where she belonged, for all time.

When they finally parted, there were snickers all around them. Tom looked defensively at Shayla and Flint, who were elbowing each other and whispering.

"Hey, this is what you two wanted! Don't be so immature."

Dominique rolled her eyes (as usual) and ran over to the two women, giving them each hugs. They were both ecstatic with relief as they held her.

Someone cleared their throat, and the girl whirled to see Yakimi standing near them expectantly. She gave him the biggest grin of all and leapt up to hug him.

"A lover, not a fighter, eh?" Orphius sneered. She shot him a glare over the Adamean's shoulder.

When she was set down, she retreated back into Tom's arms. Her brothers kept glancing over at her protectively, as though seeing her in another guy's arms was painful for them.

"Get over it," she said warningly. Tom laughed and stroked her hair, rubbing it in...just a little.

"Can we go now?" Flint snapped.

"Yes," Shayla said, beginning to turn. "The dragons are already leaving."

It was true; the flock had begun to recede, leaving the battlefield an empty, lifeless place populated only with corpses. The Red Shield survivors, if any, had already fled, its army decimated. Reyzar was crouching expectantly, watching Keller.

Keller strode in his direction, but hesitated, and looked to Dominique.

"You'll be alright?" he asked. He looked at her friends suspiciously. She nodded and patted Tom's arm.

"I think I'm good."

"You're sure?"

She arched an eyebrow.

"If you say so."

The general donned his helmet and jerked his head to Orphius. "Come on."

Dominique watched her two brothers take off to gather what remained of their now united armies, and scrambled up onto Shayla's back. Tom secured her with his arms, and she leaned back into him, closing her eyes.

Their battle was over.

Now she could rest.

21

Square One

When Dominique woke up, the first thing she realized was that she seemed floating again. That...and a crippling sense of déjà vu.

"Oh no..." she moaned.

"Ah, ssshe ssstill ssspeaksss," Poz said, with apparent disappointment. Her purple eyes looked up in distaste.

"What do you two want?"

Duna came sliding up from out of the mist. "We wanted to let you know that you have done well, daughter of Sssinge," she said. "You were brave enough to go back and lead your friendsss and family through a time of great peril."

"Thank you. Can I go back now?"

The two snake-like beings exchanged glances. "Well, you sssee..." Duna began. Dominique arched an eyebrow.

"What?" she demanded. Apprehension constricted her chest.

"There are powersss at work here, sssome you cannot even begin to comprehend. For that reassson, you mussst be sssent back to Earth."

"WHAT?"

Furious, she tried to use her powers against them, but to her horror, they failed her. Already, she felt vulnerable, weak...

Wait! Her sword. It was still at her hip. Glaring, she unsheathed it and pointed it at them threateningly.

"Send me back to Yumurango," she said quietly. Duna hung her head.

"I'm sssorry," she hissed. "Thisss isss the way thingsss mussst be. You will underssstand, in time."

"DON'T! DON'T YOU DARE-"

The next instant, Dominique found herself staring at a poster. A poster of one of her favorite actors.

A poster that was in her bedroom.

Looking around wildly, her frantic purple eyes scanned her room. Yes, *her* room. She was back on Earth!

"NO!" she wailed, collapsing onto her knees. There was no way! No way that she could have gone through all that, just to end up stuck here again...

Wait a minute. She looked back at the sword in her hand. The inscriptions on the blade shimmered oddly...

As she watched, they began to assume amorphous shapes, then more defined figures, finally crystallizing into...her friends!

Yakimi's yellow eyes stared out at her from the sword, his own sword held securely in his hand. Flint's gun was aimed with focus. Shayla displayed the usual smirk on her mouth. Orphius and Keller stood side by side, brothers at last...

And Tom stood apart from the others, staring upward, his arms crossed. A look of determination and resolve on his features.

Dominique felt that same look settle over her face, and she gripped her sword's hilt tightly. As long as this sword was still with her, she would never give up hope. She stared out her window to the sky.

She *would* find her way home again. No matter what it took. Back to her family, back to her friends, back to Tom...

Back to Yumurango.

ABOUT THE AUTHOR

Nicole Mastan began writing stories and short books when she was six years old, and has continued up until this point. Throughout her education, she has been in honors courses, and is enrolled in Honors Society at the high school level. She is currently a member of the IB (International Baccalaureate) program, and hopes that an early college level education will help her with her writing over the years. Nicole loves all types of music, parties, and all things filled with sugar. She lives in Washington State with her family and pets.

Email Nicole about the book at yumurango@live.com

Visit the Yumurango website at www.yumurango.com

www.ingramcontent.com/pod-product-compliance
Lightning Source LLC
Chambersburg PA
CBHW030342310726
48979CB00001B/154

* 9 7 8 0 5 7 8 0 1 3 0 5 3 *